Published by Ockley Books Ltd

First published September 2018

ISBN 978-1-910906-15-6

Front Cover, layout & design by Michael Kinlan
Edited by David Hartrick

Printed & bound in England by:
Biddles Printing, King's Lynn

THE GIGANTE

ROBERT ENDEACOTT

OCKLEY BOOKS

.com

Dedicated to John Charles and
his family & friends everywhere.

For Peggy,
it has been a pleasure and privilege meeting you,
and interviewing and interrogating you!

THE GIGANTE

PROLOGUE

A peaceful, pleasantly warm autumn night was about to be unpleasantly disturbed. Not long after the neighbourhood bells of St Mary's Church tolled twice in the morning of Tuesday 18th September 1956, the night sky and the clouds above Elland Road football ground took on a curious, pale glow of amber and yellow. These Northern Lights were no delight of nature; this phenomenon was disastrous.

Deep in the ground-level confines of the stadium's West Stand, corrupted wiring created a spate of sparks. In turn, these tiny explosions caused the wiring giving them life to react and smoulder. Woodwork and wallpaper ignited, tributaries and rivulets formed, trickles of fire became torrents, expanding, splintering; soon there were arteries of hell snaking through the central depths of the stand, gathering strength and momentum, fiery talons seizing, devouring anything in their path. So much wood, paper, carpeting, polystyrene, plastics, rubber, leather, fabrics, paint, fuels. All destroyed within furious minutes, the labyrinth of rooms and offices and corridors rapidly gutted. And the ruination had only just begun. In less than a quarter of an hour, the grandstand of two thousand eight hundred wooden seats and the many yards of timber flooring were ablaze. The devastation relentless, merciless.

The roof of the West Stand was an unusual structure: two conjoined, extended arches, eighty-by-ten yards of prefabricated steel covered with tarpaulin, asphalt and bitumen. The pitch-side section of the roof, slightly longer than the rear, normally served as shelter for match-day spectators standing in the paddock below. All of it would be gone in minutes, consumed by the inferno, toxic particles dirtying the Leeds air further. Fragments of debris plummeting to the ground, molten bitumen and asphalt falling on to wood below. The flames fed on oxygen and, as the fire intensified, a rush of fresh air was sucked up towards the burning roof, in effect a huge bellows in motion. The enormous furnace grew larger and hotter, flames stretched into the night sky, the unstoppable carnage spreading as a rash across the length of the roof.

Five fire engines and crews were required to extinguish the Elland Road fire, taking hours to do so. Even then, another, smaller fire reignited within the wreckage in the following days. The player dressing rooms, the club's administration offices, the directors' boardroom, the press box and the laundry room that doubled as a referee's dressing room were all destroyed, along with their contents. Ten sets of football kits, untold pairs of football boots, the physiotherapy equipment, over thirty leather footballs, hundreds and hundreds of spectator seat cushions, the lighting generators, the office equipment and paperwork – the club's *history* – all transformed to smoke. The imposing architecture of the West Stand had ceased to exist, its body gutted, its once perfect skeleton now a warped and disfigured mass of blackened unsafe metal, the vertical steel girders over-sized, used matchsticks.

A desolate picture of ruination, upsetting to behold and difficult to comprehend. But no casualties, at least there were no casualties, not even the unofficial owner-occupant of the West Stand; Blackie the cat returned a few days later, suspicious but unscathed.

A whole new stand was required. Its construction was planned to begin early the next year, 1957, with four thousand seats to be installed and the paddock standing area capacity also increased. The planning was the easy part. With a reported £40,000 insurance compensation paid to the club for the fire, over £60,000 was thus needed, and with every home game the team played without the stand and spectators there, the lost or missing revenue was near as damn it one thousand pounds. A money miracle was needed to shine on Leeds United, but miracles didn't happen, even in God's Own Country of Yorkshire.

Writing it would make him feel better. As well as, he hoped, provide comfort to those mourning his departure. An open letter to explain to them and to convey his feelings to the unhappy thousands. He was still one of them; he'd always be one of them. Putting the theory into practice wasn't such an easy task on a moving locomotive. Plus there was the small point of him not being very adept at writing. His journalist friend Ronald Crowther would publish the letter in the next weekend edition of the *Green Final* paper. All the journalists were his friends really, they had always been kind to him and they only wanted what was best for him, while of course hoping for a tasty news story or two along the way. Ronald would need to improve the grammar and the spelling but William John Charles had faith in himself to at least write honestly.

1

He never really understood it, people looking at him, studying him, photographing him, intruding on his privacy, trying to get his attention. He didn't like it either. The autograph hunters weren't so bad, only because most of them were just kids desperate for his signature and meaning no offence by it. Grown-ups were different. His unamused expression and the heavy brow weighing him down like a night-time argument should have informed them, but rarely if ever did. He was not a person to them, he was a *thing*. None of them would have believed that the unamused expression and heavy brow belonged to that odd family of shyness and wariness. How could *John Charles* be shy or wary of anything? John Charles, the King of Football?

The lack of eye contact with strangers was also a clue, one which no one ever followed, along with his awkwardness and discomfort in social occasions. At school, his old headmaster said, the boy Charles appeared permanently puzzled, as if always searching for something. On the football pitch it was an entirely different story: he was stronger, faster, nimbler, *cleverer*; he always found what he was looking for. On the field of play, this young giant – hewn from Welsh mountains – was a brilliant scholar.

◎

MONDAY 22ND APRIL, 1957

Four days after the official announcement and just one hour after the end of the Sunderland match *and* his Leeds career, Charles was departing the Elland Road stadium. He had always preferred quick exits after matches, not wanting any fuss or attention and not wanting to bathe in the filthy water of a communal bath for longer than absolutely necessary. He preferred relaxing at home with his wife and family after another strenuous, energy-sapping football match.

With Gigi Peronace in the passenger seat, Charles was attempting to ease his car through a crowd of boys congregated near the main gates of the football ground. Even with the stern instructions of a police constable and a gate-man telling them to keep out of the way, the crowd persisted in hindering the car's progress.

'Don't stop, don't stop,' urged Peronace, fearing that if Charles did stop the car then they'd be stuck there in a quicksand of well-wishers and signature demanders.

Charles had said and heard enough farewells for the day. He carefully kept the car moving, eyes to the front with a fixed smile on his face.

With a light hold of the steering wheel, only the fingers of his right hand acknowledged the noisy children. He disliked being so apparently nonchalant, it felt dishonest, but a busy night loomed ahead and he had to be punctual. Finally they stretched free of the throng and on to open road. A couple of miles and a few minutes later, Charles turned the car in to the drive of his house, 'Lynwood'. 'Stop!' cried Peronace. Charles gave a glance of annoyance; he had already hit the brakes due to the surprising presence of a person sitting on the tarmac of the driveway. The boy got to his feet, in his haste nearly falling over as he did so. He seemed about twelve years old, with bright ginger hair and a face flooded with freckles. He stepped aside to remove himself as an obstacle and Charles eased the vehicle into the driveway accordingly. Perhaps it was nervousness or embarrassment that caused the unsmiling boy's unusual behaviour.

Whichever, it didn't end there, the lad introducing himself to Charles before either man had even had time to get out of the car.

'My name is Stanley. I need to talk to you, John. I'm your friend; I have followed you since I was seven. I know that you're going to play in Italy and that you'll stay away for a few years ...'

Charles seemed to have been struck dumb by this precocious child half his size but twice as talkative. Twelve going on seventy years old. And Stanley hadn't finished ... 'I've always seen you playing with maximum effort. Now I ask you to promise me to continue to play for Juventus with the same will as when you have played for Leeds. You must do your best; it is important to the people you're leaving behind.'

Unsure how to react, Charles heard himself say, 'Okay Stanley. I promise you.'

'And you have to stay a Leeds Loiner.'

'I'm a Welshman first and foremost, Stanley, and then I'm Leeds. That will never change.' Apparently satisfied with the answer, the boy ended the conversation, 'All right, John. Now you can go. Goodbye.'

With that (and, for a twelve-year-old, a firm grip) he shook hands with Charles, at the same time hardly acknowledging Peronace's presence at all, and departed.

Late that night, on the sleeper train to London, with his mind over-busy, the irritating texture of the bedding and blankets was no help for relaxing. Better conditions, though, than in the past with fellow Swansea native John Reynolds. They would catch the overnight mail train down to South Wales from Leeds. Reynolds had been some player, a young one making a mark on the junior and reserve scene. Wise men tipped him to be 'the next John Charles'. Knee injuries decided otherwise. The train coach compartments were always crowded – the mail train being the cheapest route – and Spartan in terms of comfortable furnishings. The two Johns would flip a coin to decide who got to stretch out on the cushioned bench and who had to climb up and sleep in the luggage rack above. John C almost always won, with John R wondering if and how he had been conned yet again.

Thoughts and concerns grasped for his attention. Too many spinning plates of worry. Fatigue always brought with it unwelcome stress to twist and inflate even the slightest of matters. His body ached *inside* too, with the stark realisation he was leaving Great Britain, his home and so many friends and colleagues ... And for *God knows where*. Loss, foreboding, uncertainty, all too similar to when he'd left Swansea for Leeds that first time, along with his pals Bobby Henning and Harry Griffiths. They'd all been just kids then, nervous inexperienced kids; *now* should be different even if this time was a solo trip.

He was an uncomplicated man, his wife Peggy similar, a wise Leeds lass, strong but kind and with no edge to her personality. John took care of on-pitch business, she took care of virtually everything else. He wondered how she was feeling. Tired, uncomfortable and frustrated but radiant at the same time. With the latest pregnancy her weight had risen to fourteen stones, the same as his own weight, but he was eight inches taller and a professional sportsman. He was always relieved to know that, like his own mother, she was a strong lass, resilient, spirited. She would simply get on with life and everything it put in her way, much like so many British women had done during and following the war. As soon as he'd first seen her in the Astoria Ballroom, on that 1949 night, he'd been smitten. A fabulous girl, and his feelings for her only flourished as their time together increased; he trusted her, relied on her, needed her, and she never disappointed.

It had been a hard day, physically and emotionally. The sight of so many people with sadness in their faces and hearts, some of them actually weeping, would stay with Charles for a very long time. He had shed a few private tears too; nothing he was too ashamed of. And now he couldn't stop himself worrying. Worrying about what the journeys ahead had in store for him, in London and Italy. Worrying about what he would need to do at each airport, who he would need to see, what would happen with his luggage. And then he remembered he had Gigi Peronace with him, and his worries decreased markedly.

◎

BEFORE

The chairman had been saying it for years, football season after football season. And each time he'd said it, each time he had had to repeat himself, chairman Sam Bolton's levels of frustration increased, his facial expression failing to veil his annoyance at their ignorance and disrespect. He could hardly be criticised for this tetchiness; rival football clubs thinking they were better than his own on grounds of tradition and wealth were a pain in the neck. '*John Charles is not for sale!*' Sam Bolton would maintain. John Charles, he would reiterate, is not for sale, at any price; there is no way John Charles will be leaving Leeds United Football Club; he is under contract at Elland Road and that is where he will continue to ply his trade. John Charles, together with his charming wife Peggy, is happy here and we are happy he … *they* are here, as well. There is no chance of that situation changing. We do not want to sell him and we do not need to sell him.

The robust, pipe-smoking, football-club-running Sam Bolton, occasionally belligerent, sometimes pugnacious, always determined. Take it or leave it, that's your lot. Straightforward, honest, forthright … just like any proud Yorkshireman should be. He couldn't be faulted for his spirited attitude and determination. His response to more rumours about John Charles being sold could be seen as faultless, too, but then, crucially, came that electrical fault in the West Stand.

◎

The chairman had been saying it for months, John Charles was not for sale. Sam Bolton would rather have a West Stand comparable to the one burnt down in September than sell their best player just to be able to pay for a better football ground. Leeds United were still in Division One thanks to John Charles. They had only got to Division One thanks to John Charles. Why, asked Bolton, and not unreasonably, should Leeds United continuously fork out good money to raise and develop talented young footballers only to then sell them? In normal circumstances it was indeed a reasonable question, but these were not normal circumstances, these were circumstances in which the club was mired in financial turmoil.

The issue for Leeds United's board of directors was how to raise sufficient funds to pay for a new West Stand, one that befitted a top-tier club in a city of half a million people. They were agreed that borrowing the money was not going to happen; the club had paid more than enough debts in recent years, plus they had spent heavily on expanding the stadium seating. They needed financial assistance, but acquiring it would be difficult. Only a small percentage of the populace watched the football at Elland Road regularly, and only a small percentage of those would be able, or willing, to afford to pay more money than they already did. Nonetheless, voices of contempt could be heard whispering and gossiping in canteens and tap rooms of the town, accusing Bolton and his directors of gross stupidity and even of fiddling (*failing* to fiddle, more to the point) the insurance. Had anyone dared to say such things to his face, Bolton would have knocked their block off.

◎

At the same time as Sam Bolton kept busy trying to fend off the inevitable, John Charles sat on the upper deck of the tram, the privately delighted conductor savouring the surprise appearance of football royalty, albeit football royalty wearing grubby training gear, to such a degree that the persistent pain in his knees had vanished, along with the small matter of charging Charles for a ticket. Charles would only be on his tram for a short while anyway, just the uphill part of the run, the part in fact where Elland Road began to rise, becoming Churwell Hill, towards Morley town.

Charles wiped steam from the window to his left, smiling to himself as he peered out into the grey day to see his Leeds United team-mates enduring another long and mundane training run. Another tedious tramp in the damp and the cold through lowlands of south Leeds, through streets of back-to-back red-brick and terraced houses and workshops and factories, through clouds and mists and fumes accompanying the grim buildings and the proliferation of stout chimneys. Only the drill of running up and down the Elland Road stadium terraces pained and bored him more; even the exhausting grind of the shuttles in the mills was preferable. What was the point of running all that way up the blasted hill when he bloody lived there? No point going to work when all it meant was running back to home. They should just let him stay in bed on a morning. Regardless of the dishonest respite, he was tired and restless, his amusement betraying his cluttered thoughts.

He had only ever asked to leave Leeds twice before, more than three years ago, and then he hadn't really meant it, he had merely wanted to express his dissatisfaction with how his Leeds career was progressing. Or how it wasn't progressing, to be more precise. He wanted to see ambition from the club's rulers, ambition that would enhance the team and make them contenders for trophies. Then, Leeds had been a mediocre Second Division side, yet there were reporters in the media who had called him the world's greatest player. The world's greatest player, in Division Two? The modest Charles was embarrassed and bemused: how could he be classed as that good when he was only playing against supposed B-rated opponents each

Saturday? It hadn't been fair on him to portray him in such a way, or fair on his team-mates. It probably wasn't even fair on his opponents.

Now, Leeds were in Division One and enjoying a more than decent season. True, the side's chances of winning honours had diminished after a strong start to the campaign, but considering it was their first season back in the top flight, a mid-table finish would be a fair achievement. Charles had had another fine season, scoring over thirty goals with the campaign yet to finish; he surely would be League Division One's top marksman. A superb feat, outdoing friends and rivals like Tommy Taylor, Jackie Mudie, Tom Finney and the 'Lion of Vienna', Nat Lofthouse. His team-mates' contributions were crucial, he was always the first to tell people that, but he was Leeds United's most prized asset, undoubtedly.

Opponents feared him, comrades loved him, supporters worshipped him. There was not a centre-forward who competed harder for his team than John Charles. If only the same could be said for his efforts during training. Give him a football to train with or a practice match to play in, and he would gladly do it for hours. Make him run though – sprints or, even worse, long distances – or lift weights and work out in the gym for prolonged durations, and you could forget it: he'd much rather stay in bed. And he quite often did, much to the annoyance of trainer Bob Roxburgh, who many a time felt compelled to order junior player Peter 'Mac' McConnell to run up to the Charles residence in the nearby Heaths to get him out of bed as he was late again. Mac dared not object, though he'd query privately why Harold Williams couldn't have done it earlier seeing as the Welsh winger lived near to Charles. Charles's response to those intrusive alarm clock calls, in his sleep-affected bass-baritone Welsh accent, was usually shouted from his bedroom window, terse, virtually always using language not taught him by his mother and that would have horrified her had she known. Even more exasperating for Roxburgh now was the fact that the Charles family had moved home and lived a few miles further away. So if Charles chose to have a lie-in, the club would just have to tolerate it. The family really had gone up in the world, their current home being on higher land than the Heaths – 'Lynwood'. Whether or not the increased distance from the stadium – and thus more chance for him to sleep in – influenced the decision to move home wasn't known. His team-mates wouldn't have bet against it, that was for sure.

Alighting from the tram, and laden with the conductor's heartfelt promise of a lifetime of gratis travel if he stayed with Leeds United, Charles stood on the pavement waiting for his team-mates to reach him. They would soon be cursing him and having a go at him, the bloody great skiver, but only half-heartedly of course, player camaraderie virtually always placating and suppressing tensions and misgivings within the squad. And besides, some of the players wished they had also taken advantage of public transport; Churwell Hill was a real swine.

Although he was unaware of the exact sums supposedly involved, Charles had decided that if he chose not to join one of the interested foreign clubs, he would regret it for the rest of his life. What with the financial straits the club had sunk into due to the disastrous fire and the modest maximum wage in English football, he'd be a fool to decline the chance. Wife Peggy would back him all the way, whatever his choice, just as she had always done before. Even with their third child due soon, a new complication to add to the circumstances, Peggy recognised there were brighter, richer opportunities for her husband to take, opportunities that would benefit them all. They owned a lovely, detached home and had wonderful friends and family in Leeds and Swansea; for the time being, they couldn't want for more. *For the time being.* John's playing career would be over in less than ten years and he didn't have a 'proper' trade to rely on once those days were over. And as good as they were, all the rewards from his Leeds United employment wouldn't last very long afterwards. Italy or even Spain seemed able to provide financial security for them, *and* a warmer climate of course. It didn't seem fair but that's how it was … No one person or club was directly to blame for the unsatisfactory situation in England, it was just how a footballer's life was mapped out. This footballer though, his career route a metaphorical dead-end street, had the chance to earn richer rewards.

He deserved to be rewarded better and he and Peggy were far from alone in thinking that. It was a decade when every able-bodied person kept busy and if a person wasn't doing so then there had better be a good reason. Life and lives needed rebuilding following the Second

World War and the British people needed to help each other. Football players were no different and their efforts provided the public with entertainment and relief from the hard slog of the everyday stresses and labours of the 1950s. People understood that the best football players were highly skilled and therefore should be paid accordingly in their limited years of employment. No one in Leeds wanted Charles to leave; the numerous letters and telephone calls to his home proved that. Leeds folk were not resentful or envious, they just didn't want to see him go; he wished he could convince them that he wouldn't be away forever.

Despite the crucial contribution to British industry and The Cause of the nation by women during the war years, the predominant attitude in society was still that a woman's place belonged firmly in the home. Peggy missed full-time employment, and the pay and the companionship of colleagues. Bringing up children was harder work than a job; it certainly involved more hours' labour and less remuneration. She was a dexterous and intelligent woman who had always striven to enjoy her work and who always tried her hardest. If a job was worth doing then it was worth doing well. In her first ever occupation she showed she was a good worker, just seventeen years of age, working at a primary school in the Middleton area of south Leeds and less than a mile from the family home on Middleton Park Grove. Enjoying the job but not her employer's attitude or behaviour towards her, she decided to look for alternative work.

In what was very much a man's world, once a woman became a wife there were roles where she would be made to relinquish her career and take up her 'rightful place' in the home. When Peggy and John married in 1953, archaic bank rules forced her to leave her job with the Midland Bank on Vicar Lane in Leeds, next to the picturesque Kirkgate Market building. The office experience gained there at least made her quest for new work a formality; her new place of employment was much closer to home too: clerical work in the offices of the jam factory owned by the Moorhouse family on Old Lane, Beeston, in Leeds.

A few weeks after she had started there, John caused a commotion amongst the office girls by dropping in uninvited, wearing his training kit, and kissing the surprised Peggy over her desk. The factory-floor lads refused to believe that the famous John Charles had been anywhere near their workplace. Four years and two children later – and the third on the way – pleasingly for Peggy, John had agreed to her placing an advertisement in the local press for a home help and nanny. And now, whoever the successful candidate was to be, they might well be needed to work for the Charles family overseas as well.

◎

All the transfer rumours had affected Charles's mood, but thankfully not his performances for Leeds. His eagerness to leave had only grown stronger following Gigi Peronace's 'unofficial' remarks to him, before the 6th April game against Arsenal at Highbury. Juventus, of Turin, Italy, were willing to pay any price to get him. Football rules dictated that Peronace was not actually empowered to do such talking. Rules though, in Peronace's own cerebral rule book, existed only to be avoided or, at the least, massaged and manipulated. He informed Charles too that Umberto Agnelli, Mister Juventus, intended flying out from Italy to Belfast simply to watch him in action for Wales against Northern Ireland on 10th April. Nearly two weeks had passed since then, however – *and* it had been an uninspiring 0-0 draw – and no one seemed any the wiser about his future. No one was really telling Charles anything and, like a dark cloud, the prevailing question hovered: were Leeds intending to sell him? English football followers and observers hoped not, for the sake of the professional game and for the spirits of the British people.

In the second week of April 1957, when the presence in the Charles home front room of local and national press reporters – drinking the family's tea and coffee and eating their biscuits – seemed almost constant, progress was at last taking place. By the third week, and as if begrudgingly emerging from a veil of self-denial, Sam Bolton announced the news: John Charles would be allowed to leave the club, but only for a fee they considered high enough. No one was going to get him on the cheap and your Arsenals and Manchester Uniteds and Sunderlands and Sheffield Wednesdays and Chelseas and bloody Cardiffs could all take a running jump. They were not going to get him at all, not at any price. Yes, Charles would be sold, but only to an overseas club.

Three Italian clubs were known to be pursuing the signature of John Charles: Juventus of Turin, Internazionale ('Inter') of Milan and Lazio of Rome. Most worryingly for Umberto Agnelli, however, was the rumoured interest in the player from Spain's Real Madrid, current European Cup holders. Thanks in large part to the help of Franco's ruthless Fascist rule, Madrid were Europe's, perhaps the world's, most famous club and even wealthier than the Fiat-backed Juventus. They were supposedly ready to offer Charles the personal sum of £30,000 to sign, an astonishing amount of money when players' wages in England were less than £1,800 per annum.

Agnelli was on his way to Leeds as quickly as he could manage. Jesse Carver, restored as coach of Lazio, was already in the city and had submitted a bid of £45,000 for Charles. Leeds United chairman Sam Bolton scoffed at the offer; it wouldn't even be enough to buy Charles's boots! £50,000 was met with similar derision as 'sheer bunkum'. A great deal of money for one outstanding player yes, but John Charles was *two* outstanding players in one, a superb defender and superb striker. Lazio would not go higher; Carver's journey and hopes had been in vain. Meanwhile, Madrid's rumoured interest had been exactly that, just a rumour, as the Spanish club already possessed the maximum quota of foreign players their league allowed. And so just Inter and Juventus remained and a bidding war looking inevitable. An auction might at least ease a little the sense of loss felt by Bolton and Charles's numerous fans, except Inter then declared their unwillingness to participate in any kind of contest. They graciously withdrew their interest, much to the pleasure of Juventus and much to the displeasure of the Leeds board, who considered there to be nothing gracious at all about the decision.

Leeds United's season would culminate with three league matches to be played in the space of just four days: on Good Friday, Saturday 20th April and finally Easter Monday. To add to the peculiarity of the situation, two of the three games were against the same team. Much as he loved playing football, at this stage of a season Charles's joints and muscles were less enthusiastic about the two hundred and seventy minutes of hard exertion within four days. As it was, forty-two league games per season was a burden too many, a mad scramble as he called it, so three games in four days was plain stupid. Everyone knew it but no one ever did much, if anything, to change it. No wonder, because Bank Holiday games almost always attracted bumper crowds, which signified bumper pay-days for the notorious slave drivers of modern football, the club directors, while the men who *made* the game – the players – barely benefited. The dogs over the road in the Greyhound Stadium were treated better than that.

In efforts to elude the English press, with *Cluedo* surreptitiousness, the Italian entourage of Umberto Agnelli, Gigi Peronace and Gaetano Bolla, general manager of Fiat's British operations, drove up from the Claridge's hotel in London – in a Fiat of course – to meet their Leeds counterparts of Sam Bolton, United manager Raich Carter and director Percy Woodward, at a clandestine location in the south of Leeds. That location was the John Waddington factory based in the district of Hunslet.

To ensure he was aware of how the transfer negotiations were progressing, *if* they were progressing in reality, John Charles gratefully enjoyed the counsel of two very distinguished friends: Edward 'Teddy' Sommerfield and Kenneth Wolstenholme. During the early 1950s, as Charles rose in prominence, the pair had been good people to know. Sommerfield was a 'showbiz' agent and Wolstenholme one of the best-known and wisest sports commentators in the business. The duo arrived from London by train and were met at Leeds' main railway station by staff of the Queens Hotel, practically adjacent to the arrivals platform. Only a few people noticed them or actually knew who they were, and one of the hotel porters convinced himself that due to his dark hair and tanned skin, Sommerfield was an Italian member of Juventus's personnel. Later on waiters in the hotel, they themselves Italian, were similarly mistaken.

Wolstenholme and Sommerfield were swiftly led to room 222, where John Charles was already waiting. There, they would sit patiently until the clubs' representatives arrived, talking Charles through details of the anticipated transfer package at the same time. This would be achieved by way of regular telephone contact with Sommerfield's office in London, which provided information on such matters as the cost of living in Italy and the football players' wages, too. And all the while outside the hotel, reporters and the public of Leeds waited, like the statues of City Square, mesmerised.

The Leeds and Juventus representatives arrived at the hotel in the evening and reconvened the transfer talks in room 233, across the corridor from where the Charles triumvirate were present. Charles introduced Teddy Sommerfield as his personal manager and returned to 222. Eventually, he was summoned back to the meeting, and a further two hours' negotiations continued, primarily to listen to what personal terms Umberto Agnelli's Juventus were offering. The only serious snag would be if Juventus were relegated from Serie A to Serie B – a distinct possibility – as clubs in the Italian second tier were not allowed to sign foreign players. For Charles that actually wouldn't be a snag at all; it would be the end of the matter completely because he intended only playing in the top division of whichever country he was to end up in. If worse came to worst and Juventus did drop a division, they would at least still be able to loan him out to one of the Serie A clubs, had they bought him. But that was not something Charles was overly bothered about; he just wanted to play top-class football for whoever was paying the 'thick money' for him to do it, and Leeds United wanted a thick money transfer fee for him too, of course. Therefore, Juventus's hopes of loaning their Swedish great Kurt Hamrin to them as part of the deal were dashed. English rules would not allow such an arrangement anyway.

John Charles believed Agnelli and Peronace's assurances about life in Turin and at Juventus. He liked the stylishly attired Agnelli, who seemed a real gentleman, friendly and yet almost in awe of Charles because of his skills as a footballer. This wasn't quite like his experience of English directors, who generally let underlings know in no uncertain terms who was in charge and who had the wealth. He hadn't been an angelic child by any means, but life was quite simple with Charles: you treat people with respect and how you want them to treat you. Someone thinking they were better than anyone else because they were richer wasn't someone he wanted to know. Charles had always got on reasonably with Sam Bolton and now he actually felt pity for him. He saw hurt and resentment in the chairman's eyes and he sensed that the chairman was trying to conceal his upset at having to let Leeds' prize asset go. This wasn't really an easy situation for anyone but Bolton seemed to be really suffering, as if he felt he was somehow to blame for the 'fire sale' and that he was letting the club and the supporters down, even the country. He suspected he was being taken advantage of, losing a game of poker to a richer, big-headed cardsharp.

Charles was tired, he was hungry and he wanted to see his wife and children, even though the two boys would long be in bed. He was still a Leeds United employee and he had his playing duties to fulfil, starting with Good Friday afternoon's match at Sunderland. No time to relax. And so, satisfied that the Juventus offer was a genuine and good one, Teddy Sommerfield having explained the harder-to-fathom details of the contract for him, and satisfied that no one was being deceived or swindled, Charles provisionally signed for Juventus F.C. Provisionally ... Despite the agreement in principle, there was still a fair degree of convincing required, with various legal details needing to be finalised, and there was the matter of the Juventus team preserving their Serie A status as well. Plus he wanted to make absolutely sure the accommodation being offered, the playing terms and the city of Turin itself were all 'up to scratch'.

John even had to acquaint himself with the rules and regulations not only of Juventus Football Club but also those of the Italian Football Federation. The rules were strict and clubs were strict in enforcing them too; they had to be as the Italian Football Federation were known to be tough disciplinarians and quick to fine teams substantially. Any Juventus player not learning the rules – in effect, their duties as an employee – and then contravening them would not be able to use ignorance as an excuse. They would be punished and that was that.

Even if the stay was anticipated to be no longer than two years – he and Peggy were agreed that the main part of the children's schooling should take place in England – they were anxious to ensure the Italian accommodation was an improvement on their current home, the large and very attractive red-brick 'triangle' of Lynwood, and that really would take some doing.

He found out later that the Queens Hotel room 233 talks continued until the early hours of Maundy Thursday, 18th April 1957. The first announcement that John Charles was leaving Leeds United and would be a Juventus player next season was made to the few press men who had waited the whole time for the record-breaking news. The next day, Agnelli returned to Turin, Charles departed for Sunderland and Sam Bolton went golfing, disconsolate.

Finished writing, he felt comforted, relieved, almost euphoric. Even the physical aches had relented a touch. He was now able to relax a little more, and with the soporific influence of the gentle sway and rhythmic percussion, clatter and click-clack of the train wheels, he felt like he was floating, the tension fading ...

In his short farewell interview, which Peronace telephoned through to the Leeds newspaper from London for him, he mentioned how anxious he was to leave Leeds on good terms with the people, commenting that although the move represented a great opportunity for him and his family, it was not without a tinge of genuine regret to be leaving Leeds, both the city and the football club. Ever since his boyhood days on the staff at Elland Road he had thoroughly enjoyed happy times in Yorkshire and had appreciated the support and the good will in the area. He promised to return on visits to Leeds to see his thousands of good friends, the piece finishing with a wish that he could take his grand team-mates and the 'Yelland' Road Roar along with him to Turin.

2

John Charles was six feet, two inches tall with a fighting weight dead on fourteen stones. He knew what his fighting weight was because the army told him so when he was fulfilling his National Service duties with the 12th Royal Lancers and being trained, amongst other things, to box. It was one of the corporals, who Charles secretly called 'Corporal Rat' – a small and lean individual, as mean as the plague – who had ordered him to take up boxing. Charles really *coulda been a contender* too, for he was a fine heavyweight, victorious in every one of his nine bouts, four of them by knockout. Away from marching, cleaning armoured vehicles, making his bed, ironing his uniform, spit-polishing his boots and not having enough to eat, the army taught him a variety of useful things to set him in good stead for a life in sport, primarily pugilism. Always barked at him by the corporals, *Keep your guard up. Bounce! Balance! Be on your toes, never flat-footed. You're the target and a moving target is harder to hit. Hit, don't get hit! Rhythm and readiness – block, slip, duck. Bob and weave. Power, speed, precision ... strike!* He was told how to position his feet and his shoulders correctly for maximum effect, and how to use his centre of gravity for strongest impact.

Surprisingly, Charles's army life was at times disorganised and haphazard. On one occasion, after playing for the army football team, the players were being transported back to the barracks in Carlisle. Freezing fog made road conditions difficult and visibility poor for the driver. Their vehicle collided with another single-decker bus. Charles woke up in hospital, concussed, with a deep cut to the nose and a wound above his right eye. The doctor decreed he ought to have a few days' rest. Two days on, his boxing instructors had him back sparring and in full physical training.

In addition to the uncaring nature of instructors like Corporal Rat, another big problem in his fight career was ... Charles hated boxing. He had hated it right back to when he was a ten-year-old

Swansea schoolboy. Violence repulsed him; he hated inflicting pain on anyone and he hated being struck. He was convinced that anyone who enjoyed pain – supplying it or receiving it – was not right in the head. His pacifistic attitude bewildered his superiors, but he knew what he knew and felt what he felt. No matter how puzzled or lost in life he seemed, he wasn't a simpleton; his reading and writing capabilities needed to improve, but not his capacity for compassion. Helped by his mate Bob Mitchell, who would assist in John's correspondence with Peggy White back in Leeds, Charles's literacy was improving, but he refused to learn how to be callous. As the Charles boys grew into manhood, their father had never tired of telling them to always *play* football and not to rely on strength or aggression, 'The player who gets the goal by brute force is not a true player.'

During Charles's training schedule for his tenth official fight, the army received instruction from 'High Command' in London that he was not allowed to box any more as he was already a professional in another sport. The army had already seriously contravened the boxing association's rules.

The journey ahead still held much uncertainty and the route was undefined. The Charleses' future was still reliant on Juventus's next few match results. The negotiations, however, were complete, leaving the footballing fates to decide his immediate destiny.

They were not a secret, the contractual terms Umberto Agnelli's Juventus had promised Charles, especially when three knowledgeable English journalists were travelling on the same flights as him. The Agnelli generosity was renowned – generosity in victory – with Juventus footballers receiving lucrative bonuses and expensive gifts when impressive wins were accrued. Such extravagant gestures had not been earned very often in recent seasons. If he joined the Italians, Charles would receive a £10,000 signing-on fee paid in instalments at over £400 per month over a two-year contract. His basic pay would be £16 a week with bonuses of £40 for away wins and £28 for home wins, plus those unofficial extras when 'big' wins were achieved. On learning of the £10,000 signing-on fee, a local businessman personally offered Charles the same amount to *stay*, so keen was he to see his favourite player carry on playing for his Leeds.

There remained significant doubt over the transfer to *La Vecchia Signora* (The Old Lady) of Turin, Juventus being involved in a battle against relegation from Serie A to Serie B. The relegation battle was far from over. If it occurred, the drop would be humiliating and a disaster. Juventus weren't the only big club involved in the dogfight, but they were the only one prepared to pay a record fee for a new player for the next season. The finish of the present one was a few weeks away, and two teams would go down. Each team had five games left to play. Of the eighteen in the division, twelve were involved in the skirmish to avoid demotion. The Juventus team strategies for the campaign, implemented by the coach Sandro Puppo, had been based around technically sound but nonetheless inexperienced young players, resulting in inconsistent team displays and insufficient points accumulated. As the season went on, the players were disparaged as 'Puppo's weak puppets'. The coach was eventually sacked and the club duly mocked even more, with one newspaper even depicting *La Vecchia Signora* as a prostitute struggling to tout her wares on the streets of Turin. Puppo was replaced by Teobaldo ('Baldo') Depetrini, temporarily promoted from his role as youth coach.

The scheduled flight from London to Milan was already fully booked, so Charles needed to travel by a longer route: London Heathrow to Rome's Ciampino Airport and then the internal flight to Turin's Caselle Airport. Still in his dark blue Leeds United blazer and shirt with tie, still fatigued and uncomfortable, at least he wouldn't be lonely. In addition to his 'valet', there were three English journalists seated nearby to report on the progress of the biggest British football story of the year, perhaps of the century. They were the *Daily Mail*'s Roy Peskett, the British Broadcasting Corporation's John Camkin and Terence Elliott of the *Daily Express*. No strangers to sports intrigue and excitement, they were no strangers either to alcohol and tobacco, alcohol especially, like most press men. The flight to Rome would not be particularly monotonous. The fact that Roy Peskett, a portly, friendly man, had been born with a disabled arm made his capacity to write and drink at the same time even more impressive. And what capability he may have 'lacked' due to such a handicap, he comfortably made up for in skills as a writer and raconteur. In some ways, to Charles, he was just like Gigi, and their physical builds were not so dissimilar either, though Gigi did at least have the look of someone not always a stranger to exercise.

It was Peskett who asked Peronace about his unfulfilled career in football ... why had he stopped playing? Pleasantly surprised that someone was taking an interest in him, Peronace was rarely ever shy in storytelling, even in his second language.

'I had a bad dream, and even though it was an unpleasant dream and I was asleep, it was an awakening, a revelation. I was amongst thousands of other men, I was in a very old street in Rome. It was narrow, cobbled and perilously overcrowded. It was like a stormy ocean, of people. Our reason for being there was football, but we were not playing it; there was not a football in sight. No, we were all searching for treasures – gold and silver coins and trophies and shields. But every time I saw an item of treasure it was too far away for me to reach; there were always taller, faster, better men blocking my way. When I woke up I immediately understood ... no matter how hard and faithfully I trained and worked, I would never be a champion footballer.'

'Hell of a dream that, Gigi,' said Charles.

'Hell is a good choice of word, John. I do not enjoy the memory but it led me to a different route in my life.'

Charles abstained from any stiff drinks on the Rome flight but did share a few smokes with Gigi and the sociable reporters (which for Camkin was actually a pipe). He smoked more frequently than the British public were aware of, but cigarettes were more about helping him relax than supplying any kind of fix. The cigs helped curb his enormous appetite too, especially helpful in between football seasons when his weight gain was anything up to half a stone, prompting heavy criticism from the Leeds coaching staff on his return to Elland Road pre-season training each time. Admittedly, tobacco probably wasn't a wholly harmless vice to succumb to, but smoking sure felt better than Major Buckley's legendary prescribing of monkey glands! Aside from that, Buckley was Charles's favourite among the bosses he had worked under, instantly commanding respect, and players really did have to call him 'Sir' or 'Major Buckley' or they would be in trouble. Buckley was forthright in all of his opinions, and if one of his players was having a bad game the manager would let them know about it very audibly indeed, along with instructions on how to rectify the situation. Afterwards he would put a paternal arm around the player and encourage him and tell him not to get disheartened. Buckley's influence on Charles had been major too, particularly his demand that his players be equally adept with either foot: 'Any player with one foot stronger than the other is only half a player.' Charles had only ever played as left-half before his Elland Road arrival, Buckley immediately tested him out at right-back. To Buckley, any football player unable to trap, shoot or pass a ball equally well with either foot wasn't going to be much use.

The flight to Rome was too early for him to be boozing anyway; he needed a clear head today. Charles knew he wasn't the cleverest chap around, but he also knew how to conduct himself in front of the public and the media. *Don't say or do anything controversial or disrespectful or outrageous. And never be drunk.* During the journey, the conversation with the journalists inevitably centred upon his immediate future. Charles appeared surprised at the depth of interest being shown in his career, on a national and *international* scale.

The BBC's Peskett educated him: 'Why do you think we are all here with you, John? You are not a mere item of news you know; for many people you are *the* news.'

Camkin interjected. 'He's right, and I'm confident in saying that if you wrote your autobiography right now, even at such a young age, it would sell thousands of copies.'

Elliott agreed. 'If you just wrote about the transfer saga, people would want to read about it. I'd wager that one of the newspapers would even consider serialising it.'

'All worth serious consideration, John; you would be paid well too,' Peskett added.

'I'm not too great at writing,' said Charles, his thoughts returning to the trials of writing that open letter to his supporters.

'Hardly an insurmountable obstacle, John! There are always alternatives, always paid writers out there to help,' advised Peskett. The conversation took the form of a collective interview with Charles.

Some of the questions were easy for him to answer, others a little more taxing. All would receive seconds of consideration before he replied. He enjoyed singing more than talking unless the chat was about football, and then his confidence rose. What he didn't realise was that most people loved to hear his voice, so mellifluous and tuneful as it was, the rich deep tones complemented by the warmth of his Swansea accent. His was a voice of music and of comfort. He didn't mind talking to these chaps, *with* them, because they were not just professional reporters. He trusted them and enjoyed their company, even if he was never at ease when the centre of attention.

He was given a brief history of Juventus Football Club by the journalists, as well as of Torino F.C., which had been the greatest club team Italy had seen until the Superga air disaster of 1949, which took thirty-one lives and ripped the heart of the club apart. He was also told how the two teams shared intense but respectful rivalry. He was also told how the Juventus team had deteriorated in recent years from being one of the best top division clubs to becoming one of the worst, and how Englishman John Savage, who played for the club at the turn of the century, had obtained a Notts County kit from an English referee called Harry Goodley, from Nottingham, to replace Juventus's existing pink one. The 'new' shirts bore black and white stripes and led to Juventus becoming known in Italy as the 'Bianco-neri', the white-blacks. The contrasting stripes could be seen as an indication of the contradictory nature of the club's owners, the Agnelli family. Camkin, formerly of the Royal Air Force, enjoyed telling Charles of how Gianni Agnelli, Umberto's elder brother, had initially fought for Mussolini during the last war. Mussolini had risen to power in ruthless fashion but had gained popularity by fighting the Sicilian Mafia. Charles had not heard of the Mafia, or *Mafioso*, before. Camkin explained that the Fascists were probably more corrupt than the Mafia but at least they had supposedly made the trains run on time, a rarity in itself. Meanwhile, the family's Fiat company – founded by their grandfather Giovanni Agnelli – had practically saved the country from economic ruin, but, fabulously successful industrialists as they were, philanthropists they most certainly were not, the company earning notoriety for low pay and allowing employees to work in shocking conditions, living close to starvation levels during terrible food shortages around the First World War. Talk of politics and, to a lesser extent, war, had a depressive effect on John Charles and so he was relieved, for once, when the topic of conversation returned to himself.

'John, do you like flying? You must have done plenty of it.'

'I probably prefer travelling by road – there's more leg-room. Aeroplanes always seem to be cramped. Ferries are good, when the sea's calm.'

'Will you miss Leeds?'

'Yes, I'll miss it a lot, the people mostly. But I will be back, I'm not leaving forever, you know. Me and the wife are planning to come back while the boys, and the baby, are still young, as we feel it would be best for them to get their education in England.'

'Is Peggy looking forward to moving to Turin? If it happens.'

'She's still pregnant but excited at the same time. Neither of us really know what to expect, but Gigi has tried putting us in the picture.'

'What do you know about the Juventus players or any at other Italian clubs?'

'I've heard of a couple of their players, like Boniperti and Hamrin, and Gigi has told me that Juventus is a wonderful club to play for. Everything is better in Turin John, he always says. Everything used to be better in Rome as well, when he was trying to get me to join Lazio. I've heard of other players like the Argentine, Schiaffino, who plays for one of the Milan teams, and I've played against Ernst Ocwirk a couple of times for Wales. He was fabulous: it's no wonder his nickname is Clockwork – he was everywhere on the pitch. It's a shame that Austria play the game real roughneck; they kicked us all over the park. Ocwirk reminds me a bit of Duncan Edwards. There's going to be no stopping Duncan, I only wish he was Welsh ...'

'Have you ever heard Duncan speak? He almost sounds like a foreigner half the time!' quipped Camkin, and they all laughed politely. Edwards was from the town of Dudley in the West Midlands of England, where the people spoke with a very distinctive and at times difficult-to-understand accent.

'Would you have preferred to go to Real Madrid instead of Juventus?'

'I won't be going to Juventus remember, if they get relegated. But no, deep down I think it was always going to be Italy. I have met

Gigi and Signor Agnelli and other Juventus men, and I can't complain about anything they have said or done. I haven't spoken to anyone from Madrid, so it wouldn't be right me talking about them. It was exciting to hear they were interested but Juventus have been a great force, equally, in Italy, and I hope I can help them return to form and to winning things again. I just want to play football and test myself more.'

'How important is the increase in wages to you?'

'It isn't that much money, you know, but it is an increase and that's what matters. Leeds said they had to sell me as long as they got a fair price, so this is one of those everyone wins situations. I really hope the people in England understand my reasons for looking for the thick money; I'm not a greedy person, I'm just a normal lad from Swansea who's had to work for everything he's ever had. The maximum wage means clubs can't pay players any more money. To me that's not right. I don't understand why the players of a team that is doing well don't deserve better pay for their efforts. The crowds get bigger because of them, and the gate money rises at the same time. Who gets all that money? I'm twenty-six in December – this career isn't a long one. I have a family to support and Peggy is expecting our third baby. When an offer of more money and bonuses and other things comes in, I can't afford to ignore it. And like I say, Leeds need to sell me anyway.'

'Do you envisage any problems in playing for your country while you're playing in the Italian league?'

'Playing for my country is a great honour for me, the greatest, and Signor Agnelli promised me that he will let me play whenever possible, as long as it doesn't interfere with the Juventus club. He told me that Juventus is his priority and that it will have to be mine, but he does not want to cause me any problems. Juventus will be paying my wages so that's their right. I respect that but I'm determined to help Wales qualify for the World Cup finals next year.'

'You mentioned roughnecks before ... are you aware that such players are a prominent feature of the Italian league, especially as they play a much more tactically defensive game?'

'Signor Agnelli did ask me how I react when defenders try kicking me, and that I should give it back. He looked at me like I was stupid or kidding him on when I told him that I don't do anything, because kicking them back would just be sinking to their level. That's not what I'm about. I enjoy playing the game and helping the team; I don't enjoy violence.'

'I'm sure that Eddie Firmani could tell you, there are some real brutes in the Italian game. There is a certain degree of slyness in Italian footballers which British players don't normally possess.'

'There's more "slyness" in the English league than you might think. Early in my career I took a beating off a few strikers, like the blond fellow Dave Hickson at Everton. He wasn't sly, he was just a bully and I was only a kid. Our Jack Marsden saw him off though, good and proper, but that's another tale. The roughnecks are in the minority but they exist, plenty of them. Trying to crack your ribs or break your tibia and fibula bones by going over the ball in tackles. Or they put all their weight through the ball to do the same sort of damage. They're cowards and they're usually the first to go squealing to referees when they get the physical stuff back. Fair physical stuff, I mean. Even if it's worse in Italy, I can look after myself.'

'The goalkeepers are protected more in the Italian game; getting physical with them is greatly frowned upon.'

'Yes, I think it's the same everywhere on the Continent. It's why the Austrians started laying in to us; a couple of the Wales lads shoulder-charged their goalie.'

'Do you know the history of the Agnellis and their position as Italy's unofficial royal family?'

'No, not much really. I know they own Fiat and employ a great number of people, hundreds of thousands.'

'Well, a drastically edited history for you then: Umberto Agnelli took control of Juventus from his brother Gianni. Gianni was wounded in the war but then joined the Americans when Mussolini's number was up. Italy, and the Turin area was one of the worst to suffer, was bombed by both the Allies *and* Hitler's lot. After the war, the Fiat company was investigated for working with the Nazis, but they had had no choice so no charges were brought. Italy is not a unified country and the Agnellis are not universally loved. Turin was frequently hit badly in the war, but the country had a fairly strong Resistance movement, partisans against the Fascists and the Nazis, and the fight was strongest in the Piedmontese area around Turin. The north is wealthier than the south, which naturally creates more resentment, and northern people often see southerners as lazy and over-privileged. And the lack of unification in Italy means that, for example, Milanese people feel more Milanese than Italian, while many in the north feel they have closer ties with Switzerland and France than they do with other parts of Italy. It's a very mixed-up country.'

Charles nods even though he has forgotten much of what he has just been told.

'The average Italian dislikes politics intensely; football is much more important to them. Italian politics is inextricably linked to the last war and its causes. Mussolini, the pig, brought carnage and chaos to their country, and the Fascists persecuted people just like the Nazis did. The Torinese have a strong sense of independence about them, not entirely unlike northerners in England, John. Turin itself is heavily industrialised, not dissimilar to Leeds, but don't let that deceive you, it has much beauty and appeal ...'

'So does Leeds ...'

'True, I'm sure.'

◎

Any neutral observers in the vicinity of Rome's Ciampino Airport on that sunny Tuesday afternoon, witnessing the crowds of people waiting to greet John Charles, could have been excused for thinking Juventus were based in the Italian capital and not in Turin. The vociferous cheers from scores of the Roman public as Charles emerged from the BOAC aircraft proved how popular he was, audible even over the customary din of a busy airport and a just-landed aeroplane. And this in spite of the fact that in reality the Italian people knew very little about him.

The three journalists left Charles and Peronace to it. Charles trod carefully down the steps of the craft to the ground, relieved to feel terra firma beneath his feet again. Dazzled by sunlight and surprised by so many people waiting for him, he smiled a modest smile. Warm weather and a warm welcome, a fine start to his Italian adventure. A gathering of Italian reporters and photographers were waiting for him inside. Flashbulbs and questions burst towards him. The journey had been long and he had enjoyed precious little quality sleep. Maybe, thought Charles, this was just what it was like in Rome and Turin would be calmer, quieter, more *normal*. He acted politely and respectfully but nonetheless was grateful for the airport officials' assistance in guiding him through the physical and the bureaucratic procedures of airport *Arrivi*.

Also present in the metropolis of Rome was the Northern Ireland football squad, due to play Italy in a World Cup qualifying game at the Olympic Stadium the following day. As the Irishmen were based in the Hotel Continentale in the city, along with the three wise media men, Charles paid them a visit for a few enjoyable hours before catching the flight northwards for Turin. He knew certain players well and had probably played against them all during his career, for Leeds or for Wales. And he had often played in the same side as wing-half Wilbur Cush, his Leeds United team-mate. Gigi Peronace insisted on buying drinks for all the footballers, spending a small fortune in the process.

Anyone present at Turin's Caselle Airport that evening to welcome a simple sportsman could have been excused for thinking they were in the wrong place entirely and in fact witnessing the arrival of a living saint, Saint John Charles. Indeed, amongst the numerous black-and-white flags and placards emblazoned with encouraging messages, one banner read *Ecco il nostro salvatore!* (Here comes our saviour!). It was thirty minutes past ten when the Convair aircraft of Alitalia touched down on Turin's runway. Waiting in a private lounge room of the airport was Umberto Agnelli and a cheerful-looking, bespectacled man with black, receding hair, Walter Mandelli. Mandelli, the managing director of Juventus and close associate of the Agnelli family, was marginally older than the not-yet-twenty-three Umberto Agnelli, but his glasses and attire added years to him. Charles knew nothing about him; he seemed to be a pleasant enough fellow. In fact, Mandelli was a significant part of the Juventus framework, currently nursing a slightly bruised reputation due to his influential recommendation of Sandro Puppo's suitability as team coach.

In the public access areas were Italian journalists and photographers, and hundreds and hundreds of Juventus Football Club followers. Rome had been a pleasant reception but this was something else, something even more special, and again, all dazzling. He immediately felt he was amongst friends, that he could not go wrong with so many people supporting him, believing in him, relying on him. As he arrived in the airport terminal building, one of the first of many, translated, questions from the enthusiastic, persistent reporters was: how did he feel to be in Turin with so many admirers here?

He thought for a few seconds, smiled and then replied, in English, 'I will do my best to live up to the fame and praise.'

The answer was received with nods and smiles, but was soon history, followed by a plethora of new equally as urgent questions. There and then, Charles ascertained that Italian reporters, compared to British ones, were a different and frantic breed, buzzing buzzing buzzing.

For the duration of this stay in Turin, Charles was booked in at the beautiful Albergo Principi di Piemonte – 'principal hotel of the Piedmont region' – in the centre of the city. It was one of Turin's plushest accommodations, considered by the more refined majority as its best, a similarity with the Queens Hotel of Leeds. Because the street, Via Gobetti, was dark, the Principi seemed to glow golden and inviting. On the building's front cornice, free-standing three-foot-high capital letters in golden aluminium indicated proudly that the Albergo Principi was welcome, for Very Important People. The hotel seemed much smaller and narrower than the Queens when viewed from the outside, though the night possibly added to the aura. Inside told a different tale, almost an optical illusion. The classic floor of white marble with streaks of black running through it; bright, colourful paintings in golden frames on the walls; three-seater leather settees, similarly elegant armchairs and stylish glass-topped coffee tables. Glints and flashes of gold from various lamps and light fittings, and signage catching, distracting the eye. As soon as he had parted from Gigi and walked through the double doors of the hotel, opened by a liveried doorman, he felt again most welcome. That sensation, however, could not defeat the sudden sensation of loneliness.

A major purpose of his visit was to look at the Turin accommodation available for he and Peggy to live in, if and when the arrangement became permanent. His original task had been to choose whichever property he considered would be best for them, but he soon lost faith in himself to make that choice. He had been shown around four homes, all of them possessing certain qualities that impressed him. All the locations were attractive, spacious, in pleasant surroundings, but, unable to quite remember what Peggy had stated were 'definites' or 'maybes' for their new home, he meekly surrendered the responsibility.

It belonged, he decided, in that mythical category of 'the woman's work'. He did recall that there ought not to be many steps or staircases to negotiate, for the sake of the safety of the kiddies and Peggy too. In defence of his indecision, the fatigue from his travels and activities of the last few days hindered his already fuzzy mind. And besides, Peggy would prefer it this way; she was the brains of the marriage and the boss at home, no doubt about that. If he made the wrong decision, there would be a rollicking with his name on it due, no doubt about that either.

3

In the Churwell area of south Leeds, a young woman stepped off the local tram. Carrying a scuffed brown leather shopping bag, she approached the entrance area and front door and porch of a smart detached house. Seeing the grandness of the property close up only added to her nervousness. A white wooden plaque on the brickwork with black letters spelling 'Lynwood' confirmed she had found the correct address. She knocked gently on the door with her left hand. A few seconds passed before the door opened slowly, the eight months' pregnant Peggy Charles responding and greeting the lady. The women were almost the same age, yet without being unkind, the visitor looked considerably older. She looked, thought Peggy, tired and too thin, as though she needed a good meal and a good sleep after it. The visitor was also called Peggy. Peggy McMillan.

Peggy McMillan made a good start to her informal interview: 'I've brought some scones,' she declared. 'I hope you have butter.'

Peggy Charles, as well as bearing the considerable weight of her unborn, managed to carry baby Melvyn in her arms as she showed Peggy McMillan around their home. The size of the residence was ample evidence – if any was necessary – of her need for assistance in coping due to the imminent further addition to the family.

They sat eating buttered scones and drinking tea in the living room, seated at each end of the very large floral-patterned and very comfortable three-seater settee, one-third of a recently purchased suite. Peggy Charles had mentioned that they had better eat some if not all of the scones before husband John returned home, as he would scoff the lot if he had the chance. He wasn't even above stealing food off the kids' plates, and yes that even included baby food! The women did eat most of the scones, Peggy McMillan notably less than Peggy Charles, however, due to complaining of a stomach-ache.

'You're not, erm … are you?' asked Peggy Charles.

Peggy McMillan smiled politely and shook her head. 'No, no chance of that.'

Two-and-a-half-year-old Terry sat happily enclosed in a playpen on the carpet, in a corner near the patio doors, ignoring his toys and building blocks as the supply of Farley's rusks was much more engrossing. Not yet one and a half, his brother Melvyn now lay asleep in a pale-blue wooden cot in the middle of the room. He had not been 'down' long but already seemed to know that any chance of a nap was a chance to be grabbed.

Peggy McMillan commented that she thought the boys were behaving like little angels and then said, 'It's a lovely house you have, Peggy.'

'Thanks, it's a lovely *big* house.'

'Well you still manage to keep it spotless.'

'Not really, I'm just good at hiding the dust. It's harder to do at the moment though.'

Peggy McMillan nodded; she was still quite shy, a facet of her character which she needed to improve if she was ever going to get anywhere in life. Looking out of the patio windows, regardless of the typically grey April day outside, she praised the lovely view the room had, overlooking vast green fields stretching in a steady incline across to the Leeds 10 district, known as Middleton.

Peggy Charles responded, 'You can't see it from here but I know it's there, my mam and dad's house on Middleton Park Grove. Where I grew up, with Jeanne my sister, one year older.'

'That's nice, knowing your family's not far away.'

'And my brother Michael, I nearly forgot him. Seventeen years younger, can you believe it? Yes I suppose it is, I've never really thought about it. That's silly, I'm lying again, I think about it lots of the time.' She paused, as if silently reproaching herself ... 'Have you heard the reports we're probably moving again?'

'Because your husband is a football player with Leeds?'

'That's right. And if he does get sold then it will be to a foreign club, almost definitely one in Italy. That makes him sound like he's an object for sale in Marks & Spencer's.'

'That all sounds exciting.'

'Yes it does, doesn't it? But you know, if you got the job, you'd have to come with us …'

'God, I never thought about that!'

'Well,' Peggy Charles laughed, 'you had better start thinking about it and soon.' Peggy McMillan nodded.

'And we'd have to call you by your Sunday name, as two Peggys will cause confusion, and it doesn't take much in our house!'

Today, John Charles felt rested and well-fed, revitalised. The aches and impact pains of three bouts of football combat and uncomfortable journeys had subsided, eased by a gloriously long, hot bath in his hotel room. He had been treated so kindly and so well that he'd begun to suspect Gigi might not have been exaggerating so much after all: maybe the smoke and the rain really would be better here too. While being led to his fifth-floor suite the previous night, he had been able to smell the cleanliness and the freshness ten yards away from the door. The suite consisted of two large rooms and the bathroom, with parquet flooring of mahogany throughout, small, pretty herringbone rectangles of rusty brown. A spacious walk-in wardrobe was also all mahogany, and from there Charles had immediately put on the very comfortable white slippers provided by the hotel. The suite's bathroom was immense! Within, a large oval-shaped bath sat opposite two sink basins with faucets and plugs of gold. Mirrors on each wall, including a full-length one facing the door, nearly twenty feet away. The walls were grey marble with black and white threads running through them, silver heated towel rails and small piles of white towels at the end of the bath. Past the bath was a large shower cubicle – more like a room than a cubicle – with a frosted-glass door. Opposite the shower was a bidet and a lavatory … A strange and unfamiliar arrangement thought Charles, and not the best idea of personal privacy either. The lounge room possessed an antique but sturdy desk, on it a blotting pad and table lamp and telephone. Also there were two armchairs and a settee that did not look particularly comfortable, as well as a chest of drawers and lampstand. The bedroom consisted of two king-size beds side by side, and an identical desk together with the same paraphernalia on top.

Charles sat alone unnoticed in the restaurant area of the hotel, at a small square table in a room full of identical ones. Half a dozen or so other hotel guests sat eating; all were male, all ate alone and each wore a suit. No one was speaking. Charles disliked dining on his own, his misgivings being intensified due to his being on foreign shores with next to no knowledge of the lingo or Italian customs. But then, at last, a waitress wearing a black skirt and white blouse walked to his table.

'Coffee, sir?' He nodded and smiled shyly. The waitress, probably in her thirties, her tied-back hair adding a misleading look of officiousness, immediately softened with a smile, gestured towards a line of tables placed against the back wall, laden with white plates, glass jugs of orange juice and bowls of fruit, plus a set of four bronze-coloured containers which he'd learn were called bain-maries. She did not know the English for 'serve yourself', nor did she need to; he understood the message alright.

Mildly scalding his fingers as he opened the lid of one of the four bain-maries, the sight of a container full of scrambled eggs was pleasing. His preference was fried eggs, but this was more than acceptable. He ladled a sizeable amount on to his plate and moved to the next container. Ah – not such a satisfying sight this time: he suspected it was *meant* to be bacon, but any Italian idea of rashers was miles away from the English one. Instead there were slivers of insipid, wafer-thin ham. But at least it was meat and at least it was warm. The next bain-marie was also disappointing, though on a lesser scale; in it he found a tray of thumb-sized sausages in some kind of watery gravy with peas. On to his plate they went, regardless. The final receptacle of hot food confused him. It looked to be full of leaves, purpley black leaves. Spooning a mound out brought elasticated strands of white cheese with it too. These Italians are bloody odd, he decided, and then he noticed a small card on the tablecloth, with '*Spinaci*' written on it. Anything that was good enough for Popeye was good enough for John Charles. He found it surprisingly appetising.

His first meeting with his prospective new colleagues was to be at Juventus Football Club's training ground in Santa Rita, a district in the south of the city. The 'ubiquitous' Gigi Peronace drove him there, in a Fiat of course, a suitably new and flashy red Trasformabile. The roof of the convertible was up; Peronace did not want to attract *too* much attention to himself or his passenger. Or breathe in too much of the traffic fumes, for that matter. Their car stood out, a rare blaze of colour amidst a pale spectrum of vehicle and building exterior hues. The short journey through the centre of the city held more surprises. Coming from Swansea in the south of Wales, he was well acquainted with eye-catching, attention-demanding mountains, hills and valleys, but here in Turin the Alps felt higher and more imposing, more spectacular. They seemed to surround the city, like a huge band of grey, white-tipped clouds monopolising the horizon. He would also learn, today, that the Alps were not the only mountains in that area of Italy; that the Apennines were to the south of the city and stretched for miles. A range of hills to the east was visible too, called the Monferrato. Both were new names to him.

The supposed centre of the city appeared larger than Leeds' too, much more spread out and with wider streets and pavements, with picturesque squares ('piazzas') and arcades and colonnades (another new word for Charles, referring to the columns and pillars just about everywhere) and greenery and old, fine-looking buildings. The city centre in Leeds was a specific place, a specific location with landmarks to denote the fact. Maybe Turin was a different thing, maybe it was a city *without* a centre, with its important buildings and institutions situated across the metropolis rather than in one central area. Or maybe he was thinking too much with an already tired mind! Even though the structures and the sights passed in a blur, Charles noticed only a few houses, as if most of the population lived in blocks of flats. Arches, pillars, statues, shops, kiosks, cafés, restaurants, bars. And, just about wherever he looked, arcades. It all looked very grand yet unimposing.

Gigi interrupted his attention, 'John, you see all the covered arcades? I do not know for sure if it is true ... In Torino, in the rains, the arcades are as shelter for the wealthy people but poor people have to walk in the uncovered areas.'

Charles wasn't aware of places like this in Leeds, with the exception of the vast Quarry Hill flats, which looked to him like a massive fort from the future. Torinese buildings all had a stylishness to them that belittled many Leeds buildings, in both elegance and size. Even the building repair work taking place across the Turin terrain was easier on the eye than that back in Leeds. He assumed the repairs were connected to Second World War bombs, but he could just as easily be wrong. Charles thanked his chauffeur for the lift to the stadium, situated in the south of the city in the Santa Rita district, and recommended that he shave better next time as he was looking 'scruffy'. It seemed to Peronace, not unhappily, that he had gained a new role: that of Charles's favourite target for jest.

Today was a special day. Usually, for their training sessions, the Juventus players would change into their training strip in the locker room of the main stadium, the Comunale, and walk across the wide Via Philadelphia to the training ground known as Campo Combi. Not today, the routine was different today: they were going to be introduced to the world-famous player who had been making so much of the news. The existence of a Juventus training base was a surprise in itself to Charles. A separate football ground with better facilities to those of many established football league clubs in England, the Combi even possessed a grandstand with seating for over two thousand spectators. Peronace had explained that it had been renamed in honour of Gianpiero Combi, a former Juventus goalkeeper ('*portiere*') who had died the previous year and had won the World Cup with Italy in 1934 as well as league championships with Juventus in the 1920s and 30s. A very popular sportsman in Italy, he had been regarded as one of the best ever goalkeepers in world football, though Charles wasn't sure he had even heard of him.

While last night's response at the airport had amazed him, there were even more people inside the Comunale, now late morning. Normally, in England at least, people had responsibilities to take care of, work to go to, and children had school to attend, yet here was a crowd of a few thousand, including that ubiquitous and curious breed called the autograph hunter, the majority of them boys in short trousers. Kids had always ignored him in England, innocently, when he insisted there were other just as important players in the team whose autographs they should be collecting. It was obvious he had even less chance of getting the message across to Italian fans.

On the football pitch stood twenty to thirty men, most wearing suits, a few sporting sunglasses too, talking in clusters or taking photographs or being interviewed and photographed by reporters buzzing around, as was their wont. There was even a film crew, preparing to start 'rolling'. In the background, youth players in dark shorts and white tops casually kicked a football around, a row of sentinel cypress trees outside the stadium, overlooking the pitch. Charles spotted Umberto Agnelli in conversation with a medium-height, fair-haired man. At twenty-two years old, Agnelli was actually younger than most of the men there, which probably explained why he was socially more at ease with the players and could be more 'one of the boys' than his elder brother, Gianni. Charles recognised the man he was speaking with as Giampiero Boniperti, well known across European football, a forward who had played for the Italy national side and was the current captain of Juventus. A very good player indeed. His light-coloured, perfectly groomed hair, a dimple in the strong, prominent chin, and a high sense of pride and self-confidence about him, reminded Charles straight away of the actor Kirk Douglas. Another dapper man, similar age to Charles and at six foot tall only a couple of inches less in height, brought to mind – even more – another Hollywood star, Robert Taylor. And to think that Peggy had often said her husband resembled the young film star Marlon Brando ... *This* matinee idol he had just shaken hands with was in fact midfield player Umberto Colombo, a cheerful, sociable man. So similar to the actor was he that Charles near expected to hear him speak with an American accent. During introductions Agnelli confirmed that Colombo was the only Juventus player able to speak any English, therefore he and Charles were practically paired off from the outset. Colombo's English-language skills were elementary but a damned sight better than Charles's Italian ones.

There were too many new faces and characters for him to get suitably acquainted with at such an early stage, but the facial features of certain other Juventus footballers immediately sparked comparisons in his mind. The player Emoli, for instance, was quite short but certainly looked like he could take care of himself, as if he enjoyed fighting. Maybe he'd been a boxer, one of those 'squat' ones with a nose that looked like it had endured a few too many punches. It would be much later before Charles learned that Emoli had a strange heart condition: when physically active, his heart seemed perfectly normal, but when at rest he would sometimes complain of chest pains. Baldo Depetrini was also there. Charles likened him to a boxer too, due to his bumpy nose, but he seemed a pleasant chap nonetheless.

A moment of confusion followed for Charles; he scratched his temple though there was no itch. A Juventus football shirt was handed to Giampiero Boniperti, who was now presenting it to him. Boniperti held the shirt up to drape it across the chest of the Welshman. For a couple of uncomfortable seconds, Charles believed he was being asked to take his jacket and shirt and tie off to model the striped jersey.

Besides that moment of consternation, the overriding thing he noticed was that everyone there, either on the football pitch or in the stand or congregated behind the fencing close to the pitch, appeared delighted to see him, all of them so friendly and genuine. Even a few officious-looking men, too old and too heavy to be sportsmen, seemed pleased to meet him. No doubt they were enjoying being near the limelight, enjoying sharing praise and goodwill brought on by such an occasion despite contributing nothing of significance towards it. Some things never changed in football, whichever country. The same, in a positive sense thankfully, for the presence of lively, shrill schoolboys asking him for his autograph. A different language used but the same priceless treasure being sought: his signature in their little books. He had never really understood the fuss with autograph hunting, but neither had he resented being asked. Much better to have admirers than enemies, whatever age. Fences at the front of the terraces *was* something new compared to Britain. Not that Italian football fans were known to be violent or any more aggressive than British ones; just that they were said to be more emotional and expressive. Plus the referees in Italian *calcio* could and often did cause more controversy than their British counterparts.

Later, five or so miles away from the stadium, the Molinette Hospital became the venue for Charles's medical examination. The *caveat emptor* – buyer beware – meant that Juventus were responsible for checking on the condition and suitability of the 'item' they planned on purchasing. In professional football failed medicals meant failed transfer deals. Buying an injured footballer or at least one not 100 per cent physically fit was tantamount to buying a three-legged racehorse. Charles had paid little heed to the prospect of the medical until this point. And so now he began to worry. For, during his two years' National

Service, he had needed two operations, one on each knee, to repair damaged cartilage tissue. That was probably a hazard of being quite an all-round sportsman, though 'all-round' certainly did not apply to golf – he was pretty rubbish at that. The problematic knees were from playing too much football, boxing and basketball, and cricket in the summers. He played for Leeds United during his time in the army in the north-east of England, in addition to playing matches for the army team as well, along with Leeds team-mate Grenville Hair and Tommy Taylor of Manchester United. Charles had played at least two 'full on' ninety-minute matches every week the whole year round – severe tests of his stamina and durability. So … had the cartilage scars healed sufficiently? Or had the knees been weakened by surgery?

The examinations were coordinated by Professor Amilcare Borsotti. First, X-ray scans were taken, the images then scrutinised and re-scrutinised by different doctors. Charles was then examined by an orthopaedic expert with specific emphasis placed on testing the strength and flexibility of the knees and ligaments. He would be examined by a heart specialist also. He underwent a number of strenuous exercises for the knees, plus the lifting of weights numerous times, and then more weights, followed by long-distance treadmill running while an electrocardiograph machine measured his heart rate and activity. The numerous physical exertions were straightforward, mundane, painless, but the mental tension was high; he had been under great strain, and during the running he even began to imagine significant aches in his knees. The tests took more than two hours to complete. It felt even longer.

He ought not to have worried: Professor Borsotti and his colleagues announced that, in their many years of experience, they had never seen anyone in better physical condition than John Charles. The only thing that could now prevent him from joining the Juventus team next season was the form of the Juventus team of *this* season.

The arrival of John Charles had boosted the spirits of everyone in the Juventus camp, especially the players, who had taken the opportunity to watch him in training on the Friday, two days before the crucial match versus Napoli. He had trained with the reserves rather than the first-team squad, simply because, it was supposed, his presence could have been a distraction from the first team's plans for Sunday's tie. This explained why he did not travel with the team to their usual pre-match destination, the 'mountain hideaway' in Villar Perosa. Immediately after training on Fridays, the Juventus team would be transported to Villar Perosa to spend two nights there before every game, home or away. Charles did not realise that were he to sign for the club, he would be forced to spend a minimum of two nights away from Peggy and the kids, every single week of the season.

Everyone had read and heard how good he was meant to be; now they finally had the opportunity to see the physical proof at close range. The pace, the power, the balance, the courage, the majesty. As a consequence, the players were relishing *next* season now, confident that with Charles in their team, they would actually win trophies rather than fight against demotion. Certain members of the press had apparently concluded that because he trained with the second-teamers, he was being made to feel unwelcome. And combine that with rumours that first-teamers – led by the captain Boniperti – had ignored him, it all indicated he was being forced out before even officially allowed in. These would not be the last lies printed about him. When Gigi Peronace advised him of the claims, Charles was dismayed – probably the reaction the news inventors wanted. Peronace assured him that only a small minority of journalists and newspapers were professional liars and gutter rats, but warned that he probably should expect more similar treatment.

On the matter of professionalism, Charles was pleased to find that in Italy, with Juventus Football Club at least, the football boots they equipped him with were lighter compared to his trusty pair back in Leeds. More importantly, and pleasingly, so were the footballs, and their lacing was smaller and better concealed. This would mean much less likelihood of damage to his forehead. Peggy had lost count of the number of times he had returned home from Leeds games with bruises and cuts to his forehead that sometimes gave him a Frankenstein's Monster appearance.

The training gear in general was superior to that at Elland Road too, plus it was actually cleaned more than just once a week. At Elland Road after training, the Leeds players would throw their kit on the floor in the middle of the changing room. No matter how filthy, stinking and wet it was, the pile usually stayed there ready for use in the next training session. He discovered also that in the Juventus changing rooms were individual showers and each player had his own locker to place their personal possessions in. They were issued with lightweight clogs and a luxurious white bath robe too.

There had been a knock on his room door on the morning of Saturday 27th April 1957. Charles had still been in bed. By the time he had reached the door, the knocking had stopped but a small envelope addressed to him had been slipped under. He stooped to pick it up, and as he did so the room telephone began buzzing. The man calling him was the hotel manager, Italian but speaking perfect English. He had been very happy to inform Charles that the hotel had been contacted from England with the news that Peggy had given birth to a baby boy last night, and that mother and son were in fine health. John Charles, football's giant, wept tears of relief and joy.

Thousands of miles away back in West Yorkshire though, Peggy was in great shape but not in great spirits. As well as the weather being cool, grey and damp, she was being cared for in a cold nursing home where the staff were proficient but not particularly friendly. Close to the estate of Howley Hall in Morley, the building was a bleak and foreboding one with few home comforts and little warmth. She detested the place, so different to Mount Carmel in Armley where the nuns staying there were lovely and helpful on her two previous visits when giving birth to Terry and later Melvyn.

The Stadio Comunale was the venue for the team's home matches, including today's against Napoli on Sunday 28th April 1957. There is something rather demoralising and depressing for sportsmen to see their home stadium nowhere near full to its limit. A beautiful smile tainted by missing teeth. For much of the season, one that had started in September 1956, the Juventus side had hugely disappointed their supporters (the '*tifosi*'), their woeful campaign causing attendances to fall way below the stadium's 75,000 capacity. Today, however, Sunday 28th April, an important football match was about to take place and an important figure about to be introduced to the crowd, then paraded around the pitch like a prized racehorse.

He had rarely appeared in front of a crowd of this size before, even when representing his country. He had never appeared in front of a crowd with the vast majority applauding and cheering *him*, calling his name, albeit the Italian version.

'Gi-o-va-nni, Gi-o-va-nni!'

So many striped black-and-white Juventus flags and banners. Having to wave or salute the noisy crowd for the duration of the unofficial procession made his arms ache by the end. His mouth ached a little too, from all the smiling due to such an amazing welcome from thousands upon thousands of new friends. His eyes shone with joy, eyelids pinkened by the moisture, and his skin felt cold despite the day's warmth. He was close to being overwhelmed. It was difficult to absorb the occasion. He couldn't quite comprehend all this noise, all this enthusiasm towards him, but he felt privileged to be the subject of it all.

'Because they love you, Big John!' explained Peronace, close to shouting.

'They don't even know me!'

'This is what it will always be like, when you are successful.'

'What if I'm not?'

'Then I dare not tell you.'

'Jesus Christ, I'd better play well then.'

'Yes. And you will, I know you will.'

If Juventus managed to beat Napoli then they would almost certainly be safe from relegation, thanks in part to the Serie A fixture list having determined that most of the teams below them were due to play each other in the coming weeks. Whoever won this would be able to sleep easier. Charles was known in England to be a casual or light smoker, a man who hardly ever smoked cigarettes in public. On this day, in Turin, within the Comunale Stadium of Juventus, he was exposed by the Italian press as something of a fraud. Judging by the slowly growing pile of burnt ends at his feet where he sat watching the match, he was a man who smoked much more frequently than his reputation suggested.

Cigarettes were a relaxant for him, and any spectator with as much riding on the game as Charles had was probably in need of something to help him do just that. Without doubt the welfare of his wife and new baby boy was prominent in his mind too, though he knew they would be taken good care of. The football match, on the other hand, was much less predictable.

A torturously close affair ensued between two teams desperate not to lose. He was puzzled at the sight of the referee and the two linesmen, wearing black jackets and a white collared shirt each above the normal black shorts and socks. They looked like fussy, forgetful bank clerks. Charles, not the centre of attraction at last, was able to sit alone for most of the afternoon as just a spectator left in relative peace, the seats in the directors' enclosure not all occupied. He was a proud and thrilled young man, a father for the third time, and if Juventus won today then he would be even happier.

In what reporters described as 'The Match of Salvation', the decisive moment of the game came two minutes from full time, with the Swedish attacker Kurt Hamrin striking the single goal from close range. Hamrin was a gifted, pacey international, but had that season often been targeted by ruthless opponents. He'd had to watch too many of the Juventus games from the stands, injured. He would become another victim, of sorts, again in the not too distant future. After the match, John Charles felt rather like a spare part, a party gate-crasher who barely knew any of the guests. Standing in the humid dressing room, smiling, trying to demonstrate team spirit and camaraderie while avoiding eye contact and longer-than-comfortable gazes as players showered and dressed, was all a mildly embarrassing situation.

In the nursing home on that Sunday night, a telegram arrived from Turin, purportedly from John and possibly one of the shortest messages ever sent: 'Congratulations on birth of baby son'. It could hardly fill her with happiness, and she just knew the humourless staff there would be regarding her husband as being as uncaring and ignorant as most men.

While she was sure the majority of men could not genuinely appreciate the pain and stress women endured during labour and childbirth – together with the many weeks of post-partum – her husband certainly was not uncaring or ignorant; just a bit too laid back at times.

◎

Early in June 1957, in the polished, gleaming, immaculate reception area of the Hotel Principi di Piemonte, his luxurious home for just a few but still too many nights, Charles knew he had seen the face before but he couldn't quite put the name to it. Younger than himself, smaller and lighter (most people were. in comparison), the man had a darker complexion than his own. With acutely muscular thighs and slim frame, he had entered the hotel with a swagger and an expression of supreme confidence that could be perceived by some as arrogance. He surely was a footballer. The mass of black hair on his head created a rascallish look too, at the same time providing a slightly distorted impression of his head being out of proportion to his body. He was casually dressed, a pale-blue long-sleeved shirt, with unbuttoned collar, cream-coloured trousers and shiny brown leather shoes. Beside those leather-shoe-clad feet stood a small, brown and pristine leather suitcase on the marble floor. Accompanying him were Umberto Agnelli and Walter Mandelli. At the reception area stood Gigi Peronace, in conversation with a blonde hotel employee across the counter. The three Juventus officials wore impressive suits, Agnelli's the lightest shade and, of course, the smartest; though he could wear a postal sack and still look stylish. Mandelli happily made the introductions. 'John, to meet Omar Sivori; you will be team-mates for the Bianco-neri. From Argentina, and he too is a magnificent player.'

'And you should be grateful to him, John,' interjected the undoubtedly proud Agnelli, 'as *he* was even more expensive than you. And perhaps there will be more to come,' making a promise to no one in particular. In fact, Sivori had cost much more money than Charles, the transfer fee being equivalent to 91,000 pounds in sterling.

Charles and Sivori shared a firm handshake and interchanged embarrassed smiles. Charles's greeting of 'Hello, pleased to meet you' was met with the simple 'Hola, John' from Sivori. Neither man could speak more than a few words of Italian, but even now they each sensed the beginning of a success story: both were fluent in the language of attacking football.

Sivori had been displayed to the Juventus public in similar fashion to Charles's own introduction, on the Comunale pitch. However, in a cameo that would be regarded as ultra-typical of the South American, Sivori went some way further than Charles had. In spite of his wearing a smart suit, shirt, tie and leather shoes, Sivori insisted on juggling a football (with his left foot only) to entertain the welcoming and delighted crowd of spectators. Not with deliberate disrespect, the Italian press termed South American players as angels with dirty faces, due more to their 'spiritedness' on the pitch than their physical appearance. Argentine players were said to be highly skilled footballers, highly temperamental too. Sivori's new team-mates would learn that he was indeed a gifted performer as well as at times being cheeky and antagonistic towards opponents; they would also see that he would defend passionately any team-mate in times of aggression. Described, in complimentary terms, due to his speed and trickery, as being 'like the wind', it also applied to his being deceptive, unreliable and difficult to control.

4.

Many, many miles and so much time spent in transit, each specific stay never long enough for relaxation but too bland to keep his mind active. The next journey always too soon, he wished he could eliminate the travelling and be able to just concentrate on playing football and on seeing his wife and family and new baby, Peter. At least he was not alone – Gigi would be accompanying him, as he often did, on the thousands of miles of uncomfortable air journeys, road journeys, rail journeys or sea journeys. This dutifulness earned Peronace a variety of supposedly humorous descriptions: Charles's wet nurse, mobile butler, secretary, valet.

From Turin to Rome. From Rome to London. From London to Leeds. And finally, from Leeds to Cardiff. All within two days. On the Wednesday night he would be playing for Wales versus Czechoslovakia in a World Cup qualifier match.

For the Rome to London flight, Peronace purchased a few early Monday morning Italian newspapers. Any articles or snippets he considered of interest to Charles, sitting next to him (almost *over* him), prompted a gentle elbow nudge before Gigi related in English whatever interesting piece he had found. Other than his thoughts, Charles had nothing to really occupy his time. He smoked a few cigarettes, drank a couple of coffees served to him and generally made do with gazing out of the window. Peronace felt it his duty to keep his companion and 'client' entertained, even when Charles would have preferred to be left in peace. Today, Peronace was struggling. Not even the domestic match reports and football gossip could attract Charles's attention for more than a few seconds. Here was a rare thing: Gigi Peronace feeling inadequate, as if he were letting Charles down, until he noticed an article that he was confident would cause a reaction.

He began to relate an article claiming Juventus and Umberto Agnelli had granted Charles permission to play for Wales against Czechoslovakia in two days' time. At first, John looked puzzled, then slightly annoyed.

'What are they talking about? It's not up to them. They can't stop me playing.'

'It seems certain reporters are confused by the current situation, John.'

'It doesn't give them the right to make things up. The Wales selectors are a pain in the arse already, I don't need them putting this at my door as well.'

Agreeing with him, because Peronace *knew* Italian reporters, he could only nod in sympathy. No point in adding fuel to the fire. So, in an effort to lighten the mood, he began translating aloud another article.

'The legs of the famous footballer John Charles deserve to be insured for at least the same amount as the shapely curves of actress Betty Grable, and Juventus has asked the Welsh Federation to insure Charles for the sum of approximately one hundred and five million lira. Should the Welsh Federation refuse, it is likely that Charles will be forbidden to play for the English national team in future.'

'You've got to be joking?'

'No, no John, this is the correct translation, this is what it says.'

"*English* national team? The lads will slaughter me with this!"

◎

Ninian Park football ground, Cardiff, the evening of the first of May 1957. '*Hen Wlad Fy Nhadau*' ('Land Of My Fathers'), nation of the Daffodil, the Leek, the principal stadium of Wales overflowing, almost all of the people Welsh. The Red Dragon ('*Y Ddraig Goch*') and the flag of Wales, the glorious, legendary flag of Wales, its colours and its historic symbolism. The white, the green, the red. The white, of peace and honesty. The green, of hope, joy and love. The red, of hardiness, strength and valour. Perhaps too, white stood for the wintry peaks of Welsh mountains, the green for the valleys and hills and fields, the red for the blood of ancestors. And for John Charles, the white might represent the White Rose of Yorkshire, the red the shirts of Welsh sportsmen, the green the playing surfaces. Tonight his country's national anthem fills the evening air, a massed choir of powerful voices singing along, their bodies brimming with pride. If any native failed to be inspired by such music, it was possible they weren't actually conscious.

Although the match was a close affair, the Wales team didn't disappoint either, winning by one goal to nil over Czechoslovakia's eleven. Two points gained in the three-team table. Because the manager Jimmy Murphy considered him the best centre-half in the world, John Charles played alongside younger brother Mel in defence. The Wales players stood strong throughout, perhaps not individually as skilful as the Czechs but too resolute for them nonetheless. The visitors had been quick and graceful on the ball, but were unable to pierce the Welsh defences. And apart from a low shot from outside the penalty area which brushed the Welsh goalpost, John Charles had a relatively untroubled game.

◎

The Leeds United men travelled by ferry from Hull to Rotterdam. Thankfully the waters were calm all the way, meaning seasickness stayed away. Officially it was a football team tour, unofficially it was a short holiday for the players after a hard season. John Charles was embarrassed because that bloody Harold Williams had 'got' him again. As the Leeds players had re-grouped in one of the on-board bar areas, Harold had asked John to go and seek out the captain to ask him about the ferry's recreational facilities. John did as he was asked and went to find the captain, returning a few minutes later, red-faced and irritated. Irritated by Williams, to be exact.

'If you weren't Welsh, Williams, you'd be in the sea now!'

'Why, what's up, John?' came the straight-faced, attempted innocent response.

'I found the captain and I asked him what you told me to ask him.'

'Right?'

'He said, "No young man, I cannot tell you where the billiards table is because we do not have such a thing on board this ship."'

'Ah well, thanks for asking,' said Williams, only slightly smirking. 'You little bastard!' said Charles, grinning, while most around him guffawed.

A perimeter of trees surrounds a vast cemetery, the sound of leaves wafted by gentle breezes helping to enhance the serenity. There, amidst row upon row of white headstones belonging to the dead of war, fifteen men stand united in sorrow and respect. Heads bowed, they silently pay homage to the heroic victims laid to rest in the Arnhem Oosterbeek War Cemetery, a depressing reminder – as if one was ever needed – of the destruction brought on by the Second World War. The congregation of Leeds United players and coaching personnel look on as John Charles places a beautiful wreath of yellow and blue tulips against the humbling, towering white Cross of Sacrifice. It will be one of his final acts as captain of the football club.

The team had taken time away from a four-match tour of Holland to visit the graves of Allied soldiers, as well as the nearby landmark and battleground of Arnhem Bridge. The solemnity of the occasion added to the mixed emotions Charles already felt, knowing that he would be bidding farewell to his pals and team-mates all too soon. Being part of a team full of loyal friends and colleagues who would never stop fighting for the team's cause, and thus for you, was one of the best things on earth. The news had reached him of Juventus winning again, six goals to four against Palermo, and so it was 100 per cent certain he would be playing in Italy next season. He'd already presented goodbye gifts of a gold wrist watch to his closest friends in the team – Jimmy Dunn, Grenville Hair, Eric Kerfoot and Bob Forrest, and to two of his early mentors, chief trainer Bob Roxburgh and assistant trainer Willis Edwards. He would never forget how those friends and colleagues had made him a better football player, a better person too.

And still the ache of his absence from home had to continue; wife Peggy had their new baby Peter to look after in addition to the two bairns already, the nearly-three-year-old Terry and the one-and-a-quarter-year-old Melvyn. The assistance of Nanny Margaret was invaluable, undoubtedly, but for the baby and his brothers; father was *needed*. This absence was a frustrating state of affairs. John Charles didn't need reminding of his paternal responsibilities, but of course there was nothing he could do about it. He was travelling yet again, this time to join his Wales team-mates behind the 'Iron Curtain', just one day after his last Leeds friendly, which had been a draw with PSV Eindhoven and in which, fittingly, he had scored United's goal. Via Amsterdam and Frankfurt flights, and accompanied, of course, by

Peronace and his ever-darkening chin, Charles joined the Wales squad in Leipzig, East Germany, at the grand (in size only) Hotel Astoria where they were booked to stay for a little longer than a week. It was an old-fashioned hotel possessing scant welcome or comfort, drab accommodation set in the centre of the bleak surrounds of Leipzig city, a Second World War victim of Allied bombing and the subsequent severe Soviet Union rule. Despite sharing the same aeroplane as the players, the Welsh Football Association representatives *naturally* had things easier in Leipzig than the footballers: better grade of accommodation, better service, better transport, better expenses. Manager Jimmy Murphy often had to accompany those selectors rather than the playing squad. He disliked the arrangement but had to abide by it. They paid his wages after all, low as they were. Working also in domestic club football as assistant manager to Matt Busby at Manchester United, he knew and valued the meaning of family spirit within a football club, regardless of what level the club existed at.

Alas, he saw no such unity or camaraderie between the players and the 'suits'.

The Wales party would be away from home in Eastern Europe for nearly a fortnight, the team having two matches to contest – in East Germany and then in Czechoslovakia. In their so-called wisdom, the selectors had decreed that the sum total of thirteen players would be a sufficient number for the games. The players were not happy and, unsurprisingly, neither was Murphy. The selectors were showing their cluelessness concerning the tough physical demands of competitive football. *And* they were demonstrating gross disrespect for the players and staff too. And to add to the thirteen players' bewilderment, there were *ten* selectors accompanying them for the duration.

Although the occasion was the 'new nation' of East Germany's first ever official competitive match – thus leading to suggestions that the team was somehow inferior to Wales – they were unbeaten in friendly matches for over two years. And friendly matches were usually anything but friendly; rather they were keenly contested affairs. This match was a sell-out, with attendance in excess of 110,000 spectators. It was claimed that demands for tickets had actually been five times as many. This was all perhaps basic propaganda invented by the Russian authorities, to show the world everything was peaceful and civilised in the new nation under their rule. Regardless, it promised to be an intimidating atmosphere for the Wales team, especially with masses of uniformed soldiers in the crowd. John Charles was chosen to play in central defence again, but Mel would be up front in attack. John was assigned to mark the centre-forward Willi Troger, famous not only for his pace and scoring prowess but also because he only had one hand, having lost his right one in a grenade explosion during the Second World War.

Mel Charles's selection in the Welsh attack appeared to be a sound decision as he scored the first goal of the match after just six minutes. However, that was as good as it got, as the East Germans swarmed all over Wales to strike back and eventually win the match two goals to one. In truth, their efforts warranted a wider margin of victory; Wales had played poorly, as if all the pride shown at Cardiff against the Czechs at the beginning of the month had inexplicably dissipated. Prior to the match kick-off, John Charles, as captain, had been delegated to exchange bouquets of flowers with his opposing number as a sporting gesture between the two nations. However, as the Wales team trooped out of their dressing room – incidentally around a quarter of a mile walk away from the football pitch, the stadium was so large – a Leipzig official mistakenly gave the bouquet to Mel, thinking he was John. Though grateful for the gift, Mel had no idea what he was meant to do with the flowers and so, when the teams had taken to the pitch and the match officials and team captains were exchanging handshakes and performing the pre-kick-off procedures and the like, he ran across to a section of the terraces and threw the flowers out into the grateful crowd. A diplomatic incident was avoided and excused as a simple mistake, but John was embarrassed and furious with his brother.

Much less amusing – in addition to the Welsh display – was the post-match news that some of their players had suffered injuries. In the following days, a couple more became ill too, the number of fit players available for the next game being reduced to just ten. The selectors were forced to call up a few reserve players from Britain to travel out especially for the Czechoslovakia tie. Woeful management on their part, grossly dissatisfactory preparation. The report reaching Charles, of Juventus winning again, this time three goals to two away at Roma, wasn't much consolation for him; his spirit of patriotism was wounded and he needed a boost. They all did.

On the morning of Thursday 23rd May 1957, the Wales entourage flew the short flight from Leipzig to Prague, Czechoslovakia. They flew on an old Dakota plane converted from military use to commercial passenger transportation. The flight felt longer for a couple of the players due to their seatbelts falling apart, their consternation added to by a rough landing on a crumbling airstrip which had been over-used and under-maintained.

Prague, Sunday 26th May, Czechoslovakia versus Wales. John Charles was chosen to play as centre-forward with Mel reverting back to central defence. Given a lacklustre display from the visitors, the Czechs had little difficulty in avenging the defeat in Cardiff with a sound and straightforward 2-0 victory. It could easily have been a higher score, so inferior was the Welsh resistance. Only Jack Kelsey in goal and the younger Charles in defence played moderately well. The rest of the team, including John Charles who received no ammunition to attack, had been even direr as a unit than in Leipzig. Wales were in disarray, on and off the field of play their dreams of competing in the World Cup finals now almost certainly being dead. The following day, the players, and the officials – all together but in essence very much apart – returned to Cardiff. Gigi Peronace travelled alone back to Turin with more Juventus duties beckoning. Once the Wales-bound aeroplane had touched down, Charles would make his way out of the country and northwards through England to Leeds to meet up with Peggy and his family of now three sons. His absence during Peter's birth had been on his mind. A constant self-criticism that he should have been *there*.

◎

Neither Peggy nor Nanny Margaret had ever been on an aeroplane before. Margaret had never even been near an airport, and it was patently clear to Peggy she was far from keen on the idea of flying. She herself wasn't particularly relishing the prospect, but she was putting on a brave front, unlike Margaret who had complained again of stomach-ache and of feeling faint. Flying wasn't humanly natural and it wasn't good for the nerves – that much both women were agreed on – which explained why Peggy had absolutely no intention of ever flying without her husband being next to her. He had no choice in the matter: if he wanted his wife and their children to live with them in Italy then he had to accompany them on the aeroplane to get there. On the flight, the Charles entourage consisted of John, Peggy, Terry, baby Peter and Nanny Margaret. Middle son Melvyn was to stay in Leeds with Peggy's parents for a few weeks so that his mam could settle more easily in their new Italian surroundings. He was too young to be unsettled about the arrangement, and as long as his Leeds grandparents kept him well-fed and entertained then he would be no trouble for anyone. With luck, Peggy's brother Michael would help look after Melvyn too. 'No trouble' was a perfect description for Peter's current behaviour too. Indeed, he was less than no trouble if that were possible: throughout the flight from Leeds to London, plus the flight from London to Turin, he slept either in his carry-cot or when being held, as if nothing on earth, or indeed above it, could disturb him. It remained to be seen if his night sleeping would be affected; up until now he had been near angelic, right through from around 10 p.m. to past dawn. As for Margaret, even the gentlest turbulence in the skies appeared to add to the turbulence in her tummy. She had a paper bag at the ready the whole time, refusing steadfastly to even look towards a window.

Peggy was also nervous – the roar of the unnatural beast's take-off adding to her anxiety. She noticed the mildly discomfiting sensation of how flight seemed to numb all her senses. The constant rush of the engines filled her ears, causing her to make herself frequently yawn or gulp to 'pop' the weird audio blockage. And the enclosed cabin being dimly lit meant her vision felt weaker and her eyes drier, while her nostrils felt arid too. The whole interior of the aircraft felt synthetic and sterile, though holding her husband's hand was a human comfort at least. Even her sense of taste seemed affected.

After half an hour in the air, however, she had begun to settle. From being frightening it was now exhilarating, fascinating. She began to enjoy the flight and had become an avid cloud and sky watcher. At various junctures, as the skyscape transformed into yet another incredible new world, she would nudge her husband and say in hushed awe, 'We're so high up we're above the clouds; they look just like a wool quilt cover at home – it's like a land of snow', or, 'Look at the clouds John; they look like the beach when the tide's out.' She would comment on weird and incredible herringbone-patterned cloud structures and cotton-wool creations and explosions as far as her eyes could see, the dazzlingly white *surface* and azure horizon leaving imprints on her vision.

And when she had remarked that it was all like a new and fantastic world, John had replied, 'You always make me feel like I'm floating in the sky, Peggy.'

Again she was quite incredulous: had she *really* heard her husband say something so romantic? She looked at him wide-eyed. Alas, he shot the excitement down: 'I heard one of the Wales lads say it to an air stewardess he fancied.'

'Oh you, you spoiled it! Who was it then, that rascal Harold again?' John smiled. 'No ... he's not like that. I forget who said it. Harold will have been too busy thinking of how to make me look stupid again.'

'Really, is he that bad?'

'Yes, he's like an itch, Peg.'

'Harmless then.'

'Course.'

'Good, I think he's funny.'

'He can be. He got me good and proper with the ferry, but I never believed him about pinball machines and indoor bowls on aeroplanes. He tried that on me the first time we were on a flight together.'

Peggy chuckled. 'I probably would have believed him!'

For the majority of the flight duration, John took pleasure in holding Peter in his arms. The soothing vibrations of the voice reverberating through his daddy's muscular chest seemed to assist Peter's quest for sleep. Dad was constantly ready with the feeding bottle too, if the need arose. As well as being a good sleeper, the newcomer appeared to have a similar trait to his father and two elder brothers: that of a voracious appetite. It would not be a great surprise for him to go through six or seven bottles of formula a day. In the seat between John and Peggy sat the carry-cot. Behind them sat Margaret and Terry, the nanny having caused some embarrassment earlier by asking, a little too loudly, 'We're not flying over *Germany* are we?'

The parents were discussing their prospective new home, Peggy's secretarial skills to the fore, pen and notepad in hand.

'Address is Via Susa trentuno,' said John. 'In English – Via Susa thirty-one. They put the number after the street.'

'So you're sure I'll like it, absolutely sure?'

John nodded. 'It was the nicest apartment I saw. Or flat, I don't know what the difference is.'

'And it's big enough? Not just for us but for Margaret as well ...'

John nodded again, 'It's a quite big block of flats. Not huge like Quarry Hill but it looked to be easily big enough inside.'

'I suppose I'll be able to judge for myself.'

'You'll like it. I don't want to be in the hotel much longer.'

'You can't kid me John Charles, all that room service and waiters.'
'Can't relax there.'

'Can't steal food off other people's plates you mean.'

John laughed. 'And you and your dad won't be able to go knocking on people's doors here for the rent; it's not like Quarry Hill that way either.'

'Oh blast.'

'Via Susa thirty-one has four bedrooms, a bathroom, kitchen, dining room, living room ...'

'Any view of scenery?'

'Yes, it has windows.'

'Stop making fun of me; you know what I meant.'

'I don't remember, sorry love. It's in a posh part of Turin; I didn't take much notice of the views.'

'I hope it's not too posh.'

'It will be fine, Juventus are dead set on looking after us properly.'
'Good, I think we'll need that.'

'Hotel's posh.'

'Do you have to wear a tie for meals?'

'No, neither will you.'

'Room service?'

'I haven't used it. It doesn't feel right, people waiting on you hand and foot.'

'I'll remind you of that next time I'm cooking.'

'It's bad enough having people wait on you in the restaurant.'

'How's your Italian coming on?'

'I've tried but it's not easy. Umberto Colombo's been a big help; he speaks a bit of English.'

'Damn! I think I forgot to bring the Italian language book; it's at my mam's.'

'Get her to post it out to us.'

'Yes, I'll ask her. Is there a telephone at the hotel?'

'In the room?'

'Yes.'

'Yes. There isn't one at your mam and dad's though, Peg.'

She laughed at her own silliness. He grinned. Baby Peter stirred for a few seconds, perhaps wanting to contribute but then preferring a return to his slumber.

'It takes a couple of hours to get a connection anyway to England …' 'That long?'

'… which is why we sent you a telegram when Peter turned up.'

'Ah, we did wonder – I was nearly overwhelmed by your emotion.'

'I'm not good with words, you know that,' he said, embarrassed. He knew it was coming at some point though. 'And I didn't know what to do or how to reach you.'

'Just teasing, love. It raised a smile, we all thought "typical you". Was it Umberto Colombo who sent it then?'

'No, I was with Giampiero Boniperti, I wrote a few words down for him and he ordered the telegram. He thought I was joking when I said I hadn't sent word back. Umberto would have been out celebrating in Turin town.'

'Isn't it odd that they play their football on Sundays; everything's so quiet on Sundays back home?'

'Everything's different in Italy, Peg. Everything's better as well …'

'According to Gigi! He might be right, but I doubt it.'

'He gave me a copy of the rule book that every Juventus player has to abide by. Umberto translated some of it for me; they haven't printed an English version.'

'What does it say?'

'I don't know half of it … No drinking alcohol or dancing after Monday. And players can't go for a drive in the countryside or to the seaside without permission from the club. Even if a player has a special family occasion on, if the club tells you to go in then you go in.'

'It all sounds a bit strict.'

'Maybe it is; the club's just looking after their investments.'

◎

Exactly one month on from the arrival of the latest addition to the family, the Charles party arrived at John's temporary home of recent times, the Principi di Piemonte. Nanny Margaret, together with the boys, was to stay in an almost identical room adjacent to John and now Peggy's suite.

Two young and energetic porters, uniformly liveried in all-black, insisted on transporting their numerous suitcases up to the suite. Although their intentions were entirely honourable, it was in John Charles's blood and upbringing to disapprove of such assistance, even more so when foisted upon him. The bellboys could be very insistent, even when aware they would not be receiving any financial gratuities here; their customer had no cash in his possession (as usual). All day John had had his hands full, so to speak, trying to prevent Peggy from lifting anything of substantial weight. He did not want her to hurt or strain herself. Like most males on the planet, he had little idea of how long a woman's postpartum recovery ought to be – Peggy of course had educated him in the terminology – but he suspected just one month after the birth was still too soon to be lifting objects like luggage around. A new mother is also a formidable opponent, however, especially where carrying the new baby is concerned, and John was fighting a losing battle in that respect too.

'Have you seen the size of this bath?' Peggy exclaimed as soon as she had entered the room. And within the hour she had made full use of the hot water and the various scented soaps and bubbles on offer. Then she sat down to the task of writing to family back in England and Wales, having gathered a few postcards together from the hotel reception. The considerate staff promised they would frank and mail them for her too. One postcard bore a monochrome panoramic view of Turin; that one was intended for her parents. On it she wrote that they had arrived in Turin safe and sound in the afternoon, that it was warm weather, that Peter had not been a scrap of trouble at all so far, and that she hoped the same could be said for Melvyn back there in Leeds too. They would be looking at the flat very soon, moving in at the weekend if everything was okay, and probably choosing new furniture and the like as well.

Another postcard was written to Peggy's eight-year-old brother Michael, a photograph of Torino rather than Juventus Football Club's stadium (there were none available of Juventus's Comunale). She hoped he was helping to look after Melvyn and she told him that Terry had been asking for him, 'probably because he wants to fight you'. Her notepad of matters needing attention included arranging an appointment at the British Consulate to register and sign the necessary documentation to authorise their living in Italy. She wasn't sure which should come first, the consulate visit or the viewing of their new home. She *wanted* to get settled in to their new home as soon as was humanly possible, even though the Principi was lovely. She hoped John was right to approve of Via Susa 31. What he saw as suitable might well not necessarily correspond with her own interpretation of the word. He had never shown much taste in artistic matters, plus he could be really careless and gormless in his decision making with anything not connected to football.

They had yet to appreciate the view from their fifth-floor residence, a rather magnificent panorama of the city reaching out to the enormousness of the Alps. Picturesque, breathtaking, imposing. That picture was evolving, second by second. The lights in the bedroom, however, were on and the curtains partially drawn, and Peggy and John had been preoccupied; the dramatic scene outside had gone unnoticed. Two broad strokes of darkness: ominous clouds on high above the grey of the terrain and mountains, split by a narrow band of intense light, clear sky, causing a strange tricolour of nature. Swirls and twists in the air, a violent storm surely imminent, yet the sun would not be ignored, rays piercing the thick atmosphere, casting diagonal blurs of yellow across the scene.

They lay beside each other on one of the beds in their sumptuous, white bathrobes and slippers. They had been enjoying a rare few minutes of shared relaxation, no words necessary to show how much they'd missed each other. But then the telephone on the desk opposite, where Peggy had penned her postcards, began to ring. After a few seconds, as if only just coming to her senses, she sighed, rose from the bed and stepped across to the desk. With her right hand she lifted the receiver. Thankfully, the female caller, one of the hotel's switchboard operators, responded in English. Less thankfully, Peggy still had difficulty in understanding her message, something about a journalist wanting to speak with Mister Charles.

'I'm sorry,' said Peggy, 'he isn't available.' The operator thanked Peggy and then ended the call. Peggy stretched out on the bed, only for the telephone to begin ringing again almost as soon as her feet had left the lush carpet. She got back up and answered the call, telling a different switchboard operator that her husband was unavailable. Without fuss the operator ended the call. Within the next quarter of an hour, however, six more similar telephone calls came through to disturb what peace they were trying to enjoy. Peggy had remained reasonably calm, but by the sixth call, John had finally had enough. He demanded Peggy hand him the receiver. In English he instructed the operator to tell all journalists to refer their enquiries to the Juventus Football Club ... any interviews or meetings should be arranged only with the consent of the club. This was sensible, if slightly late, thinking on his part. He had heeded the advice of Umberto Colombo that most newspaper reporters were not to be entirely trusted and that the safest way of ensuring the truth was written, or at least that 'misquotes' were not written, was to be interviewed in person, one to one, *testa a testa*. Firmly but politely, Charles told the operator to relay the message to her colleagues: not to disturb them with any more telephone calls.

'That should do it,' he said, hopefully.

It didn't. Within the next hour came seven more telephone calls. These calls though, it transpired, were external connections. John answered each one, telling the caller, slowly in English, that they should contact Juventus to arrange any interviews with them. He assumed the calls were from newspaper or magazine reporters. It wasn't important to him, he wasn't interested in who they were or why they were calling, so each time he simply delivered his advice and put down the receiver. Finally, he took the receiver off the cradle and left it lying on the desk. Those callers were lucky he had not used language similar to the obscenities Mac had had to listen to when trying to get John out of bed on a morning.

5

The following morning they walked arm in arm along the pavement of Via Gobetti away from the Principi di Piemonte. A receptionist had helpfully plotted out the route to their destination, supposedly less than two miles on foot, on a map of the area. Peggy insisted she wanted to walk, a better way than in a taxi to discover a tad more of Turin, as well as good exercise to help her lose the 'baby weight'. Immediately it was obvious to them both that Turin was a pretty and pleasant place in which to walk. The heat of the morning sun felt just right, warm but not at all oppressive; she could get used to this. They had arranged to meet Gigi Peronace at ten-thirty. What with the commotion of the telephone calls the previous day, John had worried there would be a posse of reporters and photographers buzzing around and ready to swoop as soon as they set foot outside the hotel. Happily, he was completely wrong; in fact hardly a soul took any notice of them. A few knowing smiles and looks and nods yes, but nothing intrusive or to make them feel even the slightest uncomfortable.

Peggy was charmed by what she had experienced of Turin so far, the warm weather being just one small part of the good first impressions. The many arcades and pillars and statues. Leeds had a healthy smattering of attractive and old buildings and architecture, but here was practically brimming with visual delights, and unblemished by pollution, unlike some of Leeds' As they continued on to Via Susa and approached number 31, her glow of enchantment simply became stronger. Via Susa was a long thoroughfare possessing majestic, auspicious-looking buildings on both sides of the road.

Noticing yet more centuries-old buildings bearing scores more balconies, 'It's like something out of *Romeo and Juliet*,' she said again in wonderment, and her pleasure was heightened further still upon seeing number 31's own array of balconies and shuttered windows. All geometrically neat, small, enclosed by stone carved balustrades;

some containing bright-colour glimpses of flora and potted flowers, others merely swathed in leaves and greenery. To her they all looked beautiful.

Outside an arched entrance of the apartment block, Gigi Peronace was leaning against his car and smoking a cigarette. There are people who strive for that look of cool and sophistication. With another smart suit, expensive shirt, cufflinks and silk tie, braces too, Gigi was one of those. For some though, no matter how hard they try and how much money they spend in their quest, they never quite achieve it. Gigi was one of those people too. Fortunately he was generally spared ridicule concerning his physical appearance because he was a popular fellow. He looked at his expensive watch. Exactly thirty minutes past ten. Seeing the happy couple walking towards him – he knew *they* were cool, without their even trying to be – he flicked the butt into the gutter, casually, as he had done countless times before. 'Good morning, Mister and Missis Charles, welcome to your new home!'

'Morning, Gigi,' said John and Peggy simultaneously.

Using a key to open the large metal gates at the side of the building, Peronace led the couple to the door of the ground floor apartment. After thudding on the oak door a few times, with a strenuous twist of the handle and hefty nudge against the brass kickplate, he opened it. He then stepped back, gesturing for Peggy and John to go in before him. Inside, waiting for them, was the caretaker – he preferred the title 'concierge' – named Gianni.

They don't have these at Quarry Hill, joked Peggy to herself on first sight of the man. Gianni's sagging trousers and baggy shirt caused him to look older than his forty-two years. The light didn't help his appearance, or rather the lack of it didn't. She initially decided that the place needed more illumination. That impression would never really go away; the dim light made her feel ever so slightly gloomy too. Not that it prevented her from noticing the immaculate polished parquet flooring, the herringbone design of slim wooden rectangles, exactly like their hotel rooms, covering the entire interior. It was very appealing.

The kitchen of the property was through a doorway directly opposite the entrance. It contained a small free-standing gas cooker with a fume extractor hood installed above it. Inches below the hood was a narrow shelf holding condiments and the like, and behind the cooker was a square-shaped fireplace in the wall, no longer in use. A window overlooked the courtyard-cum-garden; Peggy peered out through it. She did not seem particularly impressed with the view. Next to the cooker was a washing machine with a circular door made of steel, and in the middle of the room there was a small dining table, complete with a cutlery drawer attached underneath and four wooden chairs keeping it company.

Gigi Peronace, considering himself surplus to requirements by now, planted himself on one, like a relieved man close to exhaustion urging the others to go on.

John Charles disagreed. 'No Gigi, we need you to translate what Gianni says.'

'Ah yes, I apologise.'

Gianni seemed to understand the conversation, nodding and nearly smiling. He then spoke to Gigi, in Italian, which Gigi then relayed to the Charles. 'There is a very good market nearby, for all your food needs.'

Each room of the apartment led from a passage running through the middle of the property. After the kitchen came the doorway to a long room divided into two, serving as the dining room and the lounge. A large rectangular table with a shiny wood surface was, Peggy presumed, where they would have their meals. At the far end was a huge and quite ugly television set mounted on a long pole in the middle of the room. A radiator, painted black and of a sleeker design than any they had seen in Britain, would struggle to heat a dog kennel, it looked so feeble. Next to it stood a wooden stool and a small table with a telephone on it.

There were three bedrooms, each a decent size, with a sufficient number of beds for the group, as well as a cot for the baby. Each had a large, wardrobe within it too; all were empty for the time being. The wardrobe in the 'master' bedroom was not a free-standing type but one affixed to the main wall. It was cavernous; Peggy had never seen one like it in a house before. The Charleses had little idea as yet that this wardrobe would become crammed with stylish and expensive garments, mainly suits for the man of the house, together with silk ties and hand-made shirts and shoes, most of them gifts from various Turin tailors connected with Juventus or wanting to gain stronger connection with them. And it would not be long before Peggy would be off out clothes shopping, and Gianni would grow increasingly annoyed – in truth, envious too – at all the mysterious deliveries to Via Susa 31 needing his attention. Meanwhile, the one bathroom contained a bath, a lavatory and, 'to bath the baby in', a bidet.

The guided tour was over and Gianni led them back to the entry door, where Gigi joined them. Outside the apartment, the caretaker locked the door and shook hands with each of the trio. Gigi promised he would contact him shortly. Once Gianni had departed, Gigi asked Peggy what she thought of the apartment.

Her reply took him somewhat by surprise …

'It's a good size, roomy enough for six of us, and the curtains and bedspreads are nice. But it's all a bit dark, Gigi, there aren't enough lights. And there aren't any carpets or rugs, not one! A bath mat doesn't count. Do you know how dangerous a polished floor is for toddlers? And there isn't much furniture; I thought you said it would be fully furnished? And the garden isn't really a garden, it's just a patch of land covered in gravel. We wanted somewhere where the boys can play football and run around …'

In all the time he had known her, Gigi Peronace decided, he had never heard Peggy Charles talk so much before. He actually was mistaken in that observation and, had Peggy known, she would gladly have put him right. He was a pleasant enough man, extremely pleasant in fact when being helped to serve his own purposes, but from their very first encounter Peggy had noticed there was no one in life as important to Gigi Peronace as John Charles. It had occurred a few times. Peggy had been talking with Peronace and, even when she had been in mid-sentence, Gigi's attention had diverted to her husband, leaving her talking to a wall or a ceiling or sparrows in the sky. Nothing else mattered to him other than John Charles, including her thoughts, words or even presence. Infuriatingly rude, yet John had claimed never to notice such poor manners.

She rounded off her remarks, noticing that Gigi seemed quite uncomfortable but not allowing him the opportunity to interject, 'But other than that, it all looks quite a nice place to live.'

Apologetically, Gigi assured them that he had taken note of their concerns and that he would get back to them as soon as possible, once he had spoken with Umberto Agnelli. And regarding any new furniture and sundries for the flat, he suggested that Peggy and John go searching in the Turin shops later on, and anything they saw that they wanted – what *Peggy* wanted – they should make a note of and confirm the details to him. Peggy told him that she had already made a decision about the furniture, and would he ask Umberto Agnelli if Juventus would be willing to pay for their lovely three-piece suite to be transported across to Italy from Leeds? Her dad worked on the railways and would quite easily be able to arrange cheap carriage.

By the time her parents set off for Turin, with Melvyn in their charge, a hefty list had formed, things for them to deliver in addition to the suite. Peggy requested a 'Speak Italian' book be brought, as well as – if there was such a thing – an Italian recipe book in English, and bottles of milk of magnesia (for the children), and if possible some custard powder, some mint and some packets of English bacon. And for the home she asked that her favourite rugs be brought over, and cushions and her Long Play records.

Though she was by nature a cheerful and relaxed person, this was a rare occasion when Peggy adopted a more sombre tone so as to ensure she was being taken seriously and listened to. Frankly, she – and John, though to a much lesser extent – were disappointed with the club: the situation was far from satisfactory. They had expected better. Gigi Peronace had understood her concerns loud and clear, and promised to improve matters. Peggy was quite relieved that he did not take any of the criticism personally, and she knew he was a man of his word. For now though, Gigi said, the Charleses had an appointment at the British Consulate to fulfil. The offices were within walking distance, but he insisted on taking them there; they did not *have* to walk everywhere after all.

While he drove, he advised them that the person they would be seeing was an Italian-English woman called Elsie McMillan, whose parents were from London but who herself was from Turin, born in the thirties. 'That's funny, Nanny Margaret's surname is McMillan as well,' said Peggy.

Gigi advised that Elsie would guide them through all the employment and immigration documentation needing their attention, as well as providing more general advice about life in Turin. Their car travelled parallel to the River Po. The midday sunshine complemented the picturesqueness of the green inclines and hillside villas across the river, the many statues and architectural delights seemed to increase in their import and relevance. Was this really the over-industrialised and grim city of Turin she had read so much about, and not some close relation to Paris or Athens? It would take a great effort to make such a setting an ugly one, though the city planners in Leeds seemed to have succeeded with the River Aire.

Gigi turned right and then left on to a street called Madama Cristina, consisting of large and important-looking buildings similar, considered Peggy, to the banks and offices in and around Park Row in Leeds. He parked the car, got out and walked around the front of the vehicle to the door of the back seat where Peggy sat. Always the gentleman, he opened the door for her to step out on to the pavement. Less than discreetly, however, he then thrust a wad of lira into her hand with the instruction that the couple should enjoy a meal or a few drinks together after their consulate meeting. Peggy protested, but he would not take no for an answer, as if planning for and knowing exactly how little Italian currency they presently possessed. Earlier in the month, back in Leeds, the Charleses' finances had been a subject of consternation for Peggy. John was owed money by Leeds United, but it appeared the administrative employees at the club had deleted him from the payroll. He had been away but had told Peggy to go to the stadium and collect his wage. It was a pleasant late-spring day and so she had walked to the stadium, wheeling Terry in his pram with her and leaving the other two with the nanny. When she reached the football ground offices, quite tired, she was sternly informed that there were no monies due to be paid. Regardless of whether or not it had been intended, Peggy felt disrespected and rather embarrassed by their stance, something she certainly did not need more of in her life.

They entered a square, compact anteroom with cream-coloured walls, lit by an attractive and yet incongruous crystal chandelier hanging from the ceiling. At the other side of a mahogany desk busy with documents and an unlit lamp sat Elsie McMillan, a petite, lively woman, similar in age to Peggy. Similar in demeanour to her too, in that all jobs were to be done as well as is possible. Above her, on the paperless wall, in a golden metal decorative frame, hung a print of Queen Elizabeth II, clad in coronation regalia. In the corner closest to her, a tall flagstaff, resplendent and proud, bearing a yellow-tasselled silk Union flag of bright red, white and blue.

'My husband Alec is a firm admirer of yours, Mister Charles, even though he's Scottish.'

John Charles smiled. Unsure what was the best response, he decided on a straightforward, 'Thank you.'

Peggy interjected, increasing her husband's embarrassment. 'He prefers to be called John. He thinks he's in trouble when someone calls him Mister!'

'Oh, okay then,' smiled Elsie. 'I prefer things to be informal too, but there aren't many times in consulate business when I'm able to ...' She stopped to look at some of the papers in front of her. 'May I ask, can either of you drive a car? The trams and buses in Turin are very efficient, but driving around by car is the best way, I find.'

'Ah well, that's a bit of a sore point with me,' answered Peggy, 'as I failed my driving test in England earlier this year. I think I was badly done to.'

'Yes?'

'I think so, yes,' said Peggy. John raised his eyebrows as if implying only Peggy really agreed. Fortunately for him, she did not notice. She continued, 'I was heavily pregnant at the time with Peter, and my tummy was touching the steering wheel. When I was doing the test I accidentally stalled the car. It was quite a jolt and it caused the examiner to bang his head on the windscreen.'

'And he failed you for that?'

'Yes. Well, that and because I was pregnant. He should have expected it.' Elsie smiled. 'It was you expecting though, not the examiner.'

Peggy laughed, even John quite appreciated the joke.

'Would you like me to help you arrange a driving test here in Italy? I believe they are supposed to be easier than the English one.'

'Yes please, Elsie.'

'Would you like some help with a refresher lesson, as it were? I drive a Fiat Six Hundred, just like so many people here. You'll need to acquaint yourself with driving on the wrong side of the road; that will be interesting for you!'

Peggy nodded enthusiastically.

'Good, allow me to make arrangements once we have you all settled in; it would be my pleasure,' Elsie said.

'Thank you, I'd like to do it as soon as we can.'

'This region is like Yorkshire in some ways: there is a large amount of industry, which seems to be all that anyone notices, yet there is so much natural beauty to see.'

'But don't be overdoing it,' added John. 'Passing a driving test isn't urgent.' Elsie agreed. 'Yes, that's also true.'

Peggy smiled. 'Thank you, I'm back to full fitness now.'

Elsie went on to ask them if they needed any help with the language and 'the ways of Turin'. Peggy answered that they hadn't got very far with learning Italian yet and hadn't really been there long enough to learn much at all about the city ... 'John always says that Italian is supposed to be easy to learn; all you need to do is add an 'ay' or an 'oe' at the end of the English words and people will understand you.' Elsie looked surprised and Peggy, in turn, looked embarrassed.

'I knew he was making it up!'

'No, no, it's not that, Peggy, not at all. I was just quite surprised because there is some truth in what John has told you. There are many connected words in the two languages, probably due to them originally being Latin or even French.'

'Well, please do say so if I can assist. This is a good place to live, but of course it can be difficult for new arrivals, and there have been so many migrants to the city, not all of them Italian. Before all the paperwork, I should tell you a little about Turin. The region we are in is called Piemonte – Piedmont in English – and Turin is the capital. Piemonte actually means 'foot of the mountain'. Turin is the centre of Italian cinema too, like Hollywood in America, so if you like the movies then the main cinema is the Lux, near to Piazza San Carlo, which is the main square for social gatherings and the like. The films are in Italian though, of course.'

'We used to go to the pictures quite a lot,' Peggy said. 'But there won't be much point now I suppose.'

John shared her disappointment.

'Do you have a radio set at all? I think you should be able to tune in to the BBC World Service, to keep up to date on the news back in England.'

'I'll put a radiogram on my shopping list, thank you for reminding me,' Peggy said. 'I need to stock up on my record collection too, and get my dad to bring all my records that we couldn't carry.'

'The layout of Turin is fundamentally a "Roman grid pattern" … in other words, it is very well planned. It has three main squares – I just mentioned Piazza San Carlo, which is very close to your hotel, and there is Piazza Castello and Piazza Vittorio Veneto.' Peggy nodded and smiled; she was very interested. John meanwhile tried to look interested, but Elsie was not fooled.

She continued. 'Have you noticed much of the architecture in the city? People will probably tell you that it is "Baroque" style, but that is not entirely true as much of this century's buildings are what is called "Art Nouveau" design.'

And then, quite unexpectedly, as if a faded thought had suddenly sprung back to life, Peggy asked Elsie if she would help them with the language by coming to their flat and giving them tuition. For a fee of course.

Elsie reacted enthusiastically, but *of course* she would not take one single penny or lira as payment! Soon they were checking dates and making social plans for the future, while John sat there, hearing but not listening, wondering when he and Peggy would be on their way. The formalities of their appointment, the whole form-filling and signing procedures, took over an hour to complete. Elsie had talked them through the details – even to the extent of informing John when his wages were paid and where to collect them – and she supplied cups of tea along the way, too. No biscuits though, to John's mild frustration.

They said their farewells and Elsie promised to contact them very soon, in addition to giving them some papers for the nanny to complete. She advised them to stay close to the riverside so as not to get lost … that way, after five or ten minutes they would reach the Piazza Vittorio Veneto, which had lots of lovely bars and restaurants if they were hungry. It wasn't as popular or as famous as Piazza San Carlo, 'the Living Room of Turin', but it was still a fabulous sight to see and the general atmosphere was always sociable. Despite enjoying a surprisingly hearty, unusual breakfast of scrambled eggs and lurid green *broccoli*, lots of it, they were both hungry again. Rare were the times when John wasn't at least peckish. Neither of them had remembered seeing or tasting broccoli before, but they agreed that it somehow 'worked' as pleasant enough breakfast manna. Elsie also warned them that while Turin might appear to be all straight lines and therefore simple to navigate, it was easy to get lost in as well. 'Try to keep the River Po to your right and keep the museum Mole Antonelliana in your sights, as it is around a kilometre away from your hotel. You can't miss it; it's over five hundred feet high.'

Their stroll along the paved bank of the delightful Po was a simple and enjoyable route, ending with a gentle ascent of the stone slope that brought them out directly opposite the Piazza Vittorio Veneto immediately before the Emanuele Bridge and its arches spanning the water.

'That's the Church of the Holy Mother then, according to Elsie,' Peggy said, looking to the other side of the bridge and the very pretty domed building resembling an observatory, with steps and pillars in front of it, together with another statue dedicated to someone or other. The whole area felt calm and casual; even the motor traffic and the trams seemed quieter and slower here. At a set of traffic lights, John and Peggy crossed the road to the piazza, the towering spike of the Mole easily visible in the distance, formerly blue sky slowly fading into grey. John scanned the magnificent square before him and estimated it to be at least the size of six football pitches. Six large football pitches at that. The area suggested the look of a vast courtyard belonging to not one but a pair of – one at each side – huge palaces. The left and nearer side consisted of a row of many arches, each representing a way in to the long and dark arcade spanning the full length of the piazza. Within the arcade were small restaurant and bar and shop frontages, some of them aglow with welcoming interior lighting, whereas others, judging by the cavern-like gloom, were not open for trade. And the arcade was suddenly not the only overcast area: slate-grey clouds now dominated the sky; light rain began to fall.

Just as Elsie had indicated, the Mole was indeed a good landmark to use for keeping track of their whereabouts, but it was not visible from under the cover of the arcade where they had just dashed, laughing, to avoid the now large raindrops suddenly splattering the area. They walked under cover of the arcade and then chose to turn left and away from the piazza. They were soon lost and in danger of getting soaked, but they could hardly have been less concerned about it.

They passed another closed restaurant, a weekday afternoon apparently not a busy enough time for Turin dining establishments in locations away from the main piazzas and thoroughfares. This closed restaurant was different, however. A curly-haired man in a yellow shirt and brown braces had been cleaning the windows of the premises, La Spada Reale. He was also wearing a white apron, bow-tied around his neck and waist, to prevent his shirt getting damp and grubby. As the Charleses walked by, their reflection caught his attention while he was polishing the pane from the inside. Turning around quickly to look more closely at the passers-by, he called to them.

'Hello. Hello?' He dropped his cloth into the steel bucket of water at his feet and walked towards them, wiping his hands dry on the apron as he did so. Thrusting his right hand forward to share a handshake, excitedly he greeted them, 'John and Peggy Charles! It is, John and Peggy Charles! Welcome to Turin, I am Juventus all my life and I know all about you. We all cannot wait for you to wake our team.'

'Thank you,' said John, while Peggy smiled politely; the rain was getting annoying now, spoiling her hair and making her feel uncomfortable.

The man spoke quickly. 'My name is Stefano; have you eaten? Ah! I apologise to you; I am Stefano and La Spada Reale is my restaurant.'

In spite of the restaurant not being officially open for business so early in the afternoon, Stefano insisted that the Charleses have a look round inside. Encouraging them to sit down at one of the tables, he persuaded them to allow him to serve them some cold dishes. There would have been hot dishes had his chef been present, but it was a couple of hours before the kitchen staff's work day began. John always preferred 'proper' meals that came as big portions on one plate rather than the antipasti or 'snacks' method of small plates with individual food items on. And *sharing* just did not feel right! Here and now, however, he had no choice … and free food did usually taste better.

As they waited, Peggy looked at the condiments on their table, the salt and pepper in containers made of clear cut glass topped with perforated silver lids. She picked the salt pot up and held it close to her eyes.

'John,' she said, 'it looks like there's a grain of rice in the salt. Why is that, I wonder?' John replied with a disinterested shrug and an exhaled 'I don't know.'

Stefano returned, wheeling a trolley laden with many small white plates. 'The rice grain prevents moisture in the salt,' and then he chuckled. 'Damp salt is for me an annoying matter in life.'

Peggy smiled. 'Ah, I see.'

Cold meat cuts and salamis, breadsticks (which John abstained from), crab pieces looking like patterned boiled sweets, lumps of *something* that both John and Peggy had mistaken for over-sized shelled boiled eggs until cutting into them and tasting the thick, glutinous Parmesan cheese filled the table. Nice enough tasting though, once the initial shock had subsided. And ribbon-thin slithers of ham, numerous green and black olives, and lots of green salad in balsamic vinaigrette. All the titbits were a tad too small to constitute a genuinely appetising meal, but John found himself sated regardless; Peggy certainly was full. Stefano, a pleasant and generous man who had studied in London, would not accept any payment whatsoever for his catering, his only request being that John and Peggy visit his restaurant again, for a proper meal. Stefano promised he would provide sumptuous food and in a special settings for them.

Next was a stroll around the shops Turin had to offer. The drizzle had dissipated but as Peggy was tired and her feet ached their browsing and compiling a list, as Gigi had suggested, were relatively token efforts. At one stage they chose a wrong turn and ended up a few hundred yards further away from the hotel than they had estimated. However, as the wrong turn brought them to the quite spectacular Piazza San Carlo, the 'Living Room', regarded as the cultural and social heartbeat of Turin, they realised they were in safe and special surroundings, and the hotel stood barely five minutes' walk away. It gave them a brief opportunity to study the majesty of the bronze statue of Savoy Duke 'Iron Head' Emanuele Filiberto as a soldier on horseback, mounted on a huge plinth which itself was atop three large steps.

'Isn't that a fabulous statue, John?' John nodded.

'Does it remind of you of anything?'

'The statue?'

'Yes, this statue …' attempting to read the nameplate. 'I think it says … of … the Duke of Savoy … Emanuele Filiberto.'

'No, not that I can think of.'

'Really? It should do. It's just like the one of the Black Prince in City Square, back home, back in Leeds. I wonder if they were related.'

'I don't know. City Square's nicer for me though.'

'Yes. But we're here now.'

6

n late June, soon after the Charles family had moved home into the new world of their apartment on Via Susa, Gigi Peronace called in to see how they were faring. Quite nicely was the answer from both Peggy and John, and Peggy revealed that they were really looking forward to their 'new' friends Elsie and her husband Alec visiting that evening, to provide some Italian-language tuition, to dine (Peggy and pasta dish-cooking were quite well acquainted now) with them and to play a few games of cards, most likely canasta.

Meanwhile, John demanded Gigi tell him why there were so many telephone calls from press reporters. How did they know the telephone number?

'I am sorry, I do not know. The reporters here are often like spies; they are cunning. I will ensure that it does not continue. Did you tell them anything?'

'Yes, I told them to ring Juventus to sort out any interviews.' In reality it had been Peggy answering most of the calls, on his behalf.

'Good, good. Do you know which publications the reporters work for?' 'One was *Tempo*, then there was *Oggi* …'

'I think there was one called *Novella*. And *Candido*?' said Peggy.

'Yes, renowned 'family' magazines here … the newspaper men will know to contact Juventus and not you directly.'

'They haven't been that annoying; at least the calls have been at a civilised hour,' commented Peggy.

And then, in one of those perfect moments of seemingly pre-planned coincidence, the Charleses' telephone in the living room began to ring. Peronace did not wait for anyone else to react or give him permission; he strode purposefully from the kitchen to the telephone to pick up the receiver and answer the call. It was obvious to the Charleses that Peronace was speaking with polite authority. After half a minute or so he ended the call with a forceful press of the receiver on to its cradle and returned to the kitchen, slightly redder in complexion.

'I have told this journalist, he is with the *Visto* publication, to never call here again, and I instructed him to inform all of his colleagues the same message,' he advised, proudly.

'Let's hope you're right,' said Peggy. 'Thank you.'

'You know where the bathroom is, Gigi; have a free shave on us,' John teased. Peronace shaped to smile; it was not a convincing attempt. He was annoyed that his friends were being treated like this; it was not impressive. After drinking his coffee, he said his goodbyes and departed. Twenty minutes later, the telephone rang again: another press man wanting to speak with John.

After lunch, Peggy enquired about the 'important-looking building' she had seen atop a high hill miles away to the east of the city. She had meant to ask him before but had forgotten. She seemed to do that quite a lot recently; it mildly annoyed her. Too far away to determine any real detail, the impression was of a huge, grey structure with a domed top, set above a vast green forest that overlooked the River Po valley area. So far, John had taken in little of the natural scenery of the Piedmont area. He shrugged his shoulders, thought for a few seconds and then speculated that it might be an old Italian church or 'something like that'.

Peggy disagreed. 'It looks a bit more exotic than that.'

There were not many things, if any, in existence with the power to bore John Charles quite as much as the subject of churches. Peggy was already well aware of that; for as long as they had known each other there had been little doubt. When they married, he had wanted to get out of the church – St Mary's in Beeston, near to the Leeds football ground – as soon as was possible once they had exchanged their wedding vows. She knew he didn't *not* believe in God, it was more a case of he couldn't be bothered thinking too deeply about religion. There was always something more relevant and interesting to think about, like football. In fact, John was – to those who knew about such things – probably an agnostic, in that he did believe there was 'a' god but wanted to see more evidence before committing himself.

She sighed. She might never find out.

He knew exactly what the sigh meant. 'I'll ask,' he promised. 'You could have asked Gigi yourself when he was here.'

'Yes, I could have, but I thought I would try and have a conversation with my husband instead,' came the dry response.

That evening, Elsie and husband Alec visited, she with a box of chocolates for the children, he with a bottle of wine for the adults. During the night's proceedings, the subject of the media was again a matter of light discussion. Both Peggy and John missed having the English dailies to read on mornings, but it was not a serious problem. 'Well, I'm in a way glad that you don't read the Italian newspapers, Peggy,' commented Elsie. 'Why, what do you mean?'

'She doesn't mean anything really, Peggy. Do you, Elsie?' asked Alec.

'No, I don't mean anything … just that gossip columns are popular over here.'

'Yes?' Peggy said.

'Yes, you know …' She paused, hesitant but knowing she had to elaborate. 'They invent news about footballers, things like that.'

'You mean saying that a player is to be sold to another club, along those lines?'

'Yes … yes, that's exactly what I mean.'

◎

At nearly ten o'clock the next Monday morning, Umberto Colombo parked his silver and black, four-door Fiat saloon car outside Via Susa 31. Gigi Peronace clambered out of the front passenger seat and walked down to the side of the building. They were quite ignorant of the fact that the John Charles of Turin was a different person to the John Charles of Leeds: he was actually just about ready. He was no longer in the habit of keeping people waiting for him. He kissed Peggy, Terry and Peter goodbye – and it felt like ages since he had seen Melvyn – and joined the two Italians at the car within two minutes of their call.

Peronace was now seated in the back seat; John obviously needed more leg-room and there was never much space in the back of a Fiat. Today was to be another hot day, the kind of heat that the working man only really appreciates when it is over. Charles liked hot weather; it made a refreshing, invigorating change from what he was generally accustomed to in Leeds or Swansea. He particularly enjoyed earning a suntan, as it made him look and feel better. Whether he would appreciate the heat so much when the Piedmont summer temperatures peaked and really began to oppress was another matter.

The hill looked closer to the Charles home than the reality of its seven to eight miles distance. Getting there by car would take less than half an hour normally, if the road traffic was kind. And the many trams. Once there the drive up the hill would take longer.

'John, did you know the Agnelli family are owners of *La Stampa* newspaper?'

'No, I did not know that.'

Yes, and I read in *La Stampa* that Signor Agnelli says you can afford to buy your own car, now you have arrived ...' Colombo said, while negotiating the various automobile obstacles and annoyances on the road around them.

'I'm no good at reading Italian, I just look at the photographs.'

'Possibly the wealthiest family in the whole of Italy, the renowned owners of Fiat, say you must buy your own car!'

'There were two new Lambretta scooters waiting for us when we moved in.'

'Ah, a whole new complexion on the matter then.'

A cough came from behind him. Gigi Peronace. An embarrassed cough. Peronace then spoke up for his employer. 'Umberto Agnelli has always been very generous with providing cars as gifts to the players when the team has done well, so I am sure you will be taken care of, John.'

There was a chance Peronace did not hear Colombo's gentle snort of derision, but only a very slight chance. 'You will need to be patient, Big John,' Colombo said. 'And I expect Gigi is sure of that too.'

'Lambrettas aren't any use to us; Peggy hasn't got a licence and I'm too big. Frank will get more use out of them back in Leeds.'

For a few moments, no words were spoken. Wearing a stern facial expression, Colombo appeared to be concentrating hard on the driving, Charles tried to take an interest in the Turin suburban scenery of apartment blocks and industrial buildings, and Peronace looked out of his side window, pretending not to be embarrassed. Unexpectedly, the car began to slow down, causing Colombo to hurriedly find a kerb-side space to park away from the road traffic. Trams whooshed by and other vehicles sounded their horns accusingly.

'Ah … we have no petrol,' sighed Colombo after they had stopped. Deciding it would be quicker if he spoke in their native tongue, Peronace asked, '*Sei securo che e la benzina che manca e non un guasto al motore?*'

Colombo replied, seemingly annoyed, '*Conosco bene la mia macchina, Gigi.*' And then, calmer, '*Abbiamo passato un distributore di benzina un chilometro fa, vai a comprare una tanica di benzina.*'

'*Se devo.*'

'*Non c'e nessun altro modo. Non ci puo mica andare John, vero. Certo che devi.*'

'*Mi aspettate qui?*'

'*Sí, probabilmente e questo che accadrà, Gigi. Le nostre opzioni sono piuttosto limitate.*' Peronace opened his door to step on to the pavement. 'Okay, I will return soon.'

'Your generosity will be recognised, thank you,' Colombo responded. Then, to Charles, 'John, I will attempt to translate … I told Gigi we have no more petrol. He asked if I was sure it was not an engine fault. I told him I know my own car, it is no engine fault. I requested he go to the petrol station and buy us fuel. He was not happy and asked that we wait for him. I said we will wait because our options are limited.'

Charles smiled.

After a few more seconds' wait, and then angling the rear-view mirror to check that Peronace was still within shouting distance, Colombo grinned, restarted the engine and then craned his neck out of the window to shout, in English, 'Gigi! I take John to buy a Citroen.' To Charles's ears, he was serious.

Colombo laughed to himself as he started to drive the car away, leaving a flustered Peronace waving his fist angrily in the air. Charles chuckled at his old friend's expense, the baritone timbre a brief and gentle drum roll audible over the engine noise.

Colombo apologised. 'I have lied, I am sorry, John.'

Charles nodded; he understood. After all, the language of 'pulling someone's leg' tended to be a global one.

Colombo added, 'We will make sure you receive a car very soon, my friend … It was too warm for Gigi and he needs more exercise.'

'He needs a shave too,' commented Charles, hand-signing the action of shaving.

◎

Previously, she had gone out shopping for essentials in Turin with Nanny Margaret. Technically, she wasn't alone now as she had Peter with her in his pram. Margaret was back at the flat, attempting to look after Terry as well as take care of herself. For the entire duration of their time in Italy, Margaret had seemed poorly, often complaining of nausea, lethargy or simply stomach-ache. Her condition seemed to have worsened in the last few days; her energy levels certainly had not improved, while her complaints of abdominal pain had increased. Peggy suspected she had lost even more weight since their first meeting at Lynwood in April. Peggy, usually a compassionate and understanding person, was losing patience with her – perhaps a product of the stress created by their still new surroundings. Something was not right about the situation and it needed to be resolved for all their sakes. Margaret would moan and groan about feeling poorly, but then refuse to take anything for the discomfort. If in fact she was regretting the move to Italy then she should have the courage to admit it rather than cause inconvenience for others.

Peggy had got up even earlier than normal so as to wash the family's laundry and, more importantly, hang it out to dry on the balcony overlooking the 'garden'. Due to a Via Susa 31 rule as imposed by the caretaker Gianni, residents had strict instructions that absolutely no laundry should be visible outside after 11.30 a.m. Naturally, Peggy did not want to offend or hurt anyone's sensibilities and so adhered to the rule, a needless pain though it was.

A few deep breaths, a check in the mirror on the wall and a stroke of the baby's head. Yes, Peggy, Peter, pram, all were ready, ready to venture from the dim light of the residence into the glare of outside and, specifically, the local outdoor market a few streets away. All the strangers and their rapid talking and their inquisitive looks, all representing a daunting experience to a newcomer. And if that newcomer was of a negative disposition it could feel worse, it could be excruciating. Peggy Charles (née White) thankfully was not a negative kind of person, and her husband deserved credit for much of that. She in fact relished a challenge and rarely felt intimidated, even as a foreigner abroad, a virtue she had most assuredly gleaned from John's sporting exploits. Plus she had a secret 'weapon' with her: an adorable little baby!

So many people wanted to bend down to smile and wave at baby Peter, and surprisingly it was the men more than the women doing most of the *melting*. Any obstacles to communication and general interaction Peggy had feared seemed to simply fade away with a baby present. It was almost as if he had developed uncanny powers of magnetism, drawing people to him. Complete strangers would stop in front of the pram, halting its progress at the same time, and crouch and begin to chatter softly, *daftly* to the child, sometimes without even acknowledging his mother. Peggy knew instinctively that none of them ever meant the slightest offence or harm, and every time a cooing Italian stranger demonstrated such affection to her baby, her own confidence and fondness for all things Torinese grew just a little bit more. In the north of England the people of Yorkshire were well known for their friendliness and sincerity, but here in northern Italy the natives seemed to be on an even higher level of kindness and consideration. And, while she would never tell anyone about it, she had noticed quite a few of the men casting the 'glad eye' her way too, another boost to her ego, especially when the admirer was handsome and smartly dressed. Normally, the image of a young mother with a baby in tow would deter men from romantic aspirations, but not here. Quite the opposite in fact, and her pulse momentarily hastened correspondingly each time the admirer was a good-looking man.

For colour and noise and vibrancy, Leeds' Kirkgate Market would take some beating, especially the indoor market and its high walls and sloping floor crammed with stalls and kiosks and people. Yet this outdoor market possibly achieved it. A constant buzz of shoppers talking and stall holders loudly announcing (Peggy assumed) their wares and prices. Never a moment of peace. On sale in the food area were fruits and vegetables and other provisions she had never set eyes on before. There were even colours of nature she had not previously seen. Certain vegetables looked to be miniature versions of something out of *Invasion of the Body Snatchers*, but she was bold enough to believe that Italian grocers would not knowingly sell anything harmful to humans or, for that matter, anything possessing ambitions of taking over the world. Aubergines of a sumptuous purple, and bright red peppers, bright green peppers, bright orange ones, and yellow ones and purple ones. Olives – there looked to be millions of them on various stalls, piled on trays or in glass jars of various capacities: pale green, dark green, black, beige. Dark green courgettes too, which looked just like cucumbers. Pasta of many different shades, shapes and sizes. The arithmetic was hard work for Peggy, trying to calculate the lira versus sterling prices while determining that she wasn't spending, or over-spending, too much. Her alarm at having to pay higher prices for butter, cheese, coffee and tea (especially, for the latter, as it was not so popular a drink in Italy as it was in England) was eased by milk, tomatoes and mushrooms being considerably cheaper to buy.

◎

Turin's second-tallest hill. Renowned for innumerable aspects of natural beauty and abundant yields of wild mushrooms, truffles and cherries. Winding roads, surprisingly wide bends and corners, small bridges, streams, greenery and flora at just about every turn, and high stone walls, iron gates and railings. Trees, so many varieties – Charles could not possibly identify them all: even a keen gardener would struggle to do so. He recognised cedars, birches, elms, willows … He hadn't learned much about trees at school, primarily because he wouldn't have been paying attention in class. Trees were uninteresting unless they were representing makeshift goalposts. He never asked questions at school, and he rarely answered any – correctly at least – either. And for different reasons, when he was employed by Leeds United, he never questioned the manager Major Frank Buckley, and in the army he never questioned his instructors, the soldiers' supposed superiors. Anyone questioning those in charge would receive a rollicking anyway, but Charles knew that the football manager and the army sergeants were always right and that it was not for him to doubt them. It was all for his benefit.

They drove by the funicular railway station, which immediately reminded him of the seaside town of Scarborough and its own funicular versions. As the car climbed the hillside, elegant villas and houses greeted them, all owners of glorious panoramic views across Turin. Although they were situated miles away from the toil and sweat of the workers, and the dirt and fumes of the city's manufacturing and heavy industry, once the car had begun its climb the improvement in air quality was distinctly noticeable. Motor traffic brings with it its own filth too, of course, but as they ascended it was almost as if they were escaping a choking, grimy existence into a purer, more wholesome level of life. A healthier, clearer perspective ... unfogged, *unsmogged*, unspoiled.

They arrived in a large square, the Piazzale della Basilica – yet more trees bordering the edges, the area almost deserted with the exception of a few nuns, three hundred yards away, dressed in all white, walking towards the front entrance of the huge building before them. Colombo parked the car under the shading boughs of a leafy tree and the duo got out.

'I am your guide for the day, Big John; I will try to inform you,' said Colombo.

Foliage and branches fending off the heat of the sun, magnificent leaves aglow, resolutely obscuring rays of sunshine but spears of heat still managing to break through. A relieving breeze to complement the shade. A pair of tiny gecko lizards watch proceedings from a low white wall, waiting for something. The colour of hazel, perfectly still one second and vanished the next. Charles and Colombo, striding away from the car, gravel and shale crunching underfoot, and pine cones all over the ground, were heading towards the spectacular domed building a couple of hundred yards away, the ornate building Charles and Peggy had spoken about. It was the Basilica of Superga. Colombo told him how to pronounce the title. Most English speakers would probably pronounce it 'super-gar' – as indeed Charles had – but the correct way was 'soo-pare-ga', with emphasis on the 'pare'. Most important though was how splendid a sight it was to behold, a handsome shape and design, and the colours – yellows and whites – magnificent against the blue sky background. Nearly Leeds United's team colours! Charles stopped, simply so he could realise a better view of the basilica, in excess of two hundred feet high he thought, from the ground up to the holy cross crowning the domed roof. He was impressed, so impressed in fact that the dramatic warrior and bird of prey statue commemorating King Umberto I to his right went completely unnoticed.

'I told Peggy that I thought it was some sort of church, but it was a guess. It doesn't look anything like as special from down there.'

More than one architectural style appeared to comprise the building's overall design. Wide white steps led up to a portico that resembled a small version of Rome's Pantheon, the white pillars supporting a triangular gable and roof serving as the entrance to the church and its enormous dome. And at both sides of the church, symmetrical bell towers, intricate but perhaps too intricate, creating a slightly untidy appearance. The walls of the building consisted of large sections of warm yellow, separated or bordered by whites and greys. Much more colourful than any church Charles had seen before.

Much like a local tour guide, Colombo described some of the Superga history, such as the Royal Crypt inside the basilica being the burial place of the majority of the ruling Savoy family since 1732, the former monarchy of Italy. That meant more than fifty tombs inside, of princes, princesses and the like. He told also of the date of construction (it had taken fourteen years to build and was completed in 1731) and that the interior of the building was very special ... if such matters personally appealed of course. He strongly suspected that such matters did not appeal to John Charles and so led him past the steps and entrance down to the side of the basilica to a long and gently sloping pathway, yet another area covered in pine cones. He was confident that the next sight they saw would evoke more reaction from Charles than any holy house ever could.

Amidst many unlit candles and holders, and a few small potted plants and a variety of claret and white silk ribbons and flags, Colombo pointed out a tombstone and dais, set against the building wall. On it, beneath a grey embossed cross, divided into three segments, was a long list of names. He described the events leading to the creation of this evocative display. During a thunderstorm and much fog and wind, an aeroplane had crashed there a few years before, into the hillside wall surrounding the basilica. The disaster had occurred just over eight years ago, the fourth of May 1949. An Italian Airlines passenger aircraft, a Fiat G212, on its return flight from Lisbon, Portugal, had been transporting players and personnel of Torino Football Club. Torino were renowned as one of the world's best ever teams. They had been led by the brilliant Erno Egri Erbstein, a Hungarian Jew who had survived the war but still had to fight against bigots in the Football Federation after it ended. They had taken part in a testimonial match for the Benfica player Francisco Ferreira, who was retiring from football. The flight was due to arrive in Turin by 5 p.m. but stormy conditions brought a premature darkness to the area, severely limiting visibility. Strong gusts of wind, heavy rain and fog further conspired to disorientate the pilot, finally bringing about the terrible accident. Everyone aboard, a total of thirty-one passengers – eighteen belonging to the Torino playing squad – perished.

'These are the names of those who died that evening. The team was called Il Grande Torino; they had already won the Serie A championship, for the fourth consecutive season. Torino was easily the best in the country, and the national team was mostly of their players. Superga was a tragedy not only for the city but also for every Italian and every football follower in the world ... It is said that five hundred thousand people gathered on the streets on the day of the funerals ...'

Colombo then mentioned he had signed professional terms for Juventus in the year after the disaster. In response, Charles revealed that *he* had made his debut less than two weeks before the disaster. His first full league match was for Leeds United against Blackburn Rovers, on St George's Day, 1949. His professional football life had just begun while for a tragic few it was about to end.

They stood by a roadside on Superga Hill, looking out over the panoramic view of the city. Below them, a hundred yards away on a verdant grass slope, a young family of five was enjoying a picnic.

'Monviso is the highest peak of the Alps; it is said to be nearly four kilometres high,' Colombo advised.

'I know that Piedmont means "foot of the mountain".'

'Nice. The highest hill, John, is Farro della Maddalena; it is over there to the left somewhere ... I am told that the Agnellis' principal home is there. They are able to look down even more on their employees, their worker ants.'

Charles nodded.

'I should not make fun; they are our employers. They have done so much to rebuild Turin and all around, and Juventus will be great again because of Umberto Agnelli, a better man than his brother. We all believe this, now you are here, as well as the Big Head.'

'The Big Head? You mean Omar Sivori?'

Colombo laughed. 'Yes! Who else has a head so large? The Statue of Liberty?'

'Ha, yes. Special ability though.'

'I agree, though he would steal the smile from a baby if it brought personal glory.'

John noticed Turin buildings and thoroughfares, row upon row upon row, neat and organised and carefully *planned*. Streets and roads, long and straight. All a huge grid. The foreground, roofs the colour of salmon and terracotta. The River Po, brought to glaring life by sunlight, lithe, twisting, weaving through the city, a slither of quicksilver. All of Turin seemed planned and placed, unlike towns and cities of England and Wales, which had a scattered, unruly look about them. Unruled, unpredictable, untidy.

Colombo asked Charles if he could see the 'Land of Fiat', the network of factories, industrial plants and mass production outlets, and the famous Lingotto building where cars were manufactured and then road-tested on the roof. Yes, the five-storey structure actually possessed a racetrack oval on the roof.

Charles stared hard but shook his head in defeat. 'No.'

'Of course you cannot see it, it is too cloudy. Chemicals and fumes. You must trust me, it is a spectacular sight when it is visible. Many men build the cars in assembly chains. The production starts on the lowest floor until it rises to the top level, where it is completed and tested around the track.'

'That must be some sight.'

Colombo nodded. 'The manufacture of Fiat cars is like our team. The creation begins at the back and it proceeds to you John, where you finish the move by scoring!'

'I won't score every time and it won't be just me who scores.'

'No, only 90 per cent!' Colombo paused, hopeful his remarks had been taken in the right context. 'Most of this city belongs to the Agnelli family, therefore most of the people work for the Agnelli family. And you and I work for them of course. The difference is, Juventus came looking, to recruit us, and what we do is not work, it is not labour. It is a privilege and honour. Thousands and thousands of the workers travel here from the south, or from other countries, to find employment with Fiat. The First World War made Fiat very rich.

'You also cannot see where most of the workers are housed because of the chimney smoke. Many hundreds of blocks and shanty towns in the proximity of the factories, built for the workers.'

'All the cranes … are homes being built?' asked Charles.

'No John, some of the cranes remove the ruins to rebuild, after the bombs of the war. Torino was hit many times because of Fiat and other connected industries. The bombs often missed and destroyed civilian buildings instead.'

'Sounds like what happened in Swansea, maybe Leeds as well. We have red-brick 'back-to-back' and terraced houses in Leeds for the workers. Some people have to live in between two neighbours as well as one behind.' His very first impressions of Leeds had been what a dirty old town it was, and that the ugly clouds of smoke and smog always failed to conceal the remnants of the devil's bombs of the last war, adding to the desolation. He recognised the shattered buildings and lives, and the subsequent years of rebuilding, repairing, replacing … similar but worse images from his Swansea childhood were imprinted on his mind. The bombings terrified him as a child and he was forever grateful for the makeshift air-raid shelter – their coal shed – at their home, as well as the sturdy oak table in the kitchen if they weren't able to make it to the shelter in time.

What Charles could see and recognise, misty apparitions, included of course in the middle ground the cloud-piercing tower of the Mole Antonelliana presiding over the skyline. His first sight of it hadn't caused much reaction; it hadn't really interested him, it hadn't offended him, it just seemed to be another old Torinese structure amongst countless other old Torinese structures. But now … now, he thought, it looked unusual, unpleasantly so, it had a mysterious edge to it, something foreboding, aggressive, sinister.

By the time he arrived home he had forgotten any such concerns. Colombo had returned him to Via Susa and parked the car in the roadside with the few others already there. On seeing the two men walk through the doorway, Peggy hadn't just smiled, she had grinned, and it wasn't just because of how handsome they were John was puzzled, it was a cheerier welcome than normal.

She stood on the tips of her toes to kiss him on the cheek, asking, 'Notice anything different outside?'

Charles thought for a moment and then shook his head. 'No, why?' 'Two cars. One's a Fiat *Familiare*, the dark blue one, and the other is a white Fiat Five Hundred. Two men delivered them; they told me they're from Umberto Agnelli, one for me and one for you. Isn't that lovely?'

Umberto Colombo nodded and chuckled. 'The Five Hundred is their newest car, very nice.' John stood still, wearing a smile and a slightly perplexed expression at the gesture.

'Ciao, John and Peggy,' bade Umberto, turning around to leave, still laughing to himself.

◎

Talks had been ongoing for weeks, clandestine though far from sinister, between Umberto Agnelli and a much-travelled Yugoslav who yearned to be the new head coach of Juventus Football Club. The much-travelled Yugoslav spoke persuasively; he talked a good talk and appeared to know more about the Juventus team than their president. He also appeared to know solutions to the problems the team had suffered with.

Ljubisa Brocic had impressed upon Agnelli the view that football – not only in the white-and-black half of Turin but in the whole of Italy – needed reinvigorating and reinforcing; it was too defensive and thus not entertaining enough for the supporters. After all, the paying public made much of *calcio*; without them the professional game would probably die, along with a part of the nation's spirit. And Juventus weren't good enough at defending anyway! Nor were the players fit enough. *His* team, Brocic declared, would be trained harder and would be instructed to attack non-stop, to thrill and entertain non-stop. His Juventus would score more goals than opponents, rather than aim to *concede* fewer goals.

A popular man of stature, respected in football for his achievements in coaching and for being strict but fair, Ljubisa Brocic also spoke English very well, possibly better than his Italian, for which he would enlist the aid of an interpreter to help translate the more complex messages he wanted to convey. That interpreter would usually be Depetrini. This prospective manager's linguistic ability represented positive news for John Charles, working hard but nevertheless struggling to learn the Italian language to a satisfactory standard. The potential new gaffer's ability to speak English meant Charles would have fewer communication issues to contend with. Brocic's reputation was a good one, and Charles expected he would get on well with him, and look up to him. Literally, he could look up to him as Brocic was actually slightly taller than Charles – quite a rarity.

Late in June 1957 his wish was fulfilled. Ljubisa Brocic, born in October 1913, would be replacing Baldo Depetrini as the coach; Depetrini would be reverting to his role as the Juventus youth team coach. He had proven he was more than competent in that role and the decision was no unpleasant surprise: he accepted it with appropriate good grace, rightfully proud of how he had completed the temporary job in fine fashion, the team's status in Serie A preserved due to improved results and displays under his tutelage. However, the ideal first-team coach for his club, decided Agnelli, ought to be more experienced, more established, and someone with a fresh, independent approach to the task. And besides, Depetrini was happier managing the youth team at this stage of his career.

On the football side of affairs, Brocic immediately got to work with the squad. He had to, there was little more than a month before the players would be on their summer vacation. In addition to Agnelli's auspicious signings of Charles and Sivori, the young goalkeeper Carlo Mattrel's loan deal with Ancona, and centre-half Rino Ferrario's with Triestina, had ended and so they were back with Juventus. Both had performed well for their 'new' teams, especially Mattrel, but Brocic needed to decide for himself.

Although Charles had been Leeds United's star player, he had also been one of the laziest when it came to training, often vying for the Worst Trainer 'honour' with a tall, young rapscallion defender called Jackie Charlton. Here in Turin, however, the summer climate seemed to affect Charles; he actually *wanted* to train, and train harder and more often too. The training routines and physical labours were no easier than those at Elland Road, but the weather damn well was! Naturally, he had yet to sample how painful the Piedmont winters could be. Though he had been resident in Turin for barely a month, the warmer climes already made him feel physically and mentally brighter, after the arduous football season with Leeds and Wales. And he looked better too, trimmer and sun-tanned, and *sharper* dressed thanks to the generosity of local tailors always keen to impress Juventus stars by way of supplying their wares as gifts. It was often said that, if the team was doing well then, as a player, everyone was your friend, but if the team was losing then you wouldn't be able to *buy* one. With luck, he would never have to find this out.

Of all the theories and ideas proposed in soccer training methods in England, Charles saw the one that proclaimed the merits of depriving players of a football to practise with as by far the most ludicrous. Worse even than the monkey glands serum. The theory suggested that players who frequently practised with a football quickly became stale and their match performances suffered because of it. Charles had always cited the 'Wizard of the Dribble' Stanley Matthews' methods as justification for as much practice with a football as possible – if it was good enough for the master then it was good enough for everybody else, and the master spent hours and hours honing his footwork, ball skills and control. After all, training did not have to be mind-numbingly mundane, and individualism should be encouraged; the sport did not need eleven robots versus eleven robots. Frequent ball practice could also improve an individual player's weaknesses. The whole point of training should be aimed at improving the weak spots of any one player. Frequent practice explained why Charles could strike the ball exceptionally well with either foot – he was not naturally ambidextrous, it just appeared that way. Practice makes perfect. His already phenomenal heading power had benefited in similar manner ... practice practice practice! It was practice – of jumping and connecting – that helped augment his already prodigious leaping ability and that had earned him the reputation of being a better header of the football than even the great Tommy Lawton. Thankfully 'ball deprivation' had not been too much of an issue at Leeds and so he had rarely toiled or had reason for complaint, though he had always felt the training routines could have been more varied.

Upon his arrival for his first training session with his new colleagues, Charles had been heartened to see that their methods included even more time with an actual football involved. The lighter leather balls here were much less prone to absorb any surface water than those in the English game too; he would not miss those ridiculously heavy ones at all, that was for sure.

Until a player is involved in the 'heat of battle', it is not really of much relevance to try and form an opinion on their technical ability. Still, from their training sessions and the in-house practice matches, Charles was soon impressed with his new colleagues; there were many fine players there. In nets the lad Carlo Mattrel seemed to be the natural successor to Giovanni Viola, who was not even thirty years old yet. Colombo told Charles that Mattrel, when a child, used to stand behind Viola's goal in every training session he could, to learn how to be a great *portiere*. Mattrel was nearly as tall and broad as Charles, and very agile; an essential quality for any goalkeeper to have. He needed to show more composure – also known as grace under pressure – but that should, would, come with age and first-team matches. He bore a strong facial resemblance to Don of the Everly Brothers, his thick hair styled in a quiff over his forehead. His singing voice wasn't up to much though! Two prominent full-backs were Giuseppe Corradi and Bruno Grazena, fast and quick-witted defenders, while Umberto Colombo and Flavio Emoli in midfield (wing-halves) were pacey *and* possessed supreme stamina. They would run all day long for the team if told to.

The exciting Gino Stacchini on the right wing, and precise, punctilious Giorgio Stivanello on the left, could both provide the ammunition Charles craved. If it was ever as consistently good as the service Harold Williams provided him, then the future would be full of goals. He hoped it would be of course, though he also hoped that the Juventus wingers would refrain from repeating Williams' witticisms about Charles's soaring reputation in football: 'I bloody made him, I did!'

Stivanello could run hundred-yard sprints in less than eleven seconds. Charles relished the prospect of connecting with a multitude of crosses from him in the new season. Kurt Hamrin was another exceptional wing man, in the class of Stan Matthews when it came to dribbling with the ball at his feet, but he would not be staying as teams in Italy had to abide by the rule on foreign players – a maximum of two – allowed in one team. Special as he was, Hamrin had less of the braggadocio about him than Omar Sivori, so he was out. Sivori was the perfect man to deliver flamboyancy to the team, something that Umberto Agnelli had insisted upon. Sivori would captivate and enchant the Juventus fans while opponents would resent his brilliance and his attempts at humiliating them by tricking them not once but twice, perhaps even more. He was famous (and infamous) for his love of the 'tunnel' or 'nutmeg', tapping the ball with his left foot through the legs of opponents and then collecting it at the other side. His right foot, though, existed primarily for standing on, more a simple appendage to keep his left foot company.

Centre-half Rino Ferrario, at around six feet tall, had a toughness about him, a look recognised by Charles as similar to a Leeds doorman intent on preventing drunkards entering his jazz club. A robust central defender – that was Ferrario's job summed up: undesirables shall not pass. Charles would have savoured a personal duel on the pitch with Ferrario; it would be *rough and tumble* but always good-natured. Ferrario's style as a player, though, Charles was less keen on. Centre-halves should be encouraged to pass the ball rather than just boot it clear, but such defenders were a rarity; first and foremost they were there as 'stoppers', as a general rule forbidden from ever dribbling or passing the ball out of defence.

Charles had dearly hoped to be playing football in Sweden, for Wales in the World Cup finals the following year, the summer of 1958. But the Welsh team's mediocrity in their qualification games meant he would have to wait a few more years for the next chance. And so, for now, he would have to make do with playing in Sweden for Juventus in their brief post-season tour of the country. More meaningless matches in which to go through the motions, though on a personal level Charles was quite excited. His excitement would dissipate as time wore on, alas. Taking part in just about any football match is more enjoyable than the daily routine of training, unless the opponents are no-hopers or there are very few spectators watching. In Sweden, the quality of the opposition might not be particularly high but the matches would be watched by enthusiastic crowds in sold-out stadia.

Ljubisa Brocic's first proper sight of John Charles in official, competitive action – albeit in 'pretend' combat – came in the opening friendly of the tour on 25th June. Juventus versus AIK Stockholm at the impressive Rasunda Stadium, which was set to be the venue for next year's World Cup Final. AIK were one of the country's better second-tier sides and the team contained eight Sweden internationals. The astonishing score-line, Juventus winning by ten goals to one, told a quite deceptive story; the hosts had continually taken the game to Juventus, only to be undone by ruthless counter-attacks. Charles scored two goals and played a part in the build-up to most of the others, of which Hamrin scored three and Sivori two. Irrespective of how the local resistance had been embarrassed, the press and the thousands of spectators were delighted with the spectacular display their esteemed guests had provided, Charles and the Swede Hamrin especially.

On 28th June in Vaxjo, on the Baltic coast and south of Stockholm, Juventus faced a 'mixed' team featuring players from Vaxjo and the Osters sports club. Charles scored three, all with his feet, in a 7-2 victory. A few days later, on 1st July, although he scored just once against Sundsvall, he played a significant part in all of the other goals, in a 9-2 victory. Their final game of the tour was against another lower-league club, IFK Umea. Watched by a record crowd of over twelve thousand, Juventus won 7-1. It actually had been quite a hard match: Umea had fielded a few Swedish internationals from other teams to strengthen their line-up. Charles excelled again, scoring four and gaining another man-of-the-match plaudit. In all the matches, just about everything he did – every shot, every header, every pass, every run, every challenge – had been praised and congratulated, including the mediocre or unsuccessful efforts. Even the coaches and hierarchy of Juventus Football Club had expressed their great satisfaction with his performances so far since joining. So, questioned Charles to himself ... was this it? Was it all going to be this easy, this straightforward, this undemanding and so very dull?

The Juventus return journey to Italy took a few hours, beginning in Lulea in the north of Sweden, via Stockholm and on to Milan's Malpensa Airport. Their twin-engine plane landed shortly after three o'clock in the afternoon. Back on terra firma of Milan, with the sun blazing down, it felt almost like they had just exited a refrigerator. There to meet them was the Juventus vice-president Remo Giordanetti, along with numerous Milanese football fans hoping to see some football celebrities. Being Milan, a city not known for its fondness of anything Torinese, this was quite unexpected. In the airport, club captain and unofficial head spokesman, Giampiero Boniperti, dealt with reporters asking for comments and quotes on the team's development. Amongst the usual type of questioning, he was asked for his thoughts on the talents of the giant John Charles. Boniperti remarked that he had seen many fine centre-forwards in his time, players formidable in the air as well as on the floor – he had seen Gunnar Nordahl 'The Fireman'; he had seen Alfredo Di Stefano, Tommy Lawton and Silvio Piola; and now he had seen John Charles. And John Charles was without doubt the best of them all.

The remainder of their journey home was completed by coach, lasting a little over two hours. As the road progressed and the Alps grew, the darker the sky became. Because of the wild nature of the elements around mountain ranges, the Piedmont area was frequently a victim of extreme weather. Today, as Charles would have (politely) termed it back in Britain, the weather was raining cats and dogs, and yet the atmosphere remained uncomfortably humid. From the coach he noticed lengthy swathes of the green landscape were flooded and swamped. He had seen similar conditions in England when on the road with Leeds United, and Harold Williams had tricked him, nearly twice in fact, first saying that the wet pastures had in fact been paddy fields, and then telling him also that there had once been a goalkeeper for Northern Ireland called Paddy Fields. And so now, when Boniperti tried claiming that there really were paddy fields on the outskirts of Turin, Charles looked dubious. Privately, he would have none of it; he wasn't going to get caught out again!

Hopeful that this filthy weather would not dampen the occasion too much, he was thinking more about being with Peggy and the boys again. Severer weather had struck while the team had been away, with millions of lira worth of damage caused already.

Inside the bus – seated alone across the aisle from Colombo and Charles – was Boniperti. He reached across again to Colombo and tapped him on the arm. Speaking in Italian he asked Colombo to relay questions to Charles. Although Charles comprehended extremely little of what Boniperti was saying, the manner in which he was speaking gave the impression that this was a forthright man full of confidence and self-belief. A man, therefore, with whom disputes were best avoided as he would be like a dog with a bone, never leaving it alone until he was happy the matter was finished with, and to his satisfaction. Charles had seen enough of him on the football pitch to know he was the perfect team captain who led by example almost always. Respectful and respected. Away from the playing surface, though, it was believed that the Boniperti family had been supporters of Mussolini's Fascists, a view that Boniperti himself was suspected of sympathising with. Thus, the Juventus players' trust and reliance in their captain was generally restricted to on-the-field matters rather than away from football matches.

'John, our captain is asking, did you use a rifle in your army training?' 'When we were having target practice, yes.'

A few more words from Boniperti … Colombo translated. 'He is wanting to know if you ever fired at a cloud.'

Charles paused for a few seconds, longer than normal … 'What? A cloud? In the sky?' Boniperti gestured to indicate he indeed meant the heavens, with Colombo corroborating.

'A cloud in the sky.'

Charles smiled slightly, 'No, my aim was never that bad. Why?'

Colombo gave the answer to Boniperti, who spoke for a few seconds more; then Colombo explained: 'On days of storm and rain like these, he says the farmers use shotguns to attempt the prevention of the storms which damage the crops in the fields.'

'What?'

Colombo nodded, 'Yes, the gunshot and chemicals can interrupt the storm clouds. They call them Cloud Shooters. The farmers shoot from the mountains and the hills …' Boniperti nodded eagerly before adding a few more words …

'And,' Colombo said, 'it is sometimes possible to hear them shooting the clouds in the night.'

Charles nodded too, apparently in agreement but in fact not believing a word of what they were telling him. He turned his attentions to looking out of the coach window again, deciding against asking the pair if they would understand him if he simply said 'Bollocks!' to them.

◎

He had passed nearby before with Peggy, but this was his first actual visit
to the Caffe Torino. He hadn't realised that 'caffe' was Italian for coffee,
assuming it meant 'café' or 'cafeteria', of which there were many – also
known as 'greasy spoons' – in Britain. The Caffe Torino reminded him
of a glorified tearoom, very much like those he'd visited with Peggy in
Yorkshire called Bettys. Nice but not really his preferred scene, much
more Peggy's sort of thing. He was mightily impressed today though;
everything about the place seemed so classy and expensive, similar to
the Principi albeit a less formal atmosphere. Even the entrance under
the cover of the arcade possessed a degree of glamour, the glow of the
immaculate window displays of mouth-watering confectionery shining
on a gold insignia in the shape of a bull embedded in the pavement.
The myth had it that passers-by were required to rub one of their feet
against the bull to bring them good fortune. Not noticing, Charles
casually stepped over it. He wouldn't have bothered about it anyway;
he wasn't at all superstitious. Inside, a lengthy wooden counter to
the left, three narrow, busy shelves running along the wall behind
it, a kaleidoscopic array of alcoholic drinks and liquor in bottles of
varying shapes and sizes. Above the shelves was another eye-catching
image of the Turin Bull, this time a circular medallion, around two
feet in diameter, and in a line at the far end next to the bar were a
dozen metal stools with red leather padded seats. Hanging from the
arched, intricately patterned ceiling were grand chandeliers, sparkling,
impressing. On the right side of the room loomed an even brighter
serving area of tall glass counters crammed with shelves of cakes and
delicacies and confectioneries and pastries. Turin was supposedly
famed for its fine coffee and chocolate, but here were many other
sweet temptations on display. And yet, in spite of all this splendour, it
was the image at the end of the room that dominated and demanded
most visitors' attention. Silhouetted against the long and high frosted
windows, was an exquisite spiral staircase. A splendid curl of marble
steps and an ornate banister leading up to rooms that many believe
belonged exclusively to Juventus Football Club.

Four waiters in identical uniforms – black trousers, black waistcoat, white shirt, black bow-tie – hurriedly deal with customers' needs, every task completed with proficiency and profuse politeness. The smattering of customers sitting at tables in the arcade have no cause to feel excluded; they are catered for with an identical degree of care and attention.

Striding by a cluster of diners seated around small square tables and the entrance to another busy room, the Juventus contingent headed straight for the staircase near the corner, a three-foot-high bronze nymph near the steps to greet them. It, she, would fit in well with the statues in Leeds near the Queens Hotel. Illuminating the back wall were small yellow lamps running parallel to the curve of the handrail – pretty and practical. Charles followed the half-dozen players up the steps, their intentions clearly being to relax and celebrate, this being the official start of their summer vacation. No one took much notice of them, something of a surprise to Charles; but then again the campaign just completed had not been one any Juventus man could feel particularly proud of. Upstairs he drank an Italian lager-beer-shandy – Moretti with lemonade stirred in – and regardless of the confusion his request had caused the waiter, the drink was pleasant enough and succeeded in quenching his mild thirst. The shandy wasn't up to the standard of a northern England shandy, but it was a creditable effort. From his first introduction as a lad in Swansea to ale, by his dad, he had never liked the taste, always asking for some lemonade to be added to his pint to help with the bitter taste. Beer and alcohol were not important to him. Flavio Emoli smiled as he spoke excitedly about something to Colombo, looking at Charles as he did so. While Charles recognised a few of his words, it was on the whole another rapid sequence of strange sounds and enunciations he had no hope of following. And so, as usual, Colombo was required to relay the message. This time it concerned famous visitors to the Caffe Torino, like Hollywood film stars James Stewart and Ava Gardner.

'Not together,' Colombo quickly confirmed. 'Ava Gardner was here early this year, with Walter Chiari who is very popular in our country. They were together in a film, and possibly more ...' and he winked. 'Have you heard of him, John?'

'I can't say I have, Umberto.'

'He is a very funny man.'

'I have heard of Ava Gardner – Frank Sinatra's wife.'

'I believe they are no longer together.'

'Ah, that's a shame.'

'Yes, yes … What do you think of this place?'

Charles considered for a few seconds, looking around the double room at the old paintings and maps and expensive mirrors on the walls, and the sunflower-yellow dining chairs placed around circular, white-clothed tables. 'I like it. It's, as we'd call it, plush.'

'Good! It is quiet here tonight but it will always be busy next season, especially when we win.'

From the ceiling hung more chandeliers, smaller ones, as well as – to Charles's surprise – a mirror ball. Although it wasn't presently in use, the tiny glinting panels were able to carry him back to the Astoria in Leeds, where he had first met Peggy, an eternity ago. Surrounded by revellers of Leeds interested only in dancing and having fun, and not in him. He had been with his best friend Peter when he met the woman who would become the centre of his life. A life which had very few pressures or concerns, and no stress.

The mirror ball prompted his departure from the Caffe Torino, a Juventus chauffeur driving him back to Via Susa 31 where he would reunite with his family and be greeted by wide smiles and heart-inflating affection. And when the children's excitement had mellowed a little, Terry and Melvyn would insist he read them a bedtime story or sing them a lullaby. The lullaby always won, usually by way of 'Sixteen Tons', which matched his baritone voice perfectly. John Charles was not a man to read bedtime stories for anyone. Peggy would stand at the bedroom door, loving everything of the scene except the choice of song.

7

Most of July 1957 had been a time of relaxation for the Juventus players and back-room personnel. With Brocic's stamina-sapping training regimes ready to be imposed in earnest on them, however, any member of the squad who had taken things a little too easy would regret it on their return to work. In previous years, when football seasons ended, Charles always put on a few pounds – even when keeping active by playing cricket for an amateur team – but not this year; this year he was slightly lighter. And now that he was starting a new term with a new team, he had quickly learned that Italian pre-season preparations were very different to those in England with Leeds. Although there was more work with the football, the sessions were physically harder, and for a *straniero* with a young family, mentally harder too.

In the run-up to each new season, Juventus transported the squad to private training camps miles away from their homes. Much of Juve's usual destination Villar Perosa practically belonged to the Agnellis; after buying Juventus Football Club in 1923, Edoardo Agnelli then funded the building of a football stadium, training facilities and accommodation there. This year Juventus's pre-season destination would be two weeks in Cuneo, less than sixty miles south of Turin, close to the border with France. Charles would be away from his wife and three young sons yet again; for all the improvements to his lifestyle, there was nothing to make him feel good about another extended absence from Peggy and the kids.

It was said there had been 'difficulties' during Bruno Nicole's transfer negotiations, difficulties being the player's apparent unwillingness to leave his club Padova for Juventus. Whether the reports were accurate or not, the player was certainly about to take 'the plunge' now, as four men grabbed him by his arms and legs. He struggled but could not escape or free himself from their grip. They were enjoying their boisterous play; he was not. In fact he was a little scared; he was after all only seventeen years old. No one there noticed his anxiety; instead just about everyone cheered to see him lifted off his feet and thrown into the deep end of the swimming pool. Laughter all around, except from the chosen individual in the water of course; he was too busy spluttering and involuntarily swallowing water. The boy was panicking because he did not know how to swim. During the commotion, John Charles rested on a sunbed. Sunbathing was mundane but the physical results made the boredom worthwhile. He had been lying on his back ignoring the fuss and incomprehensible chatter of his restless team-mates, and studying his eyelids and the strange colours and shapes the sun imprinted on his vision. First a small circle of orange stain, then red, then green, yellow and finally black, until all faded into nothing, only to then become *something*.

The sounds of laughter and the splashing of water jolted him. He looked up, shielding his eyes from the sunlight, trying to view the scene around him. He anticipated that something was wrong. Unsure what, and at the risk of making a fool of himself, he sprang into action, deciding to act first and ask questions later. Striding to the poolside, he dove in, aiming to grasp the torso of the individual thrashing around in the pool. Charles calmly and swiftly supported the lad's head above the water with his left arm and reversed him to the safety of the pool's edge. The tall Nicole was Juventus's newest recruit, amongst their most valuable assets, and they had nearly drowned him in some form of initiation ceremony!

Earlier in the year, before their match away at Padova, the Juventus players had been told, 'Beware the boy striker.' That boy had been Nicole and those players had paid insufficient heed to the warning; he played a major role in the home team's victory. This was not an acceptable or timely way of getting their own back. The transfer fee of around £60,000 for the player whose right foot contained an unerring shot was another national record. Of probable little relevance, unless he was to be tasked with the team's throw-ins, was the fact he was a phenomenal javelin thrower too. Yes, great things were expected of him, provided he lived long enough to deliver.

The scene of the near-criminal fun had been the luxurious Grand Hotel, a mountain retreat near the city of Cuneo, a highly picturesque part of the generally beautiful Piedmont region. Cuneo had been the personal choice of Brocic for his squad of players' pre-season preparation, known as a team's '*ritiro*', the withdrawal to a private base for intensive training for big matches or, in this case, the new campaign set to start next month. It was a good choice and the weather had been kind without being uncomfortably (or harmfully) hot and with notably less humidity than Turin. Twice as high as that city, the atmosphere was infinitely cleaner too, fresher, healthier, more stimulating. No expense was spared by Juventus, so the catering at the hotel and the facilities were of the highest quality. And while the Cuneo public were excited to have the team residing there, they did not encroach or try to disturb the players at work. Even the media men kept a respectful distance, eagerly monitoring the training methods of Brocic but waiting patiently for official press conferences and interview invitations.

Nineteen Juventus players – two goalkeepers, seventeen outfielders – were there for the *ritiro*, along with the customary company of the team masseur Amilcare Sarroglia (masseurs here were the equivalent of physios and trainers in Britain). Two training sessions held each day during pre-season, with athletic, gymnastic and weights exercises in the morning and various football matches and games and team-bonding exercises each afternoon. In theory the athletics labour in the mornings would tire the players, while the food and the football work after lunch would reinvigorate them. The reduced threat of heatstroke and similar afflictions allowed Brocic more time to work on increasing their stamina and pace. Although the welfare of his players was paramount, Brocic was known to favour a daily 'hard hour' as well as a 'hard day', which was normally the Friday. The hard hour consisted of non-stop drills, running and exercising, with only a few seconds' break for the players in the entire sixty minutes. The hard day was when the training sessions were designed to be their most arduous. Despite the pain, the players apparently enjoyed the increased labour, which in turn enabled Brocic to answer reporters' questions in a positive fashion.

Is he happy with his team's preparations for the new season?

Answer: Yes, very satisfied so far; the boys had responded fully to the training demands and to his new 'manifesto' of the team being more adventurous. The emphasis in the coming season will very much be on attack attack attack.

Does he think Juventus will win the league?

Answer: No, they will not win the title, but they will show it is a squad of players of great possibilities.

Will Bruno Nicole be in the Juventus first-eleven for the opening match of the season in three weeks?

Answer: If he trained well enough and showed the correct attitude and aptitude, then the chances were strong; they had not paid all that money just to put him in the youth team, after all.

Would he agree that the team appears to have an imbalance due to there being no winger on the right, and what did he propose to do about it?

Answer: You will have to wait and see. As he had said, there were great possibilities in the squad.

Are there too many attacking players in the Juventus squad?

Answer: No, he did not think so, primarily because he was inclined to the theory that in football it was much better to attack than to defend. As before, attack attack attack would be the order of the day.

Does the Welshman John speak Italian yet?

Answer: Everyone in Juventus is very pleased with the progress made by John, in all aspects of his development, and while it is to be a long journey, he does not travel alone. Such teamwork and camaraderie was what he demanded from his players and staff, not just in football but in life itself. Teamwork involved players believing in and respecting their team-mates, believing they can help the mutual cause and respecting their choices, which are for the team and not the individual. For example, it is easier for a man to pass the football to a team-mate who is facing the opponents' goal than it is to a man who is not facing the right direction.

In drawing a close to the proceedings, Brocic spoke of his unbreakable belief concerning training techniques, specifically that football players should have a football at their individual disposal as often as possible. Similar to how musicians practise with musical instruments and artists with the tools of their chosen medium, football players should train with the football. He did not want athletes, he wanted athletic football players. This would all have been music to John Charles's ears, if only he had understood the language.

◎

Enjoyable training routines, excellent treatment and service, glorious food and pleasurable surroundings notwithstanding, John Charles was in a gloomy state. As darkness descended, the more his mood beclouded. The desolation of loneliness, even within a crowd. Within it, but not a part of it. He had been unable to help himself; he had slid into a melancholia and was feeling sorry for himself. The players were permitted to spend their free time how they liked but the ten o'clock curfew meant that the free time was rather restricted, plus there was not actually much to do leisure-wise. Even the numerous birds in the surrounding woodland sounded bored and listless. A small glass of wine with the players' late evening meal was the only alcohol permitted. Brocic was by no means draconian in his ways but he was adamant that strong discipline within his men was crucial for a team to succeed.

There was a limit to how many postcards Charles could write to loved ones, and how many games of cards and frames of billiards he could enjoy. The poker with the regular gamblers Sivori, Stivanello and Emoli was entertaining but potentially too expensive, and he had never read a book in his life and wasn't about to start trying; watching Italian television was wholly pointless, of course. And so, almost child-like, he had grown bored very easily. And he had always hated being bored. Trap-door thoughts swept him back to his life in Leeds, where virtually everything was inferior to the *dolce vita* of Turin except for the social life and his circle of friends and loved ones. In Leeds, his friends – the married ones or the bachelors – had always been available practically at any time of day, for visits to the cinema or public house or Working Men's Club or café, snooker hall or even jazz club. Or just for a chat about football. He longed for a return to those simplistic times, and to people he had grown up with and experienced so much of real life with.

Here his room-mate and best Italian friend, Colombo, would try to help, even buying himself American magazines so as to improve his own foreign-language skills. Sometimes, alas, there are people who just want to be left alone. Only a harsh critic could find real fault with Charles's efforts at learning the language and the ways of Italy, but as well as being his own harshest critic he was a slow learner too. He would fail to join conversations with the players, and with every comment he failed to comprehend, his self-confidence dipped a little more. No one had said it would be easy ... no one had said it would be this hard either.

Colombo was concerned to see his Welsh friend looking so sombre. Attempting to cheer his mood, he commented that Charles's expression was like that of a melted candle, and asked if anything was wrong. Charles lied, answering that he was just tired, very tired. And then he bade his room-mate goodnight. Even with their friendship relatively young, Colombo recognised the behaviour as uncharacteristic. He knew also that it needed addressing.

Cuneo's elegant and grand sixteenth-century town hall (not as impressive as Leeds' equivalent, decided Charles) was the venue for the Juventus party's official reception held by Mayor Delpozzo. Proud to have such renowned guests staying in their province, presentations from officials representing Cuneo were to be made to coach Brocic and club captain Boniperti of locally made bronze-plated medallions, each bearing a crest of the city.

The players were content that their captain's leadership qualities extended away from the pitch to occasions like these. Given a choice, most would avoid such affairs, but Boniperti was more than comfortable with it all, almost as if he believed he naturally belonged to such occasions. After the reception, with the exception of a certain trio, the players were taken back to the training base. Charles was one of the trio and was unsure of what was happening, with coach Brocic's explanation hardly enlightening him: 'John, you will be accompanying Boni and Colombo this afternoon on another important exercise.'

Carle Hospital, built in the 1930s, served the explicit purpose of caring for children seriously ill with 'the white plague' (so called because sufferers often became extremely pale), better known as tuberculosis. Located in the hilly hamlet of Confreria, fifteen kilometres from Cuneo, the hospital/sanatorium was the temporary home for two hundred very ill boys and girls. Great progress had been made in the treatment and prevention of tuberculosis, but there was no actual, absolute cure as yet. The global situation was improving all the time and survival rates were getting higher, but the horrible truth was that many children, especially those living in the northern regions, would succumb to the disease. Nature's best defence against tuberculosis was good clean air, and this Alpine location had plenty of it of course, even with the presence of an old mineral mine in the area.

A ward sister, whose name Charles did not grasp, walked them through the Carle Hospital building to the rear grounds. She spoke to Boniperti and Colombo all the way. The journey took only a moment; Charles nevertheless was relieved to be in the open air again. He disliked hospitals and their chemical smells and cold, clinical appearance. Even the excitement of children (and of pretty nurses) failed to fully dispel the unease he felt when inside a hospital ward. Outside, within the spacious, glorious green garden and lawns, his unease was immediately superseded by incredulity. Before him, stretching across the scene like perfectly placed white stepping stones and skirting the many pairs of patio doors, was the bizarre sight of dozens of hospital beds, each containing, underneath pale-blue blankets, a child. Each and every one of those children, as well as those young patients within the hospital walls, were delighted to see these visitors. So thrilled were they to meet the players, and to be given their autographs, that members of the press would go on to claim that some of the children quite miraculously began to regain colour in their cheeks. The only people there who *really* gained rosy hues to their cheeks – and for a very different reason – were the on-duty nurses. That very different reason carried the name of Umberto Colombo, but there was no denying the spirits-raising effects on the children of the visit.

As the three Juventus men walked back to their car, Colombo sighed a contented sigh and looked at Charles at his side. 'It is a nice feeling to make the children smile, is it not?'

Charles did not answer. Had he done so he would probably have embarrassed himself, the emotion in his throat and tears in his eyes exposing him. There *were* no answers when it came to the suffering of innocent children; he could not fully grasp the cruelty of the illness or the fact that some, too many, of those children he had just befriended would not recover from the disease. He felt powerless and pathetic ... he *was* powerless and pathetic. For all the lack of wealth and luxuries in his life as a child in Swansea, his parents had ensured their children were raised in clean and healthy surroundings, even in the clouds of industrialised surroundings, and for that he would always be grateful.

Approaching their vehicle, acknowledging his friend's sadness, Boniperti smiled sympathetically and put an arm around the big man's shoulders. 'Good, good, John.'

◎

Friendly matches between club teams were of course quite insignificant in the context of sports competition, and at times only marginally more interesting than training. Friendlies also increased the risk of a player suffering an injury. Injuries could be costly to a player if they caused him to miss league matches, as only the basic wage is then paid, with the lucrative match bonuses vanishing. Charles, though, was reasonably enthusiastic and looking forward to their first such fixture of the 1957–58 pre-season. With three weeks to go before the first league match, this friendly against Biellese would be an opportunity to work hard against real opponents while learning more about his team-mates and the coach's strategy and desired style of play.

Even though he had been sad and frustrated at having to miss Terry's third birthday the day before, on Sunday 19th August, Charles mustered himself to work hard, right from the referee's first blow of the whistle through to his last, and he did learn a few things about certain team-mates, primarily Omar Sivori, though not in a positive respect. In the match, while Charles constantly searched for the right run, the right pass and the right decision for the sake of the team, Sivori was persistently selfish and wasteful, dribbling with the ball instead of providing the appropriate pass to colleagues in advanced positions, or attempting 'tunnels' to dismal effect. Individualism can be marvellous entertainment for the crowds, but it can easily be counter-productive for the team. A real problem was Sivori's frustrating habit of ignoring others' advice, his team-mates', the captain's, even the coach's. Charles never cared who scored as long as the team won;

Sivori performed as if he wanted to get every goal himself, humiliating opposing defenders and goalkeepers in the process. It was clear that if the team was to succeed in the new season, Boniperti could well be the crucial player, not just in leading it but in ensuring that the two 'superstars' in attack linked up well enough to work together for the common good.

The Biellese team, from Serie C – the third tier of the league – was comprised of young, inexperienced players. The match took place in Biella, eighty kilometres north-east of Turin and drew a packed-in crowd of three thousand. With hundreds more unable to gain entry, the crowd-pulling appeal of high-spending Juventus had satisfied the match organisers' hopes … tinged with the regret that they hadn't charged more for admission! Juventus won 5-0, though the Biellese players were not at all disgraced, especially in attack on the wings where the Juventus full-backs often found themselves pressed. Bruno Nicole, normally a centre-forward, played in the number 7 shirt on the right wing and showed enough skill to suggest he could fill the role very well. He supplied the cross for Charles's only goal of the game, a simple header (simple because it was a perfectly placed pass). After the match, Charles was lauded as comfortably the best player on the pitch. He didn't care much about that sort of thing, it all meant very little, plus he rarely agreed with singling out individuals from a team for praise. On this occasion, he felt, he had hardly exerted himself; there had been no need to: the 'challenge' had not been up to much.

John Charles believed he was in the best physical condition of his life, his fitness levels at their highest, with improved stamina and stronger muscle power. All he needed to do now was maintain it and not to sustain an injury by overdoing it or trying too hard. Physical fitness was not the same as match fitness; the footballer can be at his peak physically but for the matches his body needs to habituate to the exertions and the bodily contact of sports combat. Judging by the Juventus matches he had played in so far, he had very little to worry about on that score. Today's pre-season training would take place in two sessions, one mid-morning, the other mid-afternoon. The weather was good but not too good; there would be no need to delay the training until late afternoon due to too-high temperatures.

Despite the morning session commencing at ten-thirty, Omar Sivori had managed to be late again. Only the chickens get up at that time of day where he came from! Coach Brocic noticed these things but was happy for his captain, Boniperti, to dish out necessary rebukes. Sivori didn't really care who reproached him or who called him a bad professional; he hadn't meant to be late and after all, he was – in his own mind at least – their best player, and now that he was there what was the problem? Quit the fussing, let me show you how to play football!

Not entirely dissimilar to National Service in the army, training drills and routines in football can be mind-numbingly boring and repetitious. Fundamentally they are meant to be, so as to instil discipline into the individual, and to acquaint them with moves and habits until they become almost second nature. Football training of course is less regimental than the army but the principles are quite alike. At Leeds United, Charles had grown to strongly dislike training and he was not very good at concealing it. At Juventus, he was an improved professional – in truth he could hardly have sunk any lower! – but by mid-August 1957 he was restless again. Brocic's drills and routines were varied and, thanks to various team-bonding exercises and games, much less boring than Charles had had to endure in England. Nevertheless, they still eventually became dull. A sportsman thrives on challenges; he forever aims to achieve more by overcoming the challenges. Charles saw no challenges on the football-career horizon. It all seemed to be predictable, easier, cosier – but then came Bologna.

Juventus's second pre-season friendly took place in the evening of Tuesday 28th August in the magnificent Bolognese Stadio Renato Dall'Ara. Less than two weeks before the start of the real season. The capacity of this stadium was fifty thousand and the official match attendance was given as forty-five thousand. This was inaccurate: hordes of people gained access to the match without paying, and inside the ground the overcrowding forced scores of spectators to climb over the terrace fencing to avoid being crushed. Juventus's opponents this time around were a higher grade than previously: Bologna of Serie A. Bologna had finished last season in a creditable fifth in the division, four places above Juventus. Even taking into consideration this league table superiority, no sensible person would have anticipated the evening's final score.

The stars of Juventus were soon brought back down to earth. By half-time, they were 3-1 down, and it got even worse as Bologna scored three more in the second half, without reply. Their left-winger, Ezio Pascutti, *scorched* the defence, scoring a hat-trick and generally being a relentless tormentor. Juventus were in disarray, their so-called midfield virtually invisible, over-run by a keener, sharper team which was better organised and played with flair and gusto. Boniperti looked unfit, Sivori again rarely passed the ball and Nicole seemed this time to be unsuited to playing on the wing. Most of the players looked confused and inept, frequently straying out of position and even colliding with each other a couple of times, as if running blind-folded. In goal, Mattrel complained afterwards that the match had been his very first involving floodlights, which had near blinded him on a few occasions. Meanwhile, Charles had received minimal service from his team-mates but managed at least to score the Juventus goal, another simple header. He did not play well, he did not play poorly. Simply, without anything remotely resembling a good supply of passes, he was ineffective, the best of a bad bunch, a very bad bunch.

The calamitous score-line caused Umberto Agnelli much consternation. How the hell could they have allowed such a humiliation to happen? Had he wasted all that money on the three new players? Should he have improved the defence and the midfield instead of focusing on the attack? There was little time left to put things right, just one friendly fixture remaining. Agnelli had to be sure that Brocic understood the message that such an embarrassment must never happen again.

Brocic was suitably unhappy. Knowing that the club president – young enough to be his son but powerful enough to end his career with the stroke of a pen – was annoyed with him was not a pleasant feeling. Bad as it was, however, this result was not the first lousy score-line of his coaching career, and he doubted it would be the last. And on a brighter note, friendly defeats could help a coach learn more about his team than victories. Better the alarm bell ringing early than one that rings late or not at all. He realised that Juventus had not played enough friendly matches and thus their preparations had been lacking. Was he to blame for that? Possibly. He certainly would be held accountable if improvements weren't made, and quickly. It was essential that the players reacted to the Bologna debacle positively. If not, then it would appear they did not respect him enough and that his authority was being ignored. Brocic was not concerned about being popular with them, but he believed it was crucial for them to respect him.

The next Juventus training session was a quieter affair than normal, almost as if everyone was in a state of mild shock in the aftermath of a terrible storm. Certain players were worried that their substandard performance in Bologna would provoke Brocic's ire – and the fact was it would have been entirely justified – with stern reprimands beckoning. But that was not his way; he was a man of quiet determination and commendable self-control. No point in the coach being upset or causing upset by impulsively criticising and saying things that would be regretted later; the best way was to wait until emotions were calm and moods less volatile. Brocic preferred to wait at least a day before reviewing and analysing match performances with his players and staff, enabling him to convey his observations in a measured and tactful manner. He would choose to have a 'quiet word' with players individually during training and then address the squad as a whole. There were always players who were not in need of performance analyses, either because they had not played quite as poorly as their team-mates or because they were mature and intelligent enough to know where they had gone wrong and how to address the problems. Therefore, John Charles was surprised and disappointed to be taken to one side on the training pitch by Brocic, for a private consultation as it were.

'John, what are your thoughts about the Bologna game? Was your performance good?' Brocic asked.

'I thought it was a bad game, Mister Brocic; none of us played well.' 'And yourself?'

Charles's gaze dropped and he shrugged. 'I didn't have much chance to do anything ...'

'Because the passing was not good enough and there were not enough passes made?' Charles nodded.

'What can we do about the problem? What can you do?' He didn't know.

'John, you can, you must, communicate better. If any of our boys are not trying hard enough or not doing their job, then you must tell them. If you can see what they are doing wrong then you must explain to them. And if you are not receiving the ball when you should be, then you must demand it.'

'But they wouldn't understand me; my Italian is not good.'

'That is not a strong excuse, John. You must improve; football is not just in the feet, it is in the mind and it is in the words! You must learn the Italian language more quickly.'

'But ...'

Brocic put his hands on Charles's shoulders. 'You are wrong to object, John. Boni is the captain of course but there are other players capable of being leaders. You are one of them; the club want you to score many goals, but Umberto Agnelli has not paid all that money for you to be silent when matches are difficult.'

'I don't understand.'

'You will, you will. There is so much more to you than scoring goals. Would you rather be a sheep or a shepherd?'

Their final pre-season friendly match, on Sunday 2nd September, was against Lazio, who shared the vast Stadio dei Centomila with the capital city's other big team, Roma. Perhaps something radical was needed from the coach, by way of dropping certain players or altering the team tactics. Perhaps or not; radical changes certainly were made. Radical yet very simple: Brocic told his five midfield players to forget about running with the ball or trying to take men on, and to instead support the three-man defence. Defending is the priority; the Juventus attack can take care of itself. The middle third of the pitch would be a no man's land. When they had possession of the ball, it had to be passed accurately up to the attack of Boniperti, Sivori or Charles. With the emphasis on accurately.

The hundred-thousand-capacity stadium was approximately half filled. Judging from their lacklustre performance in the match, the Lazio players seemed to regard it as unimportant, whereas the visitors very much had points to prove. Points to prove to each other, to Brocic and to Agnelli. And prove them they did, scoring four times in a comfortable 4–2 win, all of their goals coming from slick movement, pin-point passing and proficient finishing. The interplay between Charles and Sivori had improved markedly, to such an extent that both scored a goal each, Sivori's stemming from a precise through-ball from Charles, the Argentine dancing around the goalkeeper and passing the ball into the net. The positives taken into account, the negative of conceding two goals against a 'lazy' Lazio side could not be ignored; the Juventus defending needed to improve.

The September heat had been unrelenting throughout the first week of the month; it had been a hellish few days. And today was Friday, the 'hard day', full of high-tempo exercise routines, with and without the use of footballs, eighty- and ninety-metre sprints, and races between players carrying a ten-pound medicine ball each. And gymnastics, and jumping, leap-frogging, attack versus defence, heading practice, on-the-move passing and volleying practice ... virtually non-stop for nearly three very demanding hours. Once the training was finished for the week – Saturday being a rest day – each player was instructed to take things easy, and advised to eat heartily and healthily, with no alcohol, to replenish and preserve their energy levels in preparation for the big match each Sunday.

Just three days to go to the first match of the new league season, at home to Verona. Outwardly, John Charles gave little indication as to his anticipation of his Juventus debut, but inside he was by turn nervous and excited, apprehensive and enthused. Today had been tough, primarily due to the oppressive heat and humidity. Being a Welshman and adopted Yorkshireman, he quite enjoyed this unusual sensation of burning sunshine. As his mum used to say, it was always raining somewhere, it was just unfortunate that 'somewhere' too often applied to South Wales and West Yorkshire. And after all, he liked how the Italian climate had helped him trim down in weight but become stronger and quicker; his hair was also a lighter shade, his skin tone darker, a pleasing golden brown. Piedmont had been good to him; good *for* him; and Peggy certainly had no complaints about her husband growing even more handsome.

Colombo and Charles dined in a restaurant a few streets away from the Principi di Piemont. In a rear corner of the Trattoria Toscana Biagini restaurant, seated at a round table away from the window and the view of any curious passers-by, in turns the Italian man spoke

English and his Welsh companion reciprocated by speaking Italian to the best of his ability. Conversation would be a slow affair but that was no issue; their friendship was a solid one and they enjoyed each other's company.

'Did you like your spaghetti?' asked Umberto Colombo.

'Yes, it is nice. It is always nice here, though a bit boring too,' John Charles replied.

'Yes, if a man does not love pasta, the menu lacks variety. Do you miss the cuisine of home?'

Charles smiled. 'Yes, of Wales and England. Fish and chips, fried breakfasts. Bacon especially; the bacon in Italy is not good.'

'Pasta is good for big appetites. And you John, you have a big appetite.' 'I like the food more in England. Peggy also.'

'We should build our own restaurant. We could call it Big John's.'

'Or Big Bert's.' Charles laughed.

The distraction of their usual waiter (Vittorio) carrying a neat pile of daily newspapers and weekly magazines to their table, provided new subjects of conversation. He placed the papers on the table and returned to the kitchen, arms full with their used plates and utensils. This week's publications would be even more interesting now that the new season was about to commence; there would be 'expert' opinions and forecasts on each team's chances of Serie A glory for the coming season. Colombo pulled out a few stapled titles from the stack, with large colour-photograph covers, to hand to Charles. 'Lifestyle' magazines and sports periodicals. He began reading the *Guerin Sportivo* newspaper himself, searching for articles relating to Serie A and Juventus in particular. The club's 'newsworthiness' had increased markedly due to Agnelli's exciting spending. Meanwhile Charles spent his time studying football photographs and trying to decipher the captions.

Colombo pointed to a cartoon in the newspaper amusing him.

'You know this will be the first *stagione* with television broadcasts of Serie A football matches?' He didn't wait for a reply. 'Here is two players … they are measuring the length of their football shorts. The number three player asks the number six why they are doing it. The number six player answers that it is the Knee of Modesty; we must not offend anyone watching the TV by revealing too much flesh.'

Charles nods and smiles politely. Colombo isn't fooled ... Charles either doesn't get the joke or he simply doesn't find it funny. Colombo will make sure he understands the next joke ... 'Did I tell you any of the history of our team, John?'

'A bit.'

'You know that our colours came from your Notts County football club?'

'Yes. Originally Juventus wore pink.'

'Nearly correct, the first ever shirts were white.'

'Okay ...'

'The pink shirts came next, with a black collar and a tie!'

'Strange.'

'Yes, strange. And you know our team nicknames?'

'La Vecchia Signora – the Old Lady. And the Bianco-neri ... the white-blacks.'

'Good, good. But did you know that we had a different nickname when the team first wore the stripes?'

Charles slowly shakes his head.

'Yes, instead of the Bianco-neri they were first called the Nero-bianchis.'

'Yes?'

'Yes, the Nero-bianchis. Because those first shirts had the stripes positioned differently. Instead of white and black, they were in the sequence of black and white.'

Charles sent a trademark inquisitive stare but the intrusion of a wry smile ruined the pretence ... 'I am not the cleverest man but I know when someone is kidding with me.'

Colombo laughs and slams the table with the palm of his hand in mock disappointment ... 'Ah, it was a brave attempt.'

'You will be telling me that Boniperti's Cloud Shooters story is true as well ...' Colombo paused, a puzzled expression on his face. 'But John, it is, it really is.'

Charles shakes his head again. Vittorio brings two coffees and asks if he can get them anything more to eat. Charles says no, thank you. Colombo declines, with a shake of the head.

Colombo: 'This newspaper, *Guerin Sportivo*, is published here in Turin but they do not like Juventus. They sing for Torino. They are kind to us today though, John, and here they say you are the most formidable striker of all time. I never trust them; every compliment has a thorn. They criticise Agnelli for spending lavishly on our attack and not doing a thing to cover up the weak defence. They call it madness, paying for a costly crown for the head while the feet are neglected and bare. They do not respect Brocic also, they say he is a pawn and not a coach, and that foreign coaches are bad for Italian football. But they say that you are now called King John.'

Charles shrugs away the flattery. 'Do you think they're right about a weak defence?'

Colombo shrugs his shoulders, and then smiles. 'We will learn more on Sunday, I guess. Your Majesty.'

'You should bow when you talk to me.'

'Ha, yes! My apologies.'

Margaret the nanny had slept in again, meaning Peggy had had to prepare all the bairns' breakfasts as well as her own and John's, in addition to seeing to the laundry, the washing up, the shopping and the cleaning and upkeep of the flat. Preparing breakfast wasn't a hard task, especially on a Saturday morning, but it was an inconvenience and annoying. She had her driving test coming up; she didn't need any distractions like this. Over-sleeping a couple of times was excusable, but when it gets to be a regular feature, it becomes a more serious problem. Peggy always tried to avoid confrontation in life – no good ever came from arguing when emotions were running high – but the situation with Margaret was deteriorating. John was no use at all; all domestic matters were Peggy's responsibility and so he would not even consider talking about the matter with the nanny.

Leaving her husband in charge of the boys eating their breakfast – a loose definition of the term 'in charge'; it was like the two elder boys had staged a food fight in the kitchen – Peggy walked along the apartment corridor to Margaret's room. She knocked on the wooden door with the knuckle of her right index finger, quietly but not too quietly.

'Margaret?' she enquired, and without waiting for an answer twisted the door knob and entered the room. It was cool, dark, soundless. 'Margaret?' she said again. Silence. She could not even be sure Margaret was breathing. Good God, she thought, has she died? But then came relief in the form of a pained groan from the curled-up body in the bed.

'Peggy? What time is it?'

'It's nearly half past nine.'

'Sorry, I must have missed the alarm clock.'

'Are you alright?'

Margaret yawned and slowly sat up, preparing to get out of bed … 'No, not really. I'm sorry, my gut has been giving me gyp all night.'

'Oh. Oh dear. Is it something you ate?'

'No, I've had it a while, it just felt worse last night, excruciating pain in my stomach.'

'But you're feeling okay now?' asked Peggy; she felt a twinge of guilt for asking.

'Yes, I think so … I'm really sorry, Peggy.'

'Never mind that now, as long as you're alright. Do you want an aspirin or anything?'

'No thank you. I was taking some tablets but I seem to have run out.'

'How about something to eat?'

'I'd better not …'

'You need something, even if it's just some soup …'

'Yes, maybe you're right. I don't think I can stomach much, mind you,' Margaret yawned.

'I could add a bit of pasta if you like.'

'No, please don't! I think pasta has been part of the problem, like it's just sitting there in my gut.'

After preparing a bowl of tinned tomato soup for the nanny, Peggy and the reluctant John went for a stroll and to do some shopping, wheeling baby Peter around in his pram. Margaret stayed at their home to look after Melvyn and Terry, her stomach pains seemingly having subsided. That said, there was no hiding the fact that she looked quite wretched, even paler, thinner and more tired than before. And while she wasn't exactly in Peggy's good books, her employer genuinely was fond of her; Margaret had on the whole been a great help. True, she was reasonably paid for her efforts but the relationship between a nanny and the mother of the children has to be more than just a professional arrangement. That was certainly how Peggy saw it at least. And Margaret had been Peggy's only real friend in Turin during their early days there, before Elsie and to a lesser extent her husband Alec emerged.

◎

Hours after she had sent the boys to sleep-land with a lullaby weighing sixteen tons – which naturally sounded better from their father's lips but he wasn't there to do it – and with baby Peter sound asleep too, Peggy was woken by sounds that might have been fragments of a dream of her own. She blinked at the luminous hands on the clock at her bedside. It was past one o'clock in the morning; they had been asleep for a good couple of hours. She wasn't happy to be disturbed, but at least baby Peter slept on in his cot against the near wall. Perhaps the absence of her husband had affected her sleep by creating a voice in her dreams, calling her name. That could explain it, a bad dream to make her heart beat faster, disrupting her sleep. But then she heard it again, her name being called, morosely, pained, hauntingly. Peggy realised it could only be Margaret. She quickly got out of the bed and quietly made her way to Margaret's bedroom a few paces from her own.

She switched the light on. Margaret was lying on her side, curled up again, almost in the foetal position. She uttered another long groan. 'Is it your stomach again?' Peggy asked anxiously, crouching by the bed and putting the palm of her hand on Margaret's forehead.

Margaret's temperature was unnaturally high and her hair soaked with perspiration.

'I can't move, Peggy; it hurts too much.'

'Is there any medicine you can take?'

'No ... The doctor gave me cortisone pills to take but there's none left.' 'The doctor?'

'In Leeds. I should have told you ...'

'Why didn't you?'

'I thought you might not give me the job if I did.'

'Margaret, even I know cortisone is serious!'

'I'm sorry, I thought I was getting better.'

Peggy ignored her. 'I'm going to have to ask someone; I don't know what to do.'

'Neither do I. Can you get me a doctor?'

'I'll find out,' Peggy said, leaving the bedroom.

She hurried to the living room where their telephone was, switching on the light and looking for a number in the family's address book, a small, brown leather-bound pad. Finding the number she had been looking for, she memorised it and commenced dialling. The ringing tone sounded at the other end of the line for more than a minute – an interminable time.

Finally, a female voice came through, terse, '*Sí? Chi sta chiamando?*'

'Elsie, it's Peggy Charles. I'm sorry to call you so late at night, but I couldn't think of anyone else to ask.'

'Peggy! What's the matter?'

'It's our nanny, Margaret, she's very poorly. She needs a doctor, or an ambulance, I don't know.'

'What's wrong with her?'

'Well, she has a fever … and she's in a terrible lot of pain, in her stomach. She's just told me that she used to take cortisone tablets for it but she ran out of them.'

'Cortisone? Heavens, that sounds serious; it's something to do with adrenal glands in the body not working correctly.'

'She can't seem to move, the pain is too bad.'

'Okay, she needs to go to the hospital; I will call for an ambulance. You'll need to look out for it but I'm not sure what else there is you can do for her. I would think try to cool her down and don't let her eat or drink anything other than a sip of water. I'll do it now, Peggy; you put the telephone down, okay?'

'Yes, thank you so much, Elsie. Goodnight. Sorry again.'

'No need to apologise; goodnight.'

Peggy replaced the receiver and quickly walked to the kitchen, dampening a towel with cool water. Margaret wasn't awake. Peggy sat at her side, dabbing the towel on Margaret's forehead. Thankfully, the nanny's breathing seemed to be quite normal, not that Peggy really had any idea of the condition or whether she was seriously ill or not. Less than half an hour later two ambulance men had arrived and taken Margaret away in the night on a stretcher. The children hadn't known a thing about the drama, sleeping right through it. Peggy was a mix of emotions: sad that Margaret had been so ill and taken to hospital, angry at her stupidity in not telling anyone about the cortisone and letting the problem get so bad, and above all else, relieved that she hadn't died. She could not, however, have imagined that she would never see Margaret McMillan again.

PART TWO

SEPTEMBER 1957

Curses innumerable, curses timeless. Curses of the Juventus masses, against their lowly paid livelihoods and lack of riches, and limited options and unremitting, filthy working conditions. These Juventus masses, thousands of them Fiat employees and migrants from the Italian south and foreign lands, have helped pay for the team's new, expensive superstars. They need heroes, they yearn excitement and they crave victory and success. If this team does not fulfil, there will be hell to pay and they will make sure the pretenders know it, in curses to the skies, curses to the football players. Watching the team is a release, the followers a kettle simmering, a volcano smouldering, and when victory is achieved it is elation. When not, it is fury. Summer 1957, a time of intrigue and excitement on the business side of the club, and the passion of the fans, the *tifosi*, has been building; there will be in excess of seventy thousand of them attending the team's first league match of the new season.

The blades of the ceiling fan hummed the air, cooling but never quite defeating the smell of liniment. In spite of the drama at home, Charles slept well the night before, and he had eaten well today, more food consumed than his team-mates could quite believe in truth. The waiters of the Trattoria Toscana Biagini, the team's customary late Sunday morning, pre-match meal venue continually brought platefuls to the long table and Charles had helped empty them. Had his team-mates known his appetite was actually less voracious than normal due to the warm conditions – as well as a slight case of nervousness – their eyes would probably have widened even further in wonder at his food intake.

His nervousness only increased when he saw his Juventus shirt waiting for him in the home changing room, adorning a personalised hanger in his small wardrobe. The stencilled and very bright red vinyl 9 on the shirt back was resplendent over the famous black and white stripes. His white cotton shorts and nylon socks lay folded on the seat, a pair of lightweight shin-pads on top. And his boots – much lighter and more comfortable than the near clodhoppers of home – had been placed on the floor. On the seat to his left, Omar Sivori's kit was similarly arranged, minus shin-pads which he always refused to wear, opting to play with socks rolled down to his ankles, to invite and to goad opposing defenders in a manner similar to that of a matador's rag to a bull.

The footballers sit still, some with their eyes closed, some silently praying, some taking advantage of the quiet to try and recall their instructions as well as the team's tactics for the match ahead; performers rehearsing their routines and lines. All try to relax and keep cool, a difficult task this afternoon. Charles ties the laces of his boots, while next to him Sivori spits nausea into a bucket. Charles's laces are extra-long, necessitating their being wrapped around the boot like a bandage, knotted on the top of each foot.

The team physiotherapist and masseur, Amilcare Sarroglia, walks to the main door and leans against it, a makeshift guard on sentry duties. In the middle of the room, next to the massage table, stand Brocic and Depetrini. Brocic calls for quiet and demands the players' attention to commence his team talk for the afternoon. He will repeat his instructions in English, directly, calmly, to Charles shortly afterwards.

It is the first match of the season, the visitors are the blues of Verona. 'Apart from a few of their players, we do not know so much about the team; this is their first time in Serie A. They will defend in number, in the hope of a draw. You are too good for this to happen, too strong. Today is your day. The supporters have not seen you for months; three of you they have never seen in the shirt. Thousands of them, baking in the sun and hot with expectation. Today a new journey begins. Give them hope, give them belief, give them optimism. Give them goals.'

With a smile on his face, he then steps across the room to Charles and hands him a slip of paper, 'A telegram for you, John.'

As Charles begins to read the message, his faces reddens and his eyes suddenly become moist.

'Bad news, John?' asks the concerned Boniperti, pulling the red fabric band up his right sleeve, the captaincy armband.

'No, no ...' Charles replies, almost gasping the words. 'It's from the Leeds United players; they send best wishes to me and Peggy and the children ...'

Boniperti, that grin above that chin, reaches up to ruffle Charles's hair, declaring, 'We cannot lose now boys, everything is for us!'

Everything apart from the heat, the merciless heat, good for nothing but lizards and devils!

◉

Too much sun, too little air. Too much sweat, too low energy. No shade, no respite, no escape.

The dazzling sun, scorching the terraces, the glare of thousands of white shirts. Hard ground, hard knocks, hard labour.

An early goal from Boniperti, a superb strike. Charles not involved. Stray passes, incomplete passes, intercepted passes.

Wayward crosses. Weak crosses. Not one single cross of merit or value.

Verona are not a good team, and Charles's immediate opponents are not good-natured.

When Charles has the ball at his feet, an assault on his legs usually follows. No restraint, no reprieve.

Lesions on his calves and ankles. No referee intervention. The referee's dim-wittedness knows no bounds.

Desperate to impress, Charles regularly can be heard shouting for the ball to be passed to him. Omar Sivori, Charles's Argentine colleague, appears to be deaf.

From Boniperti a successful pass of the ball to Charles's feet inside the penalty area. The supreme control in those feet. And the immediate onset of violence and continued ignorance of the referee. Charles recalls the advice: *a moving target is always harder to hit.*

It is easier said than done when the opponent is quick and cunning. Another pass of the ball to Charles's feet. The control, the perfect touch, the eluding of his marker Francesco Rosetta. *Hit, don't get hit!* The turn and the strike, of power, of purity. *This is it, this is it ...*

The thud of the ball against the crossbar. *Damn!*

Another tight duel with Rosetta, whose boots rake and stab Charles's legs. The ball deftly touched to Sivori. Sivori teases the goalkeeper, feigning to aim right, gently rolling the ball to the left. Two goals to nil.

The delighted Sivori no longer ignores Charles; he shouts and jumps with joy and hugs his Welsh team-mate.

Half-time. The long walk to the changing room.

Drinks. Cooling down, instructed to conserve their energy. The second half.

Verona score, an embarrassment for Mattrel in goal; the ball rolls through his legs. Two goals to one.

The defence creaks in the scorching sun, the barrier expanding, stretching, cracking, players' nerves splintering.

IL PRIMO

No crosses provided, Charles's team-mates on the wing are weak today, the debilitating heat sapping their legs of power. He has a bad headache, his legs feel heavy, every movement laborious, draining the energy even more.

A careful pass from Boniperti, perfect, Charles through on goal … Tired, weak, anxious. Salvation arrives, he is fouled, tripped by Rosetta. Fouled yet again by Rosetta, a penalty awarded this time. About time.

But the black-shirted goalkeeper blocks Stivanello's penalty. The football bounces out … and is returned to its rightful place with a whip-like reaction by John's right boot.

Charles shouts in joy and relief. The crowd roars, reminding him of an aeroplane take-off.

Team-mates flock around to congratulate him, the jog back down the pitch a delighted one, and exhausted.

Three goals to one.

The Verona players do not give in … Juventus concede another bad goal: 3-2.

Another pass of rare accuracy in to his feet, thirty yards from goal. The control of the ball, the acceleration, the sharp advance. And the immaculate shot.

He knows. *It is sweet, sweet, sweet.* The white goal net shimmers, the goalkeeper suffers.

No, it is disallowed, Sivori offside! In their thousands, spectators jeer and whistle; the linesman is wrong and the referee a cursed fraud!

No more drama, no more goals. The referee blows his whistle for the final time. Juventus three, Verona two.

Hundreds of those fanatical supporters wait outside the stadium after the match, as close to the Players' and Officials' door as they can. They hope to thank and congratulate the Juventus players, in particular John Charles. But the players, in particular John Charles, have been advised to stay inside until the throng has diminished. It takes longer than an hour for that to happen.

In England, Charles had always preferred to go straight home and re-join his family, especially when dissatisfied with his own performance. In Italy, he is not allowed a choice, his presence is insisted upon by his team-mates. Their first win – with him scoring the decisive goal – is high cause for great celebration: Piazza San Carlo and the Caffe Torino await.

'A good start love; you scored the winning goal,' Peggy said brightly to her husband as they lay in bed.

'I didn't play well,' came his unimpressed response.

'Did anyone? It must have been too hot; you're being too hard on yourself.'

'Doesn't matter, none of it was good enough; I have to do better.'

'But if no one else in the team plays well, it makes it all the more hard for you, doesn't it?'

'I suppose so.'

'Well then, something to build on.'

'Yes, love.'

'And a nice win bonus.'

'Yes … I'm tired. Goodnight.'

◎

Sunday 15th September, the second match, away to Udinese. Juventus Football Club charter a private aeroplane for the journey, the town of Udine a few hundred miles away in the north-east, lying between the Adriatic Sea and the omnipresent Alps, not far from the border with Yugoslavia. The Stadio Polisportivo Moretti, oval in shape and with a speedway track surrounding the pitch, is about to be filled to capacity: 25,000 spectators will attend, a record crowd. The Juventus new signings are hot news; a corresponding reception awaits them. The pristine first-choice kit again, carefully lifted out of his Juventus number 9 leather case, the boots as new, even the long laces have been cleaned. This afternoon Depetrini is absent from the changing room; he is at another game, assessing future opponents. Coach Brocic addresses the team, Giampiero Boniperti standing at his side. 'Football is a simple game but last week it did not appear so. This week the weather is cooler; there are no excuses for anything less than 100 per cent commitment. Out there you must communicate better, listen better, all of you.' He does not look directly at Sivori but they all know he is referring to the Argentine.

Sivori is not overly concerned; he has more pressing matters to deal with, primarily the pre-match nausea which has beset him again.

Boniperti nods his head. 'Yes, yes.'

Brocic continues: 'Last week was a victory but it was not well deserved. There was not enough team work and too much individualism. Team wins the day, not one man alone. The passing of the football was substandard and there were no good crosses. The referee was a nonsense but it is not the referee who creates and scores goals. Today we are not at home; today it is likely the referee will be even more inept. Today it will be tougher.' He then looks to Charles. 'John, it is likely you will be the target for more aggression here. For heading, you must raise your arms and elbows to protect yourself. Understand?' Charles acknowledges the advice while Sivori spits again into a bucket.

Brocic proceeds to remind the players of their individual and 'departmental' duties on the pitch, reiterating which Udinese players can hurt them, like the Argentine in midfield, Pentrelli, and Bettini, and Lindskog the Swede in attack – he never gives in. The left-winger

Alberto Fontanesi, quick and clever – Juventus's Giuseppe Corradi will need to be quicker and cleverer when marking him.

Excessive physical aggression towards Charles has not materialised, primarily because Udinese have had most possession of the ball. Fortunately for Juventus, they have also had the least accuracy with their shooting.

Charles's shirt is often pulled, his toes trodden on, his arms tugged, torso grappled with. All sneaky tricks of the defender's trade, the onus on the attacker to evade them … *block, slip, duck.*

His team-mates' defending has impressed Charles; they have shielded their goal superbly, particularly midfielder Colombo, who has also supported every Juventus attack. In goal, when the back line has been pierced, Mattrel has performed faultlessly.

But the dearth of service to Charles in attack has depressed him. The Udinese forwards scurry around, everything is urgent, desperation to score, and hasty and erratic. The experts reckon that fortune favours the brave … possibly, but to win a match it isn't always necessary to attack more, just to attack better.

The first half peters out, scoreless, and for Charles, chanceless also. Brocic is unworried, Be patient, he advises.

The second half.

IL SECONDO

One chance is sometimes all he will get in a match, just one. One chance, one attempt to score.

The man-marking by his *sentinella* Mario Pantaleoni has been effective, when the football has actually reached Charles.

Colombo wins another duel and smartly strokes a long, accurate pass along the turf to Charles. Charles collects the ball and quickly, smoothly, turns, enabling him to simultaneously elude Pantaleoni in a rare lapse. In his stride, Charles taps the ball with his right foot to the left flank to the demanding Sivori, and continues to advance. Sivori completes the one-two exchange, the return pass rolling perfectly in front of Charles, his marker now a mere memory. Charles is twenty yards away from the Udinese net, only the goalkeeper Cudicini in his way. Before Cudicini can decide how to block Charles's route, a low strike from the striker's right foot has flashed past him into the goal. One chance, one shot, one goal. One-nil.

Udinese strive to break through the massed defences of their visitors. Their efforts are unwelcome … they will not succeed, not today. One goal, two points.

'Thieves, thieves!' accuse the Udinese fanatics; the Juventus players do not care, they have weathered all the hosts' pressure and then taught them a hard lesson. The scorer would receive the credit for the victory: not relevant or deserved – the team's defending had earned the two points; Mattrel had been magnificent in goal. Unjust praise never beautified the unedifying truth for Charles: that of there being plenty of room for personal improvement.

The forthcoming Wales versus East Germany match, a week on Wednesday, worried him. As always, he was eager to an extreme to play for his country but he strongly suspected Umberto Agnelli would not let him, as Czechoslovakia had already won the single qualifying place of the three-team group.

Meanwhile, back at the family home Via Susa 31, Peggy had tried to tune in their posh new radiogram to a channel she could understand so as to keep up to date with how the Juventus game at Udinese was going. She failed and of course the BBC's World Service did not feature Italian football matches, so she eventually made do with playing records instead. The television would show the final scores at some stage … The turntable, housed in a splendidly polished mahogany cabinet, was soon stacked with singles; all Peggy needed was someone to dance with! Even if she had to carry her unwilling escort in her arms to do so. Terry, being the eldest and steadiest on his feet, was the ideal choice, but he often preferred to sit on the settee and laugh at his mum's efforts. Her favourite group, The Platters, seemed to be the three boys' *least* favourite judging by the grimaces on their angelic little faces, especially when the opening strains of 'Only You' sounded, which visibly upset them. Frank Sinatra was her favourite solo singer, but she didn't have many of his more swinging records; the only music with which she could persuade them to join her on the living room dance floor/rug, and enjoy themselves at the same time, was Bill Haley & His Comets.

◎

Sunday 22nd September, Juventus versus Genoa.

Brocic: 'You have not played anyone of repute so far, yet you have toiled. Too confident and complacent. The defending was exceptional last week but your passing from defence has to be better. Genoa are bottom of the division now, a false position and they will be keen to demonstrate that. They will be sore. Do not be fooled by the eight goals they have conceded in two matches; their team contains dangerous players and they are especially strong on the wings. You, Corradi and Garzena, need to be stronger; if you are in difficulties then you must tell your colleagues. The Uruguayan, Abbadie, on the right, will be a threat, and Delfino and Frignani on the left. Their supply to Corso up front needs to be prevented. Understand?'

Confirmation comes by way of players' heads nodding.

He goes on, 'And we have the best attackers in the land, but if they are not given good service it means nothing. Better crossing from open play and from corner kicks is needed. You are at home and the weather is perfect; there can be no excuses this time ... beat them, beat them well.'

Within one minute of the game, Sivori has achieved three tunnels on the same defender. Sivori has won three meals as a result of a bet with Bruno Garzena. But with fourteen minutes gone, Juventus are 1-0 down. The goal designed by Abbadie, scored by Beccatini.

And with sixteen minutes gone, it is 2-0, Corso increasing the lead. Mattrel and the defence are half asleep!

Not one pass to his feet so far, no Juventus moves of note, no interplay between attackers, no crossing, no service. Charles is not blameless in this; his marker Rino Carlini has dominated, he has shadowed him everywhere, each pass to Charles repelled by his interventions and interceptions. Tenaciously, toughly, fairly, a clean fight.

To Juventus followers there are two kinds of shot, the good ones and the bad ones. The good ones go into the net, the bad ones don't. So far there have been *no* shots at all from the home team, good or bad. Their team losing by two goals is unacceptable; unless matters improve, it could be a case of 'their' team being disowned. Whistles and jeers fill the Comunale air. These matters are, for John Charles, understandable but depressing, unhelpful, dispiriting; he'd experienced more than enough unpleasantness of this nature before, in the English game. The Torinese version is much more distracting, however, and it feels somehow more personal.

Boniperti intercepts an errant pass and sets off with the ball in his possession with a characteristically forceful, direct run towards goal. Cutting in from the right wing, he unleashes a fierce shot that sadly for Juventus flashes mere inches wide of Genoa's goal. A glorious effort for which Charles applauds the captain. The fans disagree, the screech of whistling even louder than before.

Shadows can be defeated: *block, slip, duck. Bob, weave.* A good cross, from the left wing; Stivanello. Charles jumps highest, above Carlini, above the goalkeeper, above Viciani. A deft flick with his head and the football is goal-bound ... only to bounce off the left-hand post into the goalkeeper's grasp. The crowd shows its approval, or rather it stops sounding its disapproval.

The captain Boniperti, encouraged, urges and implores the players to work harder, to continue improving.

A seductive pass from the majestic left foot of Sivori demands Boniperti to lash it. He cannot resist: the football arrows into the Genoa goal.

Half-time, Juventus one, Genoa two. The home changing room. Players sit, relaxing, drinking water or juice. Players chatter; Charles hears the name 'Ferenc Puskás' uttered a few times. He does not know why the Hungarian great is mentioned; certainly no one here is playing anywhere near that standard. Ljubisa Brocic has entered the room. He stands, silent, listening. Eventually the talking stops – he did not need Boniperti's assistance in calling for quiet but he got it anyway. The usually calm and straightforward coach is unhappy. 'It appears some of you are more interested in who is watching from the stand than in your responsibilities. Ferenc Puskás does not matter, *you* are wearing the shirt, now is the time for you to prove you deserve to ...'

The second half.

The expected onslaught from Juventus has not materialised.

And Genoa's Corso, with only Mattrel to beat, somehow shoots wide of goal. Three-one looked certain, and defeat therefore probable. And despite the miss, the crowd's whistling recommences.

Matters improve, however, challenges and links are successful, passes more accurate, player movement fluid and swift. Sivori is enjoying being the tormentor – of Genoa and not his own team-mates – and he shares the football.

Charles retreats to collect the ball on the half-way line. For once Carlini is caught unaware. Charles swivels with the football at his feet towards the Genoa end. With a sweep of the right leg he floats the ball over defenders into the path of Sivori. Sivori cushions the ball in his stride, immediately on the attack, the goalkeeper suddenly realising his realm is under threat ... he is too slow, the ball is already in the net, two goals each. Seventeen minutes left.

IL TERZO

From the right wing, Bruno Nicole attempts to despatch a cross into the Genoa area but the ball deflects out of play: a corner-kick to Juventus. Boniperti takes the kick; his strike from the corner arc flies towards the throng of players near the goal. Charles, calculating the best point for maximum impact, dives to connect with the ball. Carlini dives also. Carlini fails, Charles succeeds, with his forehead, the ball rising and spinning. Just before hitting the hard surface, he glimpses his projectile's trajectory, and just as his body touches the earth, he hears a Sivori shout of joy and the rise of the crowd's roar. The ball flew by Cudicini's despairing right hand into the top corner of the net.

Charles is delighted but unable to stand, weighed down under a pile of team-mates celebrating and congratulating him.

Now leading, Juventus finally take control of the game until the end, winning 3-2.

◎

Late in the year of 1956 and due to the collapse of social uprisings – described as a national revolution, Hungary returned to Soviet rule. The Soviet regime had proved to be oppressive for the Hungarian people, and the failure of the revolution was disastrous for many. At that time, the country's star footballer, Ferenc Puskás, was in Spain with Budapest Honved F.C., playing in the second European Cup competition, against Athletic Bilbao. In protest at the chaos in his homeland, along with some of his colleagues, he decided to stay out of the country, declaring that he no longer recognised the authority of Hungarian football's authorities. His self-imposed exile came with sacrifice: he wasn't able to see his wife and daughter, they would need to flee the country to be reunited. He had led quite a nomadic existence ever since and the national football side, the famous 'Flying Magyars', felt the loss too; Puskás was commonly acclaimed as one of the best and most exciting forwards ever to feature in world football. Presently he was unemployed, and today he was a spectator at the Juventus–Genoa game in Turin.

After the match, in the upstairs double room of the sumptuous Caffe Torino, Gigi Peronace ordered from and paid a tray-carrying waiter for John Charles's and his team-mates' refreshments. Peronace was a generous man; not though a foolishly generous one – hangers-on to the team did not benefit from his charity. A few socialites frequented the Caffe Torino in the hope of meeting the Juventus stars: businessmen and awe-struck fans, and pretty girls wanting to sample higher society and glamour. Pretty girls appeared in every bar and club in town frequented by Juventus players, such occasions providing rich resources for gossips and columnists to report salacious events, even if no such incidents actually happened.

Peggy had attended the Genoa match, taking Terry in his carry-cot, with Gigi their chauffeur for the journey to the Comunale and the return. Thanks in large part to Elsie, a great help with 'refresher' lessons as well as arranging the formalities, Peggy had passed her driving test comfortably. No one, though, had seriously expected Peggy to drive to the game; the traffic around the Comunale on match days could be a stiff challenge even for the most experienced of drivers. And Italian drivers were not renowned for their patience at the best of times. Gigi was also to thank for the hiring of a new helper for the family after the sudden departure of Nanny Margaret, now recovering back home in England. The new woman, a Torinese lady in her forties, called Lucia, was able to speak English fairly well and would work six days a week and live in with the family. Her duties would differ to Margaret's: she would be more a housekeeper than a nanny, Peggy intending to be with the children more and, now that she could drive, planning to discover more of the new land. Her self-confidence increased as a result and henceforth she would take advantage of the car at her and the boys' disposal, to explore the unappreciated Piedmont region more. Her confidence was helped by Lucia too; the feeling of awkwardness when entering fashionable clothes shops and boutiques would decrease thanks to Lucia's presence, and she persuaded Peggy that expensive *pointy* shoes were attractive and trendy. In general, Lucia's assistance would be of great value, and the impression of high worth was oddly complemented by her mouth containing an unusually large number of silver fillings. Thankfully, the boys weren't at all frightened by this sight, though John had been a tad alarmed when she first smiled at him.

Peggy was not invited to the after-match gathering in the Caffe Torino. This did not bother her; such neglect was not meant as a slight and it was generally the same in English football – team spirit, camaraderie and the socialising side of football generally being a men-only domain. She was though surprised, and a little disappointed, to see that she had been the only Juventus wife or girlfriend at the match in the exclusive but rather shabby directors' box of the grandstand. It all needed a new coat of varnish and cushioned seats; it was little better than the old West Stand at Elland Road. There was no suggestion here of Terry or herself being made to feel unwelcome; it was more a case of no one taking particular notice of them at all.

Charles and Peronace sat together at one of the small circular tables in a dimly lit corner of the room. Peronace had revealed the news to the Welshman of his enforced unavailability for Wales's match against East Germany.

'Mister Agnelli has told the press that the Juventus cause is more important at this time than Wales's. The team has not knitted together well enough and so it is essential you train with your club all week as normal, because the team needs to keep improving. He says you will be able to play for your country in important matches but this one against Eastern Germany is irrelevant.'

'Not to me it isn't.'

'No, of course, John, but he is saying that this specific match has no consequence. You realise this, yes?'

'Yes, but you tell him I'm not happy about it.'

'Naturally you are unhappy, and that is to your credit.'

'I don't feel any better for hearing that.'

'Of course I will pass your feelings on, John. Mister Agnelli does know and is sympathetic to your situation ... You did well today. When John Charles scores, Juventus win!' he continued, trying to improve the mood. 'You are pleased with the match?'

'Pleased we won, but we have not played well again; neither have I.'

'It will come; it can take time. You have scored three times, in three matches, and each goal has won the tie. Imagine what you will achieve when you are happy with how you are playing!'

A Charles shrug of indifference. 'Do you know why Puskás was here? Is Agnelli planning on buying him?'

'I do not think it is possible to buy him due to the political troubles in his country. He lives in ... in exile; he stays in this country in Bordighera but his family are not allowed to leave Hungary.'

'It's a long way to come just to watch a match.'

'He told reporters he is a guest of the cycling team Carpano-Coppi.'

'I bet someone from the club invited them.'

'I think you worry when there is nothing to worry about, John. Puskás is over thirty years old and does not look in good shape.'

'I'll believe that when I hear Umberto Agnelli say it.'

'Puskás is my shape now,' Peronace quipped.

'He still has it, Gigi, fantastic ability ... What else did you hear him say?'

'Well I could not hear everything but he did say that Sivori is a phenomenon, and a true champion, and that every pass he made in the game was perfect.'

'Maybe that's true, but he doesn't make many. Too much nutmegging. Anything else?'

Peronace shook his head and said 'No' a little too promptly. Charles looked at him sternly, a look that could petrify a statue.

Peronace fumbled. 'Ah ... He said he considered Sivori, Boniperti and Ferrario as the best players today.'

'And?'

'He said he was disappointed with John Charles.'

'Did he? Well that's great. He should keep his opinions to himself.'

When he arrived home that evening, Charles was greeted with the revelation from Peggy that Lucia had dealt with four telephone calls earlier in the evening from press reporters demanding to know what John thought about the prospect of Juventus trying to sign Ferenc Puskás. Lucia was already informed enough to firmly tell the callers to call the football club and to never bother the Charles household at home again. Her proficiency as an unofficial secretary was of scant comfort to Charles: the presence of Puskás at the match and the reactions of various people had troubled him. He cursed quietly when hearing about the intrusive phone calls; regardless of Gigi's calming words, a negative voice in Charles's mind argued that Puskás would soon be a Juventus player. And if that did happen, as far as John Charles understood it, one of the two foreign recruits – he or Sivori – would have to leave the club, even if only on loan to another Italian team.

After a few days, Puskás seemed to be forgotten and almost insignificant, as if he had vanished. No word of him was mentioned by any of the Juventus players or even in the press, and that included the newspaper columns that published 'fiction' rather than actual news. The 'Puskás matter' simply faded away ... he would return to professional football, but not in Italy.

Before he left for yet another long footballing journey, Peggy told her husband not to forget the 'small money matter' of a few months before. He hadn't needed reminding; the small matter had been a major annoyance and had darkened what were generally pleasant memories of his departure. What with all the big concerns going on in the life of the Charles family, the lack of support from his former employers was a big disappointment. Not only was he owed money; they also owed him more respect – much more. He felt he had been taken advantage of.

9

OCTOBER 1957

Juventus were in Leeds, preparing to fulfil a part of the transfer deal of John Charles's move to Italy. Charles's participation in the friendly match against Leeds United was in doubt due to a dispute over wages from his time at Elland Road. Charles (and Peggy) insisted that Leeds still owed him wages from April and May, more than £100, and unless they settled the matter he would refuse to play. No professional footballer, even the most famous and best rewarded, could afford to be complacent in their business affairs; there were always people looking for a piece-of-the-money action and to extort and deceive the fabled golden goose.

He had gained the support of the West Yorkshire press, or at least they gave the matter coverage, and that was good enough for him. It was, after all, news. They had somehow learned of the unpaid wages story and had run with it, to the embarrassment and concern of Charles's former employers. If Leeds United did not resolve the issue and it was announced that Charles would not be appearing in the friendly match, how many thousands of fans would decide not to attend? How badly would that affect the club's coffers? The Leeds directors didn't need telling the answer and they didn't want to find it out either.

For the first time, Charles was the 'social leader' of the Juventus entourage, showing them around Leeds as well as the salubrious Queens Hotel in which they were staying for two nights. He even took Mattrel, Colombo, Ferrario and Corradi – well regarded already for their style and panache – shopping on a tour of Leeds tailors and outfitters. The sixteen players on the trip, as well as club president Umberto Agnelli, coach Ljubisa Brocic and masseur Amilcare Sarroglia, had arrived a day late, their connecting flight from Brussels to Manchester Ringway delayed due to a technical fault with the aircraft. Charles had originally planned an excursion for the team to the seaside resort of Blackpool and its glorious illuminations, but it had to be cancelled.

Gigi Peronace was waiting for them when they landed in Manchester, meeting with and feeding information to members of the press while there. The latter all wanted to know how John Charles had been faring abroad. They were not particularly interested in the form of Juventus or Charles's team-mates, but they were told anyway: Juventus were top of the league and the only team to have won all their games, with eight points out of eight. John has settled down magnificently and his team-mates and the supporters love him. Last week's victory against S.P.A.L. (Società Polisportiva Ars et Labor) was the first match he had not scored in, but even so his contribution had been splendid and the team triumphed by one goal to nil. He will be even better when the Italian weather cools down; the fans will then be amazed at how great a player he is. John is in superb condition. The other teams are paying clear attention to him and there are always two and sometimes three men to mark him, but it does not seem to make any difference. The latest victory was not without cost, as some of the players are recovering from influenza and injuries. The captain Boniperti has a sprained leg, Colombo has a fever, Emoli was kicked in the face and lost three teeth, Garzena is nursing a sore knee, Sivori has a cold and Stivanello a head injury. But everyone is extremely keen to play against Leeds United.

◎

Charles did play against his former club, to the relief of the 41,000 crowd (and the Leeds United directors of course). The Leeds players and public saw for themselves how magnificent he looked: leaner, tanned, relaxed and, away from the game, stylishly dressed. The attendance was the largest gate ever for a floodlit match at Elland Road, and the highest of Leeds' season so far too.

Charles, despite scoring twice and helping create the other two goals in the 4-2 win, had a 'casual' match. It is plausible he went easy during play so as to avoid inflicting any more suffering on Leeds, their season so far having been quite wretched. Scorer of the other two goals was Sivori and he proved to be a main attraction of the match, juggling with the ball, toying with defenders and bewitching the crowd. He nearly had a fight too, with Leeds' outside-right Georgie Meek, the smallest man on the pitch. Tunnels and nutmegs charm spectators but offend their intended victim, especially when that victim is playing on his home ground.

After the match, and following the cheers and applause from the spectators, and the handshakes and pats on the back from the players, in the Juventus dressing room Charles had tears in his eyes again on hearing the crowd singing 'Auld Lang Syne' for him. If only he could play for both teams, then he wouldn't have to have any regrets!

Sunday 13th October, the Filadelfia Stadium in Turin, a cauldron of noise. Torino F.C. play host to their neighbours of barely two kilometres' distance, Juventus F.C. Five victories out of five matches so far for Juventus, ten out of ten points, another narrow home win last week, 2-1 against Padova. But while the team sat at the summit of Serie A, they had not played consistently well. Parts of the team had, the defence being the most consistent, but the stars of the high-priced attack had yet to shine, a fact observers paid the most attention to.

Brocic's instructions to his players for the match were no surprise: deal with the pressure, play a disciplined and organised game, and respond by counter-attacking. Torino were the hosts and so the onus lay with them to take the game to their visitors, especially given that the match was a local derby, and one of the most competitive rivalries in Italian football. For each set of supporters, it was imperative their team won. And the players of each team were acutely aware of the *tifosi*'s feelings on the matter. If Juventus were to lose, the players would be best advised not to show their faces around the town for a while.

Brocic outlined Torino's main threats, their danger men, though the Juventus players already knew as much and possibly more about them than he did. Torino's most influential player was the French midfielder Antoine Bonifaci, the central mastermind, similar to Boniperti's role in the Juventus side. In attack was Giancarlo Bacci, their big striker with a healthy scoring record. Brocic's own options in attack were limited today due to the absence of Sivori, who had a calf muscle strain as well as a heavy cold. Reliable midfielder Antonio Montico replaced Sivori, with Bruno Nicole switching to centre-forward, Charles to inside-forward and Boniperti to the right wing.

Boniperti was loathed by followers of a few opposing teams, particularly Torino's. Edoardo Agnelli had bought Juventus in the 1920s and had demanded that every Juventus player conduct themselves to the highest standards possible, on and off the football pitch. Many football supporters regarded the attitude as pompous and degrading, and Boniperti's apparent aloofness seemed to epitomise the insulting snobbery. For years they had taunted him with the nickname 'Marisa', a woman's name. Boniperti's hair was almost always perfect, and his thighs long and muscular, but the reason for the nickname was that a young lady, the then 'Miss Piedmont', presented flowers to the captains of Novara and Juventus before a friendly match. She wore a Juve shirt, a deed calculated to infuriate some of the locals, who reacted by calling Boniperti 'Marisa' in as mocking a fashion as they could muster, and they had done so at every possible opportunity ever since. Naturally he did not like it at all, but he found solace through playing even better than normal, harnessing energy from those insults from the terraces. .

The Torino tide towards the Juventus goal pressed strongly the defence needing vigilance and resilience, their resistance likely to be key to the team's fortunes. Rino Ferrario excelled in defence – courage, conviction, strength – the watching manager of the Italian national side simply had to be impressed with the centre-half's performance. Ferrario was one of those warrior-like stoppers who regards every goal conceded as a painful, insulting assault on his pride.

Wave after wave of efforts to break down the Juventus wall. Ferrario reigns: absorbing, repelling, deterring, combating. Jab, thrust, foot in, fend off, head clear, shut out, never give up. Goalkeeper Mattrel likewise stands tall; today he feels as though nothing will get past him.

Torino's Gianfranco Ganzer marks Charles, exerting strict surveillance, nullifying every threat Charles has so far presented. The threats have been few in number due to the paucity of supply. Bruno Nicole is young and inexperienced; he has much to learn.

When playing as a centre-forward, being greedy with the ball can at times be appropriate, but not all the time. Nicole needs to remember he is not the only Juventus player with dynamite in his boots.

Nicole receives the ball outside the box. *Pass it Bruno, pass it!* He does not pass; he fires a low strike instead, once more straight at the goalkeeper. Charles is available again unmarked.

Nicole receives the ball inside the box. He side-foots a low shot, straight at the goalkeeper. Charles is free and onside, and ignored.

Nicole, a good player, but by repeatedly making wrong choices he is in danger of becoming a bad player.

Boniperti links up with Charles in a swift one-two exchange. Boniperti strides into the penalty area, the ball at his feet and only the goalkeeper ahead of him. '*Marisa!*' comes from the terrace crowd behind the goal ... Boniperti advances and strikes with the outside of his right foot, fooling goalkeeper Rigamonti, who dives right while the ball is driven leftwards, but out for a goal-kick. Whistles, howls, ridicule, '*Marisa Marisa!*'

A high pass to Charles standing five yards outside the Torino box. He jumps a few inches to head the ball gently down to Boniperti, perfect for volleying. He connects cleanly, purely, powerfully. The pace of the ball exposes the goalkeeper's slow reaction but the ball skims the crossbar and lands in the crowd. At least, with a little good luck, thinks Boniperti, it will smack one of his grinning tormentors in the face.

In and around the centre circle, a mill of bodies and legs, a melee tangling for the football. It ricochets free along the grass into the Torino half. Charles is the quickest to respond. He sprints towards it, legs and arms pumping high. Torino's defender Evo Brancaleoni sprints too, from the opposite direction, the ball between them. Charles reaches it a fraction before Brancaleoni ... an inevitable, thunderous collision. Charles is faster and stronger ... and now through on goal with the ball waiting for him. Brancaleoni had fallen, his head struck accidentally by Charles's right elbow. The pain and blood suggest Brancaleoni's nose is broken. He lies on the ground, stunned, winded, hurt, while Charles has the simple task of running on and scoring past Rigamonti in goal. But Charles stops, choosing to ignore the possibility and instead kicking the ball to the side of the pitch and out of play, before turning around to crouch next to the casualty. Omar Sivori is angry and bemused, demanding to know what Charles is doing and why; his team-mate could have gone on and scored. Has he lost his mind?

Rigamonti walks from his goal-mouth, clapping his hands as he does so in appreciation of Charles's actions. Soon, virtually everyone in the stadium joins the applause, calling Charles's name; cheering him, cheering the compassion, the true spirit of sport.

IL QUARTO

Another skirmish for the football, close to the half-way line. Boniperti manages to trick three Torino players by back-heeling the ball away from them to the left wing, resulting in Stivanello being unleashed. Stivanello dashes thirty yards with the ball before curling a low cross into the Torino box. Nicole meets the ball with power and precision, a graceful, fluid action. There is too much power, too much precision, and the ball smacks against Rigamonti's chest and rebounds away before he can get his hands to it. It bounces out straight to Charles, and the Charles retort is emphatic, unsympathetic, dramatic: 1-0 to Juventus.

Hundreds of supporters returned from the match and congregated in Piazza San Carlo soon after the finish of the derby match. Supporters of both teams. Their team's victory gave the Juventus faithful the 'bragging rights' for the time being, yet something else had *really* impressed and moved the people. Something else had happened on the pitch that afternoon to almost unite the opposing factions of the city, the atmosphere in the square being that of friendly rivalry, many of them singing not for their team but the praises of someone now christened 'Il Gigante Buono': John Charles, the Gentle Giant.

Juventus's next game is away to Milan, the reigning champions of Serie A. The team will travel south by rail, first class of course, the journey of ninety or so miles to last a couple of hours. They will be hopeful of maintaining their 100 per cent successful start to the campaign. Milan are near the foot of the league table and generally not in good form.

Shortly after one o'clock in the morning of Sunday 20th October, when everyone in the home is asleep, Peggy wakes suddenly. She thought she had been dreaming it, but the telephone in the living room really was ringing. She wrenched herself from the cosiness of their bed and walked barefoot out of the room to answer the phone. Had she thought more about the late hour, she would have begun to worry that awful news from Leeds was about to be relayed to her. It could only be bad news at that time of night! But as it was, she was barely awake enough to even start wondering.

'Hello,' she croaked into the receiver.

There seemed to be no one on the other end of the line. She spoke again, her throat clearer now ... still no answer. One last time, she enquired, 'Hello, anyone there?' Whoever was responsible for making the call, then ended it.

It didn't take long for her to return to the land of slumber, only for her sleep to be shattered again by the sound of the telephone less than an hour later. She wanted to ignore it but of course could not. She probably should have, as only silence met her response again.

Sunday 27th October, Juventus at home to Internazionale, the blue half of Milan, known as the *Nerazzurri*, the black and blues. Juve midfielder Giorgio Turchi replaces the injured Flavio Emoli, and Montico and Gino Stacchini are in for Nicole and Stivanello respectively. Last week, Stivanello damaged his left knee in the mud during the 1-1 tie against the black and reds, Milan. More than eighty thousand spectators had watched John Charles generously set up Sivori's goal to put Juventus one goal ahead, only for the hosts to equalise in the second half. The saturated pitch hampered the chances of high-quality football and there were periods of play spoiled so much as to make the contest a lottery. And though they were powerful organisations off the field of play, both Milan teams were enduring disappointing times on it, so last week's draw was a disappointment for Juventus. They were anticipating better fortunes against Inter.

Inter begin the game in determined, ebullient fashion, chasing, harrying, hurrying. Juventus seem to be thinking about what they have had for lunch, each man immediately put under pressure when they have the ball, and then relieved of it.

Only three minutes in and Inter's Lorenzi blasts a beautiful half-volley into the top-right corner of Juventus's net.

A great goal. This is suddenly looking harder than the Juventus players expected.

IL QUINTO

Charles strides at pace towards the Inter penalty area; behind him quicksilver Sivori makes use of the football.

The football is assigned to the left side of the pitch, Montico in possession. He traps the ball, searches for a team-mate and then lofts a long and high cross into the penalty area. Almost instinctively, Charles likes the look of the pass; he senses, he expects, he *knows* that the football will be his. Out-anticipating and out-jumping the two defenders supposedly marking him – Bernardin and Vincenzi – he meets the delivery with his temple, the ball flashing towards goal, bouncing in off the woodwork and levelling the scores. Parity; one goal each.

Inter are not deterred, they continue to close down the home team, meaning there is scarce space for Juventus manoeuvres or the orchestrated passes from Boniperti. In the line of Inter's midfield, Arcadio Venturi snaps at the feet of Boniperti like an unleashed terrier. As a result, Boniperti and Colombo are hardly able to venture out of the centre circle, the main scene of combat. And captain Boniperti is becoming increasingly annoyed.

It is the kind of tackle that Charles detests seeing. And the fact that it is his captain who has committed the lousy foul makes it even harder to accept. Inter's Venturi had over-run the ball and Boniperti had pounced, his foot connecting with the top of the football and then more forcefully into Venturi's knee. Venturi was carried off the pitch for treatment to his injury, returning a few minutes later heavily bandaged and practically incapacitated. It was now, in effect, eleven men versus ten for the remaining hour. The Juventus attack benefited, with Sivori able to run at Giovanni Invernizzi more, and Charles able to receive more ammunition, his marker Giorgio Bernardin struggling to handle him.

Half-time, one goal each.

The second half.

Sivori continues to be a nuisance to Invernizzi. Too much of a nuisance in fact; it is no longer constructive or entertaining, it is like tormenting an innocent for no good reason. Too many tunnels, too much goading … Sivori is trying to humiliate the popular Invernizzi. Sivori ignores his captain and his team-mates' instructions to just pass the ball.

IL SESTO

Boniperti's high diagonal pass misses the targets in the Inter box but Corradi stretches to reach it, managing to bring the ball down skilfully, close to the left corner flag. He taps the ball to Sivori, who advances fleet-footed into the area before touching it to Charles directly in front of goal. It would actually be harder to miss the target than not, and so Charles slams the ball home, the second Juventus goal. He shakes Sivori's hand in acknowledgement … Sivori embraces him in congratulation.

Sivori adds a third goal three minutes from time, an individualistic effort which pleases him so much he celebrates by throwing the ball into the excited crowd.

10

NOVEMBER 1957

The problem with skill is that there are opponents intent on suppressing it. The problem with power is that there are opponents intent on reducing it, by whatever means necessary. Possessing extraordinary skill and power, John Charles is aware that he is always a target. Being so is not a serious problem when he is able to see the opposition challenges approaching; he can brace himself. It is an entirely different story when the threats are unseen and the actions committed by cowards. Sunday 3rd November, one step forward, one step darkness. The ancient town of Vicenza, three hundred kilometres-plus to the east of Turin. The Stadio Romeo Menti is full to its fifteen-thousand capacity, with hundreds of Vincenzans locked out. It is the home of the football club L.R. Vicenza, and as today sees the visit of the aristocratic Juventus it is an arena of malice.

The Vicenza team begins the match like a cyclone; the Juventus players are slow to react. It seems inevitable that the first goal is a matter of *when* rather than *if*. Four minutes pass and that first goal arrives, scored by Vicenza. The noise of spectators celebrating sounds more like a crowd of fifty thousand than fifteen thousand. The visitors are suitably jolted. They respond at last; finally they are activated.

A hefty pass across the ground to Charles. The defender assigned to mark him, Remo Lancioni, does so literally, in one move clipping and gouging Charles's right knee from behind before prodding the football away with the sole of his studded boot. It is a foul, a sly, bruising foul, yet the referee seems to miss it, choosing also to ignore Charles's pained enforced stumble and the angry claims of Boniperti and Sivori. A frantic clearance is made from the edge of the Juventus penalty area, the ball projected long and high above the middle of the pitch. It will land in the Vicenza half of the pitch and the vicinity of one defender and one centre-forward, Lancioni and Charles. Even with Charles's height and jumping power, the defending player is normally the favourite to win the ball in such situations. Nonetheless, Lancioni uses cunning, his main objective being not to beat Charles to the ball but simply to give Charles a beating.

The ball plummets, directly towards the perfectly positioned Charles. Lancioni is three yards behind him, preparing to use the advantage of a running jump. The referee watches the football as it descends. John Charles watches the football as it descends. Remo Lancioni watches John Charles as the football descends. Charles is set to win the ball with a header directed across to Boniperti twenty feet away. But Lancioni leaps, bodily hammering into Charles while punching the back of his skull with the knuckles of his right fist. Senses stunned, Charles is floored by the impact; the immense force with which his head hits the surface compounds the situation – he is unconscious, lying prone on the ground. The referee, Signor Righi of Milan, saw nothing but a robust, *innocuous* clash of heads and an honest clearance of the football by the defender. All innocent in his view. The innocence of a coward, innocence of malevolence. Play continues and Lancioni saunters up to the half-way line to stand parallel with his fellow defenders across the pitch, acting as if nothing has happened. Charles lies where he fell, face down on the ground; he has not moved. Lancioni's indifference to the damage he has caused convinces spectators that Charles is unharmed and feigning injury. Whistles and insults emanate from the terraces; their player cannot be guilty of anything! Charles of course knows nothing about it; he is only now returning to consciousness.

Out of necessity rather than compassion, once he is made aware of the situation, the referee pauses the match to enable Charles to receive medical attention from the Juventus physio.

Charles is sitting up, the offensive smell of ammonia inhalant assisting his awakening, Amilcare Sarroglia waving the small bottle under Charles's nostrils. 'John, you okay? John, John? You hear me?' Charles hears the voice, unsure at first who it is addressing. He is groggy but feels pain, great pain. He recoils from the ammonia and he winces. 'My ear, my ear!' Sarroglia dabs cold water on the player's forehead and nape of the neck. The back of Charles's head throbs sore and he can taste blood, back teeth cutting his tongue when he hit the earth. It is his left ear, though, causing the most discomfort. He gingerly probes it with his fingers; it must have taken the brunt of the impact as his head slammed into the soil. He is helped to his feet and tells Sarroglia that he is not hurt, just like a child would who does not want to lose face in front of his friends.

The referee restarts play, Charles is dazed but determined to stay on the pitch, insisting that he is okay. Deep breaths and taking it easy for a few minutes will ensure his recovery; he will soon be able to contribute to the Juventus cause again. And his goals will teach that bastard Lancioni a lesson or two.

Soon, another airborne clearance plummets towards Charles in the middle of the pitch. He will not attempt to win this one – his head still aches and his limbs feel weak. His new-found enemy Lancioni has different ideas. Wickedness in mind, viciousness in action, he jumps towards the football and pummels into Charles at the same time, punching him in the back of the head again also. Somehow, instead of recognising an assault, the referee adjudges Charles to have won the header and deems that his slow motion fall to the ground stems from the force of the ball. Charles is just conscious enough to cushion his fall with his right hand this time.

After more treatment from Sarroglia, he returns to the contest but is angrily instructed by his captain to remain on the right wing to stay out of harm's way. Although he is present, it is really ten versus eleven men now; Charles is useless, wandering around dazed and punch-drunk.

Half-time arrives. For Charles, the interval is a haze.

The second forty-five minutes of the match takes place, also a haze. At the end of the match, jubilant fans, some waving large red-and-white-lined banners, run on to the pitch to celebrate and to mock Juventus for losing to the humble and poor Vicenza club.

In the changing room, Charles is helped to get washed and dressed and then taken by ambulance to the hospital, Clinica Elidea. He will have to get a later train than his team-mates back to Turin, the doctors insisting he stays overnight for observations. Sarroglia and Gigi Peronace remain with him, and Gigi swiftly finds a public telephone so as to call Peggy before she hears any wrong or exaggerated reports about the injury.

A nurse shines a torch in Charles's eyes each hour, even waking him up to do so, in order to gauge the pupillary reaction of his eyes. Eventually, and with the concussion gone, Charles is restless. Slowly rising from his bed, he pads across the room to look out from his hospital room window. He notices it has been raining. A solitary street-lamp shines, its milky white light reflecting in a puddle; it glows on the wet pavement. His thoughts return to winter afternoons in Leeds with Peggy, walking along Boar Lane and Briggate in town, huge department store windows illuminating the wide pavement slabs and inviting passers-by in.

Because he was finding it just about impossible to sleep, he asked the nurses, in Italian, if he could go home because he was feeling fine now, he had recovered. No matter how sincere and imploring, his request was always declined, each nurse advising him that the doctor was the only person with authority to make that decision. The doctor would always be there 'soon', but in fact never materialised until after sunrise. Finally, Amilcare Sarroglia arranged for Charles to be discharged and then taxied from the hospital to the railway station to board a train home to Turin. They arrive at Torino's Porta Nuova railway station in the early afternoon.

When the Juventus team wins, the players attract the admiration and friendship of countless people in the city, but when the team loses they can't even *buy* a friend. Not much notice, and very little welcome, was evident in Turin last night when the train carrying the Juventus entourage arrived. And it was a similar situation today, to a lesser extent; no one cared enough to greet John Charles or to see how his injuries were. No one except his darling wife of course. Peggy had also endured a restless night worrying about him and she was insistent on meeting her husband at the station. She runs down the platform to meet and hug him as he disembarks the train carriage, as though he were a war-time hero returning home from duty.

Diagonal arrows of rain beat against the windows of the Biagini restaurant as Umberto Colombo and John Charles chat and drink coffee, a few sports papers and magazines strewn on their table. It has been raining heavily across the Piedmont region almost non-stop for two whole days now, the troubled skies suggesting the eerie gloom belongs to night and not afternoon. Colombo and Charles have eaten, a plate of mushroom risotto and lasagne verdi respectively. Charles will never be fluent in the Italian language but he manages to 'get by', and his reading proficiency has steadily improved since the advent of his and Peggy's lessons with Elsie. With Colombo, help is usually at hand anyway if there are words or phrases proving too difficult to work out. He needs no help with the front-page headline of *Il Calcio e Il Ciclismo Illustrato*: '*David e Golia!*', referring to Vicenza beating Juventus 2-1 four days ago, Juve's first defeat of the season. The paper had been quick to liken the result to David's heroic killing of Goliath, pointing out the interesting fact that the scorer of the crucial second goal, Tony Marchi, was in fact Juventus's player loaned by the club to Vicenza. The original deal taking Marchi from Tottenham Hotspur to Italian football had been another brokered by Gigi Peronace, earning him a generous percentage.

'These reporters have forgotten the Bible if Vicenza are heroes due to winning our match,' commented Colombo. 'David fought fairly against Goliath, not like a cheating, rabid dog.'

'Tony Marchi isn't a dog, Umberto.'

Colombo grinned, 'Okay, John, okay: with the exception of Tony Marchi.'

'And Lancioni is more a pig,' added Charles.

'True, true, and his wife probably beats him and makes him clean their home ... How is your head? You still have headache?'

'No, I've got two bumps on my head and my ear and jaw are still sore, and I cut my tongue, but no headache.'

'You are resilient.'

'I was used to it in England; footballs are heavier and the leather laces on them can cut you.' Even if injured, Charles would have tried to keep it secret, such was his eagerness to redeem himself in the next match. He would lose out in pay too if he didn't play. He could afford that, but he did not want to. And in certain cases, such as the 'bigger' or more important matches, unofficial bonuses from wealthy local businessmen and Juventus acolytes were a big boost, often more lucrative than the players' weekly wage. The next match, against Lazio of Rome, was one of those bigger games ...

'I did not see Lancioni attack you.'

'Neither did I.'

'We will ensure you are avenged when Vicenza come here.'

'I'll do it myself; he'll get what's due to him.'

Colombo merely smiled, doubting his gentle friend's words. Charles's expression though, showed his resolve; he truly meant it.

◎

If the Vicenza match somehow suggested to other teams that the best way of dealing with 'the Charles threat' was by foul and violent means, it was likely he would be in for a torrid time. He already knew that defenders were often happy to tread on his toes, pull his hair and elbow him to the head in their efforts to defeat him, but that was 'part of the game'. A grimy, dishonest part of the game, but one that happened regularly and had to be accepted, if begrudgingly so. Sunday 10th November would bring Lazio to Juventus's home; the two teams shared a strong rivalry. If Charles was to receive more over-aggressive attention from Lazio's defenders, it would suggest they had taken encouragement from Lancioni of Vicenza. That would not be a good thing!

After three days of downpour, Ljubisa Brocic addressed the Juventus team prior to the match against Lazio, their tenth of the campaign so far. He held a wire-bound notebook containing many lines of handwriting. Fearing at first they were about to receive a lengthy lecture, the players were surprised to learn that the coach had written down various criticisms and slurs from articles published about the team following the Vicenza defeat. Brocic normally hid his emotions well, but the veil was slipping – he was aggrieved and vexed. He spoke loudly: 'It *appears* the newspaper reporters believe the defeat last week was fully deserved, and that the Vicenza players were heroic in their deeds. It *appears* I am not your coach but just your gym teacher. You are the pupils who do as you please and refuse to listen. And it *appears* some of you dislike me ...' He points to Sivori.

'You most of all, Omar.'

Embarrassed, Sivori smiles sheepishly; he has read the same, untrue reports.

Brocic continues. 'And you Big John, you are apparently fat and unfit and, above all, you are soft, you pretend to be injured rather than have the courage to fight back.'

Charles shakes his head in disgust. He doesn't need any more grief in his head; he has already suffered physical and mental pain and has since been told he is not permitted to play for Wales in the coming match on Wednesday against Scotland, too.

Brocic continues. 'And Boniperti, he is no longer good enough – he is too old and also a bully ...' Boniperti's face is red; he grins a cold grin.

'I am disgusted and I am offended by this scandalous nonsense. Not for myself but for you! It *appears* these reporters have no ink in their pens; only urine. It is up to you.' He flings the notebook to the floor and walks to the door. The notebook lands with a slap and slides towards Boniperti's feet. Boniperti grinds it into the tiled surface with the studs of his right boot.

A match of the aquatic kind, the incessant rain saturating the pitch and preventing, ironically, free-flowing and fluid football. Nevertheless, the Juventus and Lazio players provide an exciting spectacle for the spectators who braved the rain.

Charles wears the number eight shirt, he is an attacking midfielder, playing behind the centre-forward for this game, Nicole. Agnelli, anxious for Charles to avoid aerial challenges due to his head injuries, suggested he *not* lead the front-line. Brocic agreed it was the right approach and so Charles would, in theory, be more a creator than a finisher today.

It proved to be a fine decision; Charles ruled the midfield – he was faster, fitter, cleverer than everyone around him.

The two teams competed like heavyweight boxers, by turn probing, testing, attacking each other. Juventus, though, were the quicker and more proficient boxers.

Flashes of brilliance from both teams, splashes of comedy, like Emoli crashing a long-range thunderbolt against Lazio's crossbar, and then slipping and falling into a puddle.

IL SETTIMO

Goalkeeper Mattrel rolls the ball out to his right-back Corradi. Unopposed for forty yards and counting, Corradi advances down the wing with the ball almost magnetised to his feet. He is in the Lazio half and is still running. He nears the corner of the Lazio penalty area … the Swede Selmosson blocks his way. *Nessun problema.* A swift interchange between Corradi and Nicole in support cuts out that obstacle, the threat eliminated in a second. With the soaking ball Corradi progresses into the area; close to the touch-line he despatches a firm low cross into the goal-mouth. The pace of the slippery ball makes it practically impossible to grab; goalkeeper Lovati can only parry it away from his goal. The ball demands attention, eight yards out from the goal. Charles, quickest to it, blasts the ball into the net. A gift, but no one cares: Juventus are leading.

A few minutes pass and nothing of consequence occurs, the pitch a human traffic jam, but then left-winger Gino Stacchini makes it 2-0 just before the interval. Somehow managing to stay on his feet despite two attempts to chop him down, he releases a rocket into the top-right corner of the net.

Half-time. Two-nil to the hosts. In both dressing rooms, fresh dry kits await the players.

Less than five minutes into the second half, pressure from a reinvigorated Lazio pays dividends, albeit via a deflection from Corradi. This should make the tie tighter, more interesting …

The Lazio players, however, fail to build on the fortunate foundation, as if satisfied to have scored just the once.

Like the clouds, play simply passed by, as ordinary and grey as the sky, until, in the last few minutes of the match, a special goal from Sivori – dribbling through a crowded penalty area before smashing the ball home as if Lovati did not exist – seals the impressive win.

◎

Finding it difficult to relax after the match, John decided that his and Peggy's stay in the Caffe Torino was not to last very long, despite an endless supply of celebratory drinks being offered to them. Peggy did not mind where their time together was spent; she was just happy to have him all to herself, and Sunday evenings with her husband were happy indeed, even more so if he had managed to score a goal or two. During the previous week, she had remembered the date, 5th November – known in Great Britain as 'Guy Fawkes Night' – when bonfires were built and burnt and fireworks ignited in commemoration of the Gunpowder Plot of 1605, recalling Guido Fawkes and associates' attempt to blow up the House of Lords in London. She had asked John what he thought of her idea of asking caretaker Gianni if they could build a small fire in the garden of Via Susa 31 to celebrate.

'It's a stupid idea', was her husband's response, probably much politer than what the caretaker's would have been.

◎

Away to Bologna, Sunday 17th November. The improved display last week indicates – say the experts in the media – a comfortable win this week for Juventus, the components of the expensive machine at last starting to work smoothly together, beginning to *click*.

This could even be a shooting gallery for the Juventus big guns, predict experts.

John Charles has learned to never trust an 'expert', especially those paid to make predictions.

In the forty-sixth minute, Boniperti serves centre-forward Charles with a pass of delicate finesse, which allows Charles to swoop towards the Bologna goal. The perfect timing of his run combined with the precision of Boniperti ensures the Bologna offside trap is undone. Charles is in yards of freedom, the Bologna half virtually his own. He is through on goal, he is in the penalty area. A drop of the shoulder, a spy's glance, a rapid dance of feet, the killer kick, softly stroking the football into the net, goalkeeper Santarelli bamboozled and defeated. It is, though, only 2–1 to Juventus.

By the hour mark, Stacchini and Boniperti have made it 4–1 to the visitors. Stacchini has been a revelation … but the team becomes complacent and fails to create more chances. The machine has stalled while the Bologna players fight harder, their livewire midfielder Luigi Bodi prominent in his determination. They are awarded a penalty kick for handball in the Juventus area – Bodi succeeds with the kick, Bologna trail two goals to four.

Nine minutes from time, Stacchini latches on to a loose clearance in the Bologna half to shoot home, but Charles is adjudged, wrongly, to be offside – the goal is ruled out.

Three minutes later, the hyperactive Bodi punches Juventus's Emoli unconscious. Bodi is sent off, Emoli is carried off.

Two minutes later, a cross from Bologna's Bernard Vukas is driven into his own net by Corradi. One goal now separates the teams; Juventus are quaking. Fortunately, Bologna have nothing more to offer; they are spent.

Juventus return to Turin, with hundreds of their supporters who had travelled the three-hundred-plus kilometres for the match, with the victory. Eleven matches played, Juventus top of the league table; lying second are Fiorentina one point behind, and third placed are Napoli four points behind.

◎

In the darkest hours of Sunday morning 24th November, Peggy's sleep is disturbed, rudely awoken by the sound of the telephone ringing. She cannot bring herself *not* answer it; ignoring it would only run the risk of the infuriating ringing continuing all night. She gets out of bed and trudges into the living room to take the call, not surprised at all, just annoyed, at no reply when she asks who is calling. Exactly one hour later, another 'silent' telephone call is received … this time Peggy reacts by responding and then leaving the receiver off its cradle.

◎

Before the kick-off, a minute's silence is held in memory of Gianpiero Combi, the former Juventus goalkeeper who died last year. And to commemorate Combi's contribution to Juventus Football Club and the national game, the Premio Combi prize has been specially created, to be awarded to the best goalkeeper in Serie A.

With a virtual invasion of ten thousand Napoli fanatics in attendance, and numerous coloured balloons and clouds of firecracker blue and purple smoke above the pitch, expectations in the stands and the *curva* are growing of a memorable spectacle. The Napoli team has performed well in the league so far, causing their 'under-fed' supporters to dare to dream of success.

IL NONO

Two minutes of the second half go by, concerted pressure from the hosts. John Charles jumps highest to plant Stacchini's corner-kick into the net; it is the equaliser. Now let justice begin its course; it is the least Juventus deserve. In spite of being the stronger team they had trailed to Luís Vinício's tenth-minute goal. They had bombarded the Napoli goal with shots, sorties, headers and crosses. All to no avail; goalkeeper Ottavio Bugatti had been magnificent – brave, strong, acrobatic, quick – and all while suffering with Asian flu and a high temperature. Twice Charles had been shocked to see his own headers not result in goals, so good were Bugatti's reflexes. Efforts from Stacchini and Boniperti – 'certain goals' – suffered the same outcome thanks to the keeper's brilliance. If he played as well as this regularly, the destination of the Premio Combi award was a foregone conclusion.

Bugatti's team-mates take inspiration from his display, clinically counter-attacking the Juventus back line and eventually scoring two more goals. Three-one to Napoli, and it is Juventus's first home defeat of the season.

◎

Because of international duty for certain Italian players at the club, the following Sunday was fixture-free. Juventus's next league game wouldn't be for two weeks. Nevertheless, a busy schedule had been set for the players – excluding those on national team duties, Bruno Nicole, Giuseppe Corradi and Rino Ferrario – with another visit to England to play a couple of friendly matches.

During that same week, the ruling body of international football – FIFA – held an emergency meeting in Zurich to discuss a certain, serious sporting quandary: the Asia–Africa section of the 1958 World

Cup qualifying competition. In short, a conflict dating back to 1947, when the United Nations partitioned Palestine (into an Arab state and a Jewish state) meant that dissatisfied Arab nations were refusing to play against Israel's national side. Only last year, the 'Suez Crisis' occurred, and while this Arab–Israeli conflict lasted only months, the ceasefire remained an uneasy one.

On the Thursday evening, Juventus beat Sheffield Wednesday 4–3 at the Hillsborough stadium, Charles scoring twice, with over forty thousand attending the match – a veritable feast of exciting football. Sivori entertained the crowd, even if his many attempted 'tunnels' became tiresome and the press accused him of not taking the game seriously enough due to wearing his socks rolled down.

11

DECEMBER 1957

On the cold, north-east-of-England Monday night of December 2nd 1957, as the floodlights glowed through the sea mist and the famous 'Roker Roar' strove to motivate the local team, Juventus defeated home team Sunderland 2-0. More than fifty thousand spectators were there, to see a keenly contested friendly and Omar Sivori score both goals in what was a fine if unimportant individual performance. A relatively unenthusiastic John Charles had an unremarkable game, well-marshalled as he was by the home-team centre-halves.

Two nights later, at a packed stadium in Windsor Park, Belfast, an eagerly awaited World Cup qualifying match between Northern Ireland and Italy is downgraded in status to that of a mere friendly due to severe fog preventing the match officials from flying to Belfast via London in time for the match. The only alternative would have been for a local referee to officiate, but the Italian contingent declined the suggestion. Many of the spectators were unaware of this until they arrived at the stadium, a conspiracy thus being widely suspected: the paying public were being conned out of their money. The Italian team were already assured of an unfriendly reception due to claims in the British press that the players were cheats who used 'pep drugs' to enhance performance. And as the match progressed, certain Italian players, including Rino Ferrario, proceeded to play roughly, inciting retaliation not only from opposing players but from numerous spectators too. At the final whistle, hundreds of them invaded the pitch and the unfortunate Ferrario was set upon, kicked and punched. Back in Italy he gained the nickname the 'Lion of Belfast', but his conduct here, and the consequences, meant that very few would agree with the accolade; he had caused much of the trouble and had got his just deserts as a result. Away from the trouble, a good game of football occasionally emerged, ending in a 2-2 draw.

Fog around Heathrow Airport had failed to lift by the Thursday, causing the Juventus team's flight to Turin to be cancelled. The only alternative was to sail by ferry from the south coast of England to France, then to reach Paris and complete the journey home from there by rail, constituting much more uncomfortable travel time than anyone would wish for. This they did, however, arriving in Turin on the Saturday morning, the players fatigued and unsettled.

◎

The home league game against Atalanta, Sunday 8th December. A bitingly cold afternoon, the Juventus faithful hoping for exhilaration and victory to warm them up. The early stages showed promise.

In the second minute, Charles brings a long cross from left-back Garzena under control with his chest, then strikes a low left-footed shot that beats Boccardi on his line but also the far post. Two minutes later, Charles connects sharply with a short pass from Nicole, only to shoot straight at the goalkeeper.

Juventus's passing of the ball has been slick and their advances on goal achieved easily, but then errors begin to be made and passes go astray, wrong choices are made and a general lack of effort typifies too many of the players, as if they expect to win without expending much energy in doing so. Atalanta, of course, have different ideas.

The Juventus fans are becoming impatient. No goals in a lacklustre display is unacceptable, a lack of excitement inexcusable. Boniperti is having a poor game, Nicole would struggle to keep control of a brick and Umberto Colombo labours like an overworked steam engine. Sivori is the main culprit though, frequently wasting possession by trying to beat opponents instead of passing the ball, as if trying to be the constant centre of attention. In terms of quality, Charles is the only player who looks anything like his normal self today, but the two chances he missed have made him cautious; for him it is looking like one of those days when his 'shooting boots' are misfiring.

Boniperti is tackled yet again by a blue and black. Such a crime has occurred too often! And the more he toils, the angrier he gets. And the angrier he gets, the louder he becomes. Not such a bad thing when it is the captain of the team getting louder, but the more he shouts the less a certain Argentine listens. Sivori gleans a perverse pleasure in ignoring Boniperti; no one has the right to tell him what to do, even when he is performing so miserably.

LA DECIMA

On the left wing, twenty yards from the penalty area, Stivanello is fouled. Boniperti takes the free-kick. Charles is stationed a few metres away from the left goalpost. Boniperti floats a pass towards the danger zone, but it appears to be under-hit and thus easy to defend. Inexplicably though, the flight of the ball deceives centre-half Franco Vittoni. He misses it completely, embarrassingly. And anticipating the unexpected, reading the situation astutely, is Charles. With perfect judgement, he stoops to head it goalwards. Goalkeeper Boccardi's left fingertips brush the ball but fail to halt its gentle roll across the line.

L'UNDICESIMA

Three minutes on, Boniperti feeds Nicole who, unusually for today, retains the ball, runs at his marker Livio Roncoli, fools and outpaces him, and then pulls back a low cross into Atalanta's area. Astonishingly, with the ball only a few inches above the ground, Charles dives to head it, and the ball speeds as a bullet into the net. Two-nil.

Half-time. Juventus are two goals in front, a begrudging lead. Spectators applaud as the teams leave the pitch, the likelihood being that the applause is aimed more at warming the fans' hands than praising the football players.

The second half deteriorates into an even poorer show than the first. Despite the score standing at 2-0 to their team, the Juve fans are restless and bored, dissatisfied with the quality of the team's play. *What the hell is wrong with the players? Do they not give a damn?* As the monotony continues, whistles of disapproval from the terraces increase.

Charles is worried. Are they whistling him? The answer is no; in fact he is the single shining, albeit flickering, light in the gloom of the Comunale pitch. Sivori had dazzled in Sunderland, but today he is a hindrance, driving his team-mates to despair.

IL DODICESIMO

A counter-attack from Atalanta fails, the ball booted clear by Emoli. Bruno Nicole races to it, arriving marginally before Roncoli. Roncoli, caught flat-footed somewhat, can only watch as Nicole swiftly whips a cross into the area for Charles to head-flick the ball gently out of the goalkeeper's reach and into the net. Three-nil to Juventus and a hat-trick for Charles, all of them headers. Hat-tricks are unusual, headed hat-tricks rare indeed. The stadium buzzes in wonder at the feat and at how on earth Juventus are beating a team by three clear goals when virtually all the players have under-performed. Charles runs to Nicole to congratulate him and to thank him for providing the straightforward opportunity – hoping, wishing, for more of the same.

Juventus remain top of the league table; no one quite understands how.

A variation in training again for the players, a 'private' friendly held at the Combi training ground on Thursday 12th December, three days before the big encounter, of first versus second, Juventus versus Fiorentina. The Thursday opponents were non-league Pinerolo, a town not far away from Turin. Snow and rain through the week created awful pitch conditions but Brocic and Depetrini were satisfied that the match – a comfortable 3-0 win – was a worthwhile exercise, and there had been no new injury or fitness concerns to report. If anyone had a reason to complain about staging a needless match in numbing temperatures then it would have been Brocic, having to try to beat off the cold while the players – and Depetrini, who refereed the game – ran around keeping relatively warm.

La Viola – the purple shirts of Fiorentina – host Juventus in the Stadio Comunale, Florence, before a capacity crowd of 70,000 people. The home fans sense a small upset on the calcio horizon, justice to be done, Juventus to be shown up for what they really are: over-priced impostors.

LA TREDICESIMA

Eleven minutes after Fiorentina's Argentine maestro, Miguel Montuori, opened the scoring, Boniperti has the ball in his possession and that rare commodity of space in which to use it. He centres the ball with his glorious right foot. Goalkeeper Giuliano Sarti's timing is poor; he leaps to intercept the ball but misses it completely, grasping at air. The ball drops behind him, between Sivori and Charles near the penalty spot. Charles is quicker to react and promptly jabs in the equalising goal. It is an unexpected, unwarranted development in the proceedings, but serves to jolt the visitors into a stronger sense of confidence and endeavour: they begin to take the game to the hosts, to press for another goal.

Ten yards outside the left angle of Fiorentina's penalty area, Stivanello is tripped. Free-kick. Boniperti stands with Stivanello, planning. The referee blows his whistle, Stivanello taps the ball to Boniperti; he immediately returns the favour. Stivanello is in the process of hitting a cross into the area, but Fiorentina's Giuseppe Chiappella dashes in to block the ball with the studded sole of his right foot. Excruciatingly, the full force of Stivanello's left foot smacks into Chiappella's boot studs. He is badly injured and he's out of the game, for today and for weeks more, with a broken metatarsal bone, severe bruising and damage to soft tissue of his foot. His withdrawal weakens the team and is a contributing factor to their eventual defeat. As hard as they resist the waves of purple shirts, the Juventus defence eventually cracks, Giuseppe Virgili poaching the winner late on, past the also injured Mattrel in goal.

A captivating match and, even taking into account Juventus's bad luck, a fair result. For many in attendance, however, events off the pitch ensured the score-line was viewed in starker perspective.

Fiorentina's 'Marathon' stand is a two-tiered uncovered terrace that accommodates thousands of spectators; it holds the enormous 'Tower of Marathon' too. The front area of terracing is dominated by the higher section, the two tiers being divided by a protective railing spanning the full length. The stand was full for the game, and within the crammed upper terracing, a violent dispute between two men – their reasons not known – causes panic in the crowd, people pushing and shoving to avoid the fighting, which causes unfortunate individuals to be crushed against the railing. And then a long segment of the railing buckles and gives way, and scores of people plunge over the edge into the front tier a few metres below. The match is held up for a few minutes while the police and officials and medical staff of the Red Cross and Green Cross try to tend to the many injured. More than a hundred people are hurt, and fifteen of the casualties hospitalised. Mercifully no one dies as a result of the accident.

Juventus remain top of Serie A above Fiorentina, but are now ahead by only a solitary point. The crowd scenes shocked the footballers and personnel, and with that stand being at the side of the pitch, the disturbing events on the terraces were all too easy to see. Had Juventus won the match, Charles would have felt guilty 'celebrating' at a time when the catastrophic events unfolding there could easily have resulted in numerous deaths. The clouds in his mind partially dissipated with the World Cup news that FIFA had decided to create a 'play-off' match for Israel to compete in, due to those Arab nations refusing to participate. And, because Wales had finished second in their three-team group, they were entered into a special draw: the first team drawn out of the hat would play Israel in that two-legged decider, the winners of which would qualify for the finals in Sweden. And it was the name of *Wales* that was drawn out – they'd been gifted another chance.

The Charleses were back in Leeds for a few days over the Christmas period, set to return to Turin on Boxing Day. The family crammed in to Peggy's parents' house in Middleton, a few miles' walk from Elland Road. John would have loved to watch his former team-mates in action, but the football calendar had contrived to ruin his chances, and Peggy would not have allowed it anyway; it was Christmas Week after all! As it was, Leeds United were away in both games, to Sunderland and then to Leicester City, so he would not have been able to attend even had he been permitted to … and Leeds would be defeated in both.

In the early afternoon of Christmas Eve, Peggy interrupted John's reading of the *Daily Mirror* newspaper – the sports pages, naturally – by dropping his grey fedora on to his head.

'Come on love, we're going for a walk.'

'Where to?'

'You'll see: surprise treat for you.'

'Christmas?'

'No, birthday. You've already seen your Christmas presents; I spent most of this week wrapping them!'

December 27th would be John's twenty-sixth birthday. He would be back in Turin then, sorry to be away from Leeds again but also relieved that his time there had not been long enough for homesickness to really bite. He would have felt a little more sadness had they spent Christmas in Swansea rather than Leeds. Peggy and John were both in heavy coats to ward off the chill, and he was wearing a stylish fedora hat just in case anyone recognised him and wanted too much of his time. As it was, the people of Middleton had their own lives to lead – a well-dressed couple walking down Middleton Hill to Beeston was not much to wonder about, especially the day before Christmas Day.

Their walk was about a mile, past the enormous white water tower that looked like an overgrown chess castle, down the hill, between the long lines of trees and the golf greens, until they arrived at their destination, the glorious lettering high in the grey sky, a glow of electric crimson to brighten the scene and the spirit.

'Can't remember the last time we went to the pictures,' John said.

'No, me neither. But that's where we're going today; is that alright?'

'Course love, if you want to; what's on?'

'See the advertisement? It's a war film, *The Bridge on the River Kwai*.' 'Right.'

'I bet you don't remember the first film we ever saw together,' Peggy said teasingly.

'How much?'

'How much what?'

'How much do you bet me?'

'The price of the tickets.'

'Right. It was *The Happiest Days of Your Life* and it starred Alastair Sim, and we watched it at the Scala in town. I got us in for nothing.'

'How on earth do you remember? I thought I was the only one who remembered things like that!'

John smiled and winked at her ... 'Your mum knew as well.'

◎

Very soon after the Fiorentina match, Omar Sivori had been granted special permission from the club to travel home to Argentina. The reason being ... he was getting married, to his sweetheart Maria Elena Casa. While Juventus had shown good grace in allowing him to do this, they had issued strict orders that he be back in Turin in good time for the next match, against Sampdoria on Sunday 22nd December. Any honeymoon would have to wait until the football season was over. Sivori, and wife, returned on the Friday, happy, excited and very tired due to the many hours and miles travelled. Consequently, he was a major doubt for the match, but then came the announcement that the game was postponed, both teams having players on international duty. On that Sunday, in icy conditions, Italy's World Cup qualifier against Portugal took place at the San Siro Stadium in Milan. With Juventus's Corradi and Ferrario playing, Italy won comfortably 3-0, meaning they needed just to avoid defeat in their last group match, the rescheduled tie in Northern Ireland.

12

JANUARY 1958

T he 1st January 1958, a friendly, Juventus versus Casale F.C. at the Comunale. Like Pinerolo, Casale were another minor league club based in the Piedmont region. The weather was still interminably, painfully cold, but at least the sun shone, a slight improvement on the snow and ice that had caused the postponement of the league tie against Sampdoria on 28th December. The friendly was held at the stadium, with an attendance of more than four thousand people. The three main Juve men – Sivori, Charles and Boniperti – played well, as if the time off had benefited them. They passed the ball to each other quickly, accurately, incisively. Perhaps there had been New Year's resolutions made, players vowing to be more cooperative and team-spirited, or perhaps newly married life was helping Sivori to settle and to mature.

Back at the Charles's residence, Via Susa 31, John had spent a couple of hours being interviewed (and photographed) by two reporters representing *Tempo* magazine. Gigi Peronace had been in attendance, there to offer any help with translations and the like if needed. It hadn't been; one of the journalists had arrived prepared with his interview questions written in English, just in case his own normally proficient command of the language eluded him. Peggy tried to wriggle out of being photographed by lending a few pictures from her family album, but the reporters succeeded in catching her on lens a couple of times nonetheless.

◎

'*Il gigante buono*' was one hell of a title, and after the match against Sampdoria on the afternoon of Wednesday January 8th, a couple more names were added to John Charles's canon … 'the King of

Football' as well as 'Juventus's Emperor'. The rescheduled tie, with a two-thirty kick-off time, had the even more unusual feature of being broadcast live on television too, and now that he was to be on TV, Peggy Charles's thoughts of her husband having film-star looks seemed considerably less fanciful.

His old friend from England was in the Sampdoria side, striker Eddie Firmani. The two knew each other from their times in the English league, and the chances were that they would be vying for this season's title of *capocannoniere*, the top scorer in Serie A. Chatting before the start, Firmani told Charles that he would be facing a fine Sampdoria defender by the name of Gaudenzio Bernasconi, who, if he had been a few inches taller, would have had the ability to be one of the world's best ever centre-halves. Charles nodded politely and said he looked forward to a good contest with the player.

Another Juventus player in receipt of a new nickname was the left-back Bruno Garzena, christened by fans as 'The Hawk' due to his speed and sharpness in defence and supporting the attack. In spite of scant critical recognition in the sports press, keen observers of Juventus appreciated that he had possibly been the most consistent performer in the team so far. And in the twenty-sixth minute of the match it was Garzena who swooped to intercept the ball in midfield and then descend impetuously towards the Sampdoria goal. His trickery helped him beat both Farina and Marocchi in the left corner of the pitch near the penalty area. Looking up to gauge the situation, he then curled a low pass across the goal-mouth, which cut out keeper Bardelli and presented the stretching John Charles with an empty net to fill. Good fortune, though, shone on Sampdoria as the ball hit a divot, bounced up onto Charles's shin and then rolled out of play. Charles was nonplussed, embarrassed and disgusted with himself, not quite believing he had missed the opportunity. Getting to his feet he was greeted by Bardelli grinning at him. Omar Sivori, feeling the man's pain – he was, after all, no stranger to such shame – jogged across to his team-mate and planted a kiss on his cheek in sympathy. Team spirit and camaraderie is a fabulous virtue to have in any side, but this show of affection was a little too much!

Before the thirtieth minute of the game is completed, a through-ball from the subtle foot of Stacchini sets Charles in on goal. With a shoulder-barge he out-muscles Bernasconi, but the defender Marocchi then plunges in to knock him crashing to the mud. A clear foul … a whistle blow … the referee's dramatic gesture … a penalty kick awarded. Corradi takes the kick and scores with aplomb; Juventus one goal ahead. For Sampdoria, Eddie Firmani has hardly been near the ball, such is Juventus's dominance.

Before long, Charles runs with the ball towards goal, Bernasconi matching him stride for stride, anticipating the chance – if such a rarity was to arise – to steal the ball away. But then Bernasconi feels a stab of pain in his left thigh. It could be his hamstring or muscle tear or even a rupture … whatever it is, it is certainly painful, and suddenly he is unable to run and cannot stop himself hurtling to the ground, yelping as he hits the soil.

IL QUATTORDICESIMO

A few seconds past an hour of the match played, the wise Boniperti plants a careful surface pass into the Sampdoria area. It is intended for Charles and he is onto it in an instant … too quickly in fact, for he begins to stumble. Falling but still managing to poke the ball with his right foot, he urgently bends his leg to avoid impacting into Bardelli, while the ball sneaks under the goalkeeper's body and rolls into the net. Bardelli resents the goal but appreciates Charles's efforts to avoid hurting him.

IL QUINDICESIMO

Three minutes on, Stacchini is in a one-on-one confrontation with the goalkeeper but nudges the ball too far. The keeper blocks but cannot stop the ball rolling away, directly to Charles, who has an empty net before him. No mistake this time: he casually side-foots the ball and makes it 3-0 to Juventus.

IL SEDICESIMO

In the seventy-second minute of the match, more evidence of Juventus's domination as Nicole lobs the ball high from an acute angle across and over goalkeeper Bardelli towards goal. It bounces up off the crossbar and gently drops to the awaiting Charles to score an even easier goal than his second, thus completing his hat-trick. The score is now 4-0; a late strike from Okwirk makes the final tally 4-1 to Juventus.

◎

The Juventus players had finally boarded the bus to take them the short journey to the Caffe Torino, the driver having sat patiently for well over an hour, so many people having waited around to cheer the players and get their autographs after the splendid victory. The most sought-after man of the moment was *Il Gigante*. John Charles, for many, is now a sporting god. Boys and men shout his name, complimenting him, praising him, idolising him. He appreciates the warmth of their comments, even though he understands hardly any of the words; he winks and smiles in gratitude, his cheeks reddening. On the bus, adjacent to an open slide-down window, with Colombo sitting next to Charles, a young scamp clambers up the side of the bus to position his face in the aperture. He begins talking cheerfully, excitedly, to the hat-trick hero, an entire flurry of incomprehensible language ... Colombo assists by translating: 'The boy is requesting that you continue to score more goals like you have today, and he is asking if you were hurt when you missed the one in the first few minutes.'

'No, no ...' smiles Charles, still mildly uncomfortable.

The bus's engine starts. Colombo tells the child to leave them be now and to climb down carefully.

'Ciao!' grins the departing boy.

Charles asks Colombo if the child should be in school on a Wednesday afternoon. Possibly, he is advised, though school would have finished hours ago. Besides, *this* is an education; the boy might one day play football for his occupation, and so the players are helping to teach him. Behind Charles sat The Hawk, Garzena. Laughing, he patted the Welshman on the head and called him 'Hollywood John'. To Charles's relief, the new nickname stuck for no longer than the duration of the journey to Piazza San Carlo.

The plan for the squad's 'training' tomorrow comprised mainly relaxing, and massages and sauna treatments, to rest, recuperate and re-energise the players after today's exertions. And so, most of them socialised and celebrated more than they perhaps should have, in the upstairs room of the Caffe Torino. The Juventus side of the city was a very happy one, and the champagne and cocktails flowed, admirers wanting to buy the players drinks for performing and winning so well, hoping vainly to somehow share the euphoria of victory and be part of the victorious Juventus team. Turin revellers, even on a Wednesday night, want to mingle and to share the bonhomie that a good win brings. Fashionable, wealthy, young, attractive, vivacious men and women desire to be a part of the picture, a picture that can easily become distorted due to jealousy and mischief-making. Gossip and rumours start this way, even when the targets, such as John Charles, are entirely innocent.

Umberto Colombo enjoyed John and Peggy's company; he wished only that it was in another venue – the Caffe Torino was a little too refined for his liking, too 'middle class', too sterile, too insincere. He much preferred the less formal establishments like the Bar Leri close to the Porta Nuova station, where he could relax and enjoy himself more. And he was never particularly concerned about gossip, primarily because, as a single and popular young man who worked hard and played hard, aspects of it were likely to be true!

On the subject of rumour, Charles was told of an article in the sports magazine *Il Campione* which declared that Gigi Peronace had arranged secret negotiations with Manchester United to bring one of their players to Juventus. That player was amongst the world's best, perhaps *the* world's best, midfielders: Duncan Edwards. The transfer would supposedly take place after the World Cup finals in June, and Edwards would cost over £100,000. The report claimed Juventus would be allowed to field another foreign player by then as Sivori would be classed as dual nationality. What a signing it would be, though Charles's best pal might view the situation differently: Colombo would probably be the unfortunate chosen one to make way for Edwards' inclusion in the team.

◎

No game scheduled for Juventus on Sunday 12th January, as Italy were completing their tie against Northern Ireland on the 15th, while Charles had long travels ahead on the Sunday also. Umberto Agnelli had kept his word and allowed Charles to represent Wales in their 'second chance' play-off qualifier against Israel on the Wednesday, the first leg taking place in Tel Aviv. Leaving Peggy and the kids always tore at Charles's morale, but when it was to represent his country the sadness was superseded by the pride. Playing for Wales had been a childhood dream and he would make sure his sons grew up in no doubt of its significance or of the immense pride he felt at being the youngest ever player to be capped by the Welsh national team.

His arrival in Tel Aviv was three days before his team-mates' (and the waste-of-time mob of selectors), but at least he had his ubiquitous 'butler' Gigi to keep him company. He was grateful for his presence. The people of Tel Aviv were excited at the prospect of seeing *the* John Charles in person, and the higher the excitement in seeing him, the less he savoured it. He loved the atmosphere of playing in front of big crowds in packed stadia, but such clamour anywhere else he could happily do without.

He did not score in the match; he did not play well either, marked as he was throughout by two, sometimes even three, defenders. He disapproved of that sort of attention as well, though it created the advantage of other Wales players being left unmarked and thus freer to push forward. And Wales were not 'John Charles F.C.'; the team had other fine players capable of inflicting considerable damage on the opposition: the Allchurch brothers, the captain Dave Bowen, and Cliff Jones, Terry Medwin, and of course John's brother Mel. Although the heat in Tel Aviv made the going tough for their lungs, and the pitch was rock hard and uneven, Wales earned a relatively easy win, 2-0, goals coming from Bowen and Len Allchurch.

They had fared much better abroad than their Italian counterparts in Belfast, Northern Ireland winning 2-1 and sealing the Italians' absence from the forthcoming World Cup finals in Sweden.

Charles emerged from the Israel match uninjured. He was tired though, very tired, and the uncomfortable hours of travelling back to Italy would be no help at all: the aches and strains of sporting combat would take longer to fade. As Juventus were due to play Roma in the capital city on the Sunday, he arrived there late on the Thursday, in good time. He would wait for his club team-mates to arrive; even with Peronace there to keep him company, it was again too much time away from his loved ones.

The attendance of ninety-thousand-plus spectators for the Roma–Juventus match meant record gate receipts for an Italian league match, and by the time the game had finished, Roma F.C. were doubly happy. The home supporters had been served with exceptional value for money as their team triumphed 4-1. In the second half, after being brought down in the penalty area yet again, and seeing the referee dramatically declare 'No foul!' yet again, Charles got to his feet and admitted defeat. 'This is Roma's day.'

The referee played well for Roma, in the opinion of Ljubisa Brocic after the match, as he had ignored countless fouls on his players, Charles being the main recipient, three such incidents having occurred in the Roma penalty box. Juventus chief Umberto Agnelli showed good grace in defeat but privately he was riled with his team's display and John Charles's obvious fatigue. Brocic was left in no doubt of the strength of Agnelli's dissatisfaction, though he reminded Agnelli that Charles had not been the only Juve player on international duty overseas: Corradi and Ferrario were both tired too after playing for Italy. Brocic was himself then reminded by his employer that everyone expected more from John Charles, because he was *the* John Charles and had cost such a large amount of money.

The Juventus team flew back to Turin that same night, tomorrow being their usual day off. Charles, though, decided he would go into work to train alone, for no other reason than the belief that he had not played well enough in recent matches. Nothing overly strenuous or energy sapping, but practice makes perfect and all that. Besides, he fancied a sauna, a sensational way of soothing aches and pains, especially during winter.

◎

The groundsmen had long been hard at work battling winter's influence in the hope of ensuring the Verona versus Juventus match avoided postponement. They succeeded, partly thanks to laying large sheets of tarpaulin down the sides of the pitch and spreading lots of sawdust on to the playing surface. The result was that the wings were icy but in a healthy enough condition to play on, while the centre of the pitch, from one goal to the other, was a mix of frozen mud, snow and sawdust. Treacherous but officially not too treacherous.

Whatever credit was given to the ground staff before the match had probably dissipated by half-time due to Verona being one goal behind, thanks almost entirely to the state of the pitch, specifically the goalmouths. From just inside the area, Sivori had half-volleyed on goal, but the shot was mishit and weak, enabling goalkeeper Gianbattista Servidati to watch unconcerned as the ball bounced in towards him meekly. Except ... three feet away from him, its last impact point was a tiny ridge of frozen mud and on contact it ricocheted and veered to the right of the now hapless Servidati, instead of continuing on its initial course leftwards. A bizarre goal, a sheer fluke that almost embarrassed Sivori enough to stop him celebrating scoring it ... but not quite.

IL DICIASSETTESIMO

In the sixty-first minute, Charles runs on to a thoughtful Colombo through-ball. Thanks to better anticipation and acceleration, he has a yard start on the two defenders on his trail. Within seconds he is close to the Verona area. Servidati hurries out from his goal, to try and grab the ball or at the very least narrow down Charles's sight of the net. Both objectives fail; Charles prods the ball with the outside of his right foot, its momentum helped inadvertently by the goalkeeper's left hand. The ball bobbles towards the post, bounces off it and settles just across the line, as Giuseppe Corradi gets there in case of any doubt. Two-nil to Juventus.

Ten minutes on – Ghiandi exploits hesitancy in the Juventus defence to reduce the deficit: 2-1.

Corradi has been non-stop for the entire match, hoping for redemption following his poor performance in Rome. Today he earns a just reward by scoring Juventus's third goal, which, it transpires, is decisive, despite a Garzena own-goal in the last minute that makes it 3-2.

13

FEBRUARY 1958

After watching her husband play in Juventus's pragmatic 2-0 win over Udinese, another separation from the man of the house for Peggy and family was taking place. Never any complaints from her; their being separated was all a part of professional football, compensated by the pleasant lifestyle and the high standard of living it brought them. The one aspect of life in Italy that Peggy could not take to was the harsher weather, specifically the winter cold, crueller as it was than Yorkshire weather, which itself was not renowned for its mildness.

With John due to be away for a week, Peggy arranged her own break to coincide: she would spend a few days in warmer climes with the three boys. Elsie had told her how pleasant the 'Italian Riviera' on the Mediterranean coastline was, the temperature there always being pleasantly a few degrees higher. Their destination town was Bordighera, overlooking the Ligurian Sea, renowned as well – said Elsie – for its beautiful flora, including mimosa, which happened to be one of Peggy's favourites. Even more pleasingly, Juventus F.C. kindly provided the services of one of their chauffeurs to drive them there and, later in the week, bring them back.

Had the gossips in the press known about her vacation, they could have added two and two together and made at least five by scandalously linking Peggy's visit to the fact Ferenc Puskás resided in Bordighera. As it was, gossip columns were relatively peaceful for the time being. Film star and well-known Juventus fan Sophia Loren was romantically linked to John Charles, even though they had not even met yet. Elsie had told Peggy that another Italian beauty, Gina Lollobrigida, was reportedly interested in John as a personal escort too. Peggy believed nothing about the reports, responding with a smile and the remark, 'Just let them try anyway.'

Over a thousand kilometres away in Cardiff, on the Wednesday night of February 5th, Jimmy Murphy's Wales team played Israel in the second leg of their qualifier tie. While he didn't score, Charles's influence on the match was major. In the seventy-fifth minute, Israel goalkeeper Chodoroff, who was having a fine game, leapt to try and catch a high cross and collided with Charles trying to head the ball, culminating in both men landing awkwardly with tremendous force. Charles was winded but unhurt whereas Chodoroff suffered concussion, a broken nose and a sprained shoulder. He played on, in considerable discomfort, and Wales went on to score two late soft goals, through Ivor Allchurch and Cliff Jones. While the conditions were entirely opposite to those in Tel Aviv, the match outcome was the same, and now Wales had qualified for the World Cup finals. The Welsh players and fans were almost as thrilled as if they had won the trophy.

Shortly after the match, Charles managed to elude the celebrating crowds and, with Gigi Peronace, drove from Cardiff to his birthplace Swansea, staying in a hotel for the night with the intention of visiting his parents the following day, Thursday 6th February. John would be fulfilling a promise to his mother, accompanying her on an afternoon shopping trip for wedding gifts for Mel, who was getting married in March to fiancée Vera. It would in fact be a triple wedding ceremony, as Mel's team-mates Don Pearson and Jeff Rees were marrying their own sweethearts at the same time, the three couples all due to honeymoon subsequently for a few days in London.

John and his mother were in a Swansea store, she looking for things to buy, he taking scant interest in the proceedings. Shopping was right up there with exploring churches in terms of entertainment value, but at least his mam seemed to be enjoying herself. While she was inspecting items of crockery and dinner services – and hoping in vain for support from her eldest son – John noticed a news vendor standing outside on the shining wet pavement, selling late editions of the local newspaper. Business seemed brisk. It was already getting dark and the electric lights from the shop served to enhance the faces of the people near to the big window panes. Charles wasn't able to determine exactly what the vendor was repeatedly announcing, but judging by the expressions of concern and shock on the faces of people buying copies, he sensed something was wrong, very wrong – something really bad had happened.

He used some of his mother's coins to hurriedly buy a paper, as the vendor continued to shout the headline news: 'Air disaster latest!' Charles scanned the front page and then he understood the commotion and the looks of horror on people's faces. The Manchester United team had been involved in a deadly accident at an airport in Munich. He felt ill.

The earliest news from Munich was that there had been eleven deaths when the aeroplane had crashed on take-off in icy conditions. The newspaper did not name the victims. Charles had an awful, unsettling thought that his old pal Tommy Taylor – who he had served with in the army for a year – was one of the casualties. He wondered how Tommy's mum would be feeling ... the haunted look on his own mother's face would be insignificant in comparison. Tommy Taylor was a cheerful fellow who liked to laugh and joke, and a great player too. And most importantly, a dear friend. Roger Byrne similarly; he would also have been involved.

Charles's father and Gigi were listening to the radio when John and his mother returned home. Their sombre faces needed no explaining. The radio reports revealed that seven of Manchester United's players had died immediately in the disaster: Eddie Colman, Liam Whelan, David Pegg, Mark Jones, Geoff Bent, Tommy Taylor, and team captain Roger Byrne. Duncan Edwards was badly hurt too, though the details were sketchy. Amongst the other hurt players were Albert Scanlon, Bobby Charlton, and Johnny Berry and Jackie Blanchflower, whose injuries were said to be career threatening. A number of journalists had died too, together with airline crew and Manchester United officials. Manager Matt Busby had suffered fractured ribs, a punctured lung and leg injuries; he was in a critical condition.

Soon after the news reached Italy, Turin in particular, Lucia, alone in the Charleses home, began to receive telephone calls from the ignorant and the curious – and a few concerned people – wanting to ask if Charles had heard about the air crash. By the time she had retired to her bed, she had deemed it necessary to take the telephone receiver off its cradle.

◎

Ljubisa Brocic was concerned about Charles; it was plain to see that the terrible events in Munich had upset and affected him psychologically. He looked troubled, tired and pale – somehow gaunt too, as if he had lost pounds in weight in a matter of hours. Brocic told him he would absolutely understand if he said he would prefer to miss the next Juventus match, and that Umberto Agnelli would support him whatever he decided. Charles thanked Brocic for his consideration, declaring that he thought the best way to deal with it all was to 'carry on' with life as normally as he could. If he did not play in the match then he was of the opinion that he would be letting a lot of people down.

Sunday 9th February, just three days after the disaster, Juventus were away to Genoa. Torrential rain and a sky blanketed by dark clouds mirrored Charles's spirits. Juventus won the match 3-1, with little significant contribution from Charles. Everyone there – the players, the officials, the press men, the many thousands of spectators – recognised he had other matters on his mind, troubles in his heart. As far as it was possible to do so, they shared the same troubles. No one criticised, no one complained, and the compassion and generosity of spirit needed no translation. Charles knew everyone supported him, sympathised with him. In Turin, at the same time, Torino were playing Napoli, and a minute's silence in the stadium was held before the start of the match. It was a deeply emotional time for everyone connected with Torino F.C., united in grief.

The train carriage of the funicular railway on the ascending track of Superga Hill possesses a predominantly wooden interior, mainly pine, the seats being predictably uncomfortable for both John and Peggy Charles, the only passengers this early morning. The windows are closed to keep what precious little warmth there is inside the carriage. The climb is slow and the view from the carriage at times vague due to morning mist; always interesting nonetheless. Gardens and villas and houses; pastures, roads, allotments and thick woodland. Stone bricks and imperfect walls border the track, with huge hewn slabs and cut boulders defending the line. Various types of ivy coat the walls, moist, dark green moss beneath. The carriage enters a tunnel, electric lighting weakly resisting the darkness. The tunnel is not a place suitable for claustrophobics.

The darkness seems to act as a prompt for John to speak. 'I still can't believe it, love.' Peggy squeezes his hand. 'I know, I know, it's awful.'

The latest news concerning the Munich air disaster remained deeply distressing, with Italian press reporting that Duncan Edwards had undergone a six-hour operation in an effort to halt his deteriorating condition, which included the amputation of his left leg. The claim that Edwards had subsequently said that he would have to get a new job only made the situation appear even more depressing.

◎

While Charles struggled with depression, and Sivori was niggled by a slight thigh-muscle strain, the rest of the team appeared to assume increased responsibility, as if to prove there was more, much more, to the side than just two very expensive imports. For all the positive reviews the team's strategy of attack had gained, Juventus also had the reputation of wanting to walk across the finish line instead of running. The theory was somewhat refuted, however, against S.P.A.L.

LA DICIOTTESIMA

The seventy-fifth minute. From left to right, Boniperti swipes a diagonal pass into the penalty area for the head of the monumental John Charles. Charles wins the header and nods the ball down to Sivori in the goal-mouth to volley on sight. The snap-shot, though, is blocked and spins back out in Charles's direction, towards the dead-ball line. Instead of allowing it to go out for a corner-kick, he decides to lash it with his right foot. Despite the crowd of players in front of him and the acute angle he shoots from – not to mention the goalkeeper and a defender standing on the line – the football somehow pierces the human wall to hit and stretch the net, adding to a first-minute strike from Boniperti and a second-half pile-driver from Umberto Colombo to make the score 3-1 to Juventus.

The emotions, the euphoria, the memory of his Manchester friends … the tears are unavoidable. Charles runs back towards the centre circle, Sivori running and jumping like a child alongside him, an arm reaching up to his Welsh friend's huge shoulders. Charles stops on the half-way line, and looks up to the grandstand, searching for wife Peggy. Today is the 16th of February: Peggy's birthday. He sees her, sees she is smiling and looking straight back at him. He raises his left arm and waves to her, as if to say *'That's for you, love.'* She was surprised he had even remembered, this month of all months and with so much to distract him. What she didn't know was that Gigi had reminded John of the date earlier in the week, only for John to forget again until the memory hit him just as the brouhaha following his goal snapped him to clearer senses. Few if any people noticed John's tears, Peggy included, but she nonetheless *knew* he was weeping and she privately wept with him.

Five days later came the shocking, awful news that Duncan Edwards had died; his resistance had finally faded. Before Juventus's match at the weekend against Padova, Charles was politely asked for his thoughts on the matter. He was sickened by the news of course, and wondered if the misery of the crash would ever stop. In English, and with his voice strained with emotion, he replied, 'I am always flattered when you say good things about me, but if you think I'm a decent player then you should have seen Duncan Edwards. He had everything and his death is a tragedy for the world of football.'

Subsequently, with what some observers would regard as terrible and thoughtless timing, press reports appeared within days suggesting that Manchester United now intended to buy Charles from Juventus Football Club.

14.

MARCH 1958

L ast week, Juventus had drawn one each with Padova, a more than satisfactory result as well as a clear signal they deserved their position at the top of the table. Padova remained second in the table but had never looked like beating Juventus, and the draw ensured a continuing gap of five points between them. Though none said it as yet, most observers believed it would take a minor miracle for Juventus to be overtaken.

It was exactly that kind of attitude – over-confidence, cockiness, arrogance – which seemed to characterise the team's performance in the first half of their following match, against Torino.

The players' insouciance in those first forty-five minutes of play did not go unnoticed despite earning themselves a two-goal lead. 'Complacency is a crime,' Ljubisa Brocic warned during the half-time interval. 'If you continue like this there will be changes for the next match.'

The second half saw a rejuvenated Juventus performance: dynamic, flexible, harmonious. A real team effort, synchronised and fluid, Boniperti – the piston and architect – leading by example as the best captains do, supported by the tireless Colombo. It was the triumvirate of Boniperti, Colombo and Charles who dictated things, with the tormentors Sivori and Stacchini relishing opportunities to run at and take on defenders. Torino became virtually irrelevant; the Juventus engine had moved up two gears.

IL DICIANNOVESIMO

The sixtieth minute. Cometh the hour ... Perfect close control and sharp interplay between Boniperti and Sivori and then Charles ... smart thinking, swift action, incisive passing, capped by a *smash*, and it is 3-0 to Juventus.

CHAPTER FOURTEEN

IL VENTESIMO

During the last ten minutes, on the edge of their neighbour's penalty area, using the same human weaponry, another manoeuvre of virtual geometry culminates in Charles striking the ball so powerfully it almost takes Torino keeper Rigamonti with it into the net.

Juventus are 4-1 winners.

◎

Sunday 9th March, Juventus play host to Milan, the red and blacks, the *rossoneri*, in the twenty-fourth match of the thirty-four-match season. A chilly and very windy afternoon, gusts of wind often spoiling the chances of attractive, precise football. The first half of the match is notable primarily for the superb performance of Juve's fourth-choice goalkeeper, twenty-one-year-old Luciano Alfieri in his debut game. The Milan team is toiling in the league but faring very well in the European Cup competition; having disposed of West Germany's Borussia Dortmund in the last round, their semi-final opponents will be a new-look Manchester United, in May.

IL VENTUNESIMO

Most people watching failed to see one of Milan's centre-halves – number six Eros Beraldo – pushing Charles in the back as the two men waited for a Juventus corner-kick to arrive. Fortunately for Juventus, the referee was one of the few who noticed the infringement, and despite heated protestations from the Milan players, he awarded a penalty kick.

Charles takes the penalty. Having never missed one in his professional career, he is not about to start today, his fireball of a hit burning Alfieri's left hand and rippling the goal net.

No Milan capitulation; they search for an equaliser, giving the Juventus defence no time to relax. Only when Milan lose possession or miss the target do Juventus manage any more forays, and those few occasions are counter-attacks.

Charles pursues a loose pass in the Milan half. If he gets to it first he has clear route to goal and only the keeper to beat. He pictures the sequence of success in his head. When Charles sprints, he is a human maelstrom of pumping limbs; only a brave man confronts such power in motion. Milan's defensive-midfielder Mario Bergamaschi is one such man and he is in pursuit. With great pace he reaches Charles. As he draws level and alongside him, his head also meets Charles's right elbow with great pace. Bergamaschi is hurt and left stunned and prone on the ground; Charles is at liberty to continue, but instead of running on and scoring, his concern for his opponent wins out. Kicking the ball away from goal and out of play, he rushes to the injured player and kneels at his side.

Sivori is sceptical. 'John, what are you doing?'

Charles replies, 'He's hurt.'

'He is okay.'

'Shut up, Omar!'

Bergamaschi's swollen eye is testimony to the truth. He was unlucky to get hurt, his team being similarly unfortunate to lose the match.

Juventus's next match is against the other Serie A club from Milan, the blue side, Internazionale. They are experiencing a mediocre season in the league, so the capacity attendance of over ninety thousand spectators is a surprising bonus for the home team's owners. Both Milan clubs regard Juventus as intense rivals; there are few teams they want to beat more, apart from each other of course. Unofficially, Umberto Agnelli typically adds spice to the Turin–Milan rivalry by awarding lucrative bonuses to his players if they win or, very occasionally, if they at least avoid defeat. This explains the players' ecstatic reactions when Sivori cracks in a shot from the edge of the box to level the scores after Juventus had gone behind early on.

That joy proves short-lived as Inter score again soon afterwards: 2-1 by the interval.

The half-time break.

IL VENTIDUESIMO

Five minutes into the second half. Outside-right Gino Stacchini has the ball at his feet, close to the corner flag, about to punish left-back Guidi Vincenzi. Inches from the touch-line he outwits and outpaces the defender before despatching a hefty cross into the penalty area with the inside of his right foot. The ball curls in at pace directly towards Charles's head; he is alone and has a clear sight of the ball on its approach. Inexplicably though, he jumps early. Realising his mistake he thrusts his head down, practically stooping in mid-air. Goalkeeper Ghezzi guesses he is beaten before Charles even connects with the ball, a torrent of abuse leaving the goalkeeper's mouth shortly afterwards as he berates his defenders for allowing Charles all the space he could desire. Two goals each.

The match ends 2-2, one more point accrued towards Charles winning a trophy in his first season. Hearty congratulations from his team-mates and some unexpected extra cash to go in his coffers to give him more spending power for a gift for Peggy on their fifth wedding anniversary.

Good news for Mattrel, Corradi, Garzena, Emoli, Ferrario, Boniperti and Nicole too, all called up for the Italy national squad for a match against Austria next weekend. Oddly, the consistently good form of Stacchini and Colombo has been disregarded by the selectors.

◎

The team preparation for Juventus's next match should have made for much easier work than normal for Ljubisa Brocic: the Juventus players, particularly Colombo, Boniperti, Sivori and Charles – especially Charles – had for months harboured all the motivation they needed. That motivation was of course revenge, for the opponents were L.R. Vicenza, against whom Charles had been battered unconscious. The player responsible had been their centre-half, number five Remo Lancioni. Although his close team-mates had doubted him, and gently mocked him for saying he would seek personal vengeance, Charles genuinely had been intent on exacting physical retribution on Lancioni. But then the Manchester tragedy occurred and everything changed.

Even more astonishing than there being six goals within the first twenty-five minutes of the game was that three of them were scored by the same player.

The animalistic behaviour was missing. The only similarity with animals was that Vicenza's centre-halves played like headless chickens. Vicenza's main tactic had been to place two defenders each on both Charles and Sivori, the consequence being that the other Juventus attackers benefited from having a more liberated role. Good players exploit such opportunity. Boniperti, Stacchini and Nicole were indeed good players. The Vicenza defence was in disarray for long durations of the game.

VENTITREESIMO

Advancing towards the Vicenza area, Sivori weaves through defenders as if they don't exist, the ball seemingly belonging to his left foot. Unselfishly, he passes short to Charles, whose back is to goal. Charles taps an immediate return to the Argentine. The ball bounces up unexpectedly ... unexpectedly, pleasingly, irresistibly, and so Sivori unleashes punishment with his left foot (of course). In goal, Pietro Battara is on better form than his defenders, and he leaps to protect his domain, quickly repelling the missile. But only to the extent of a few yards, nine in fact, and straight to Charles, twelve yards out. A right-footed whiplash follows and the ball nestles in the goal net. Four-two to Juventus. Charles reacts to his goal modestly and respectfully, and with only a cursory glance of disdain at his former aggressor, who is not worth the trouble. Sivori, however, has other ideas. Scorer already of three goals, which will rise to four, he congratulates Charles and celebrates his friend's strike with a gesticulation towards Lancioni and a loud insult, the loose English translation being: 'Take that you bastard!'

15

APRIL 1958

Due to the team's general excellence this season, the lead-up to the away game against Lazio was the reward of a few days in the picturesque Adriatic seaside resort of Rimini in the Emilia-Romagna region. Only light training and a casual friendly match against a 'Romagna Select' team took place, though the players had the formal boredom of a civic reception in Rimini to also attend. Bruno Nicole stayed in Turin for treatment on a muscle tear, his absence allowing Giorgio Stivanello to return to the side on the wing. During the match, which Juventus won 4-3, an accidental collision with an opponent had winded Umberto Colombo, so he was taken off as a precautionary measure, replaced by midfielder Antonio Montico. Colombo's injury was not serious, and he recovered swiftly. He was relishing the prospect of playing against Lazio in the Eternal City, a highlight of any season, competing in front of a huge partisan crowd.

The Juventus entourage were staying in a high-class hotel in the San Mauro area of Rimini. As usual for away trips, Colombo and Charles roomed together. Also staying in the hotel, the players discovered, was a beautiful French model. She and Colombo were soon acquainted, very closely acquainted in fact. Colombo, a proud, carefree bachelor, did not return to his hotel room until the early hours of Friday morning. As a result he was a few minutes late for breakfast. None of the players or personnel objected to this, coach Ljubisa Brocic even smiling at him as he sat down at the dining table.

◎

Early Sunday afternoon, when Brocic read out the team sheet for the afternoon's match against Lazio, Colombo's name was not included.

When asked the reason for the omission, the coach told the player that it was felt he needed a rest as he was not in the best condition to play in this match. Colombo knew Brocic was not being entirely truthful; it seemed clear that he had been coerced into dropping him from the team as a reaction to his *brief encounter* at the hotel and his late arrival for breakfast. Team captain Boniperti denied discussing the matter with anyone outside of the squad, while Omar Sivori smiled, sympathised and recommended to Colombo that he be 'cleverer' in future in such affairs. Colombo was well aware that he had only himself to blame, but he resented the hypocrisy and the underhand way in which he had been treated; he strongly suspected – to the point of being as certain as he could be without actual proof – that the decision was not based on football reasons or any issue over fitness and had come from the Juventus board of directors and not Brocic. The board included Gianni Agnelli, that well-known womaniser.

Lazio took an early lead in the match – an undeserved lead, for it was not a good Lazio side. The goal served only to irritate the league leaders, spurring them into rectifying the situation quickly: they grabbed control of the match, attacking at speed in dynamic, intricate patterns and triangles. Lazio were chasing shadows for much of the time.

IL VENTIQUATTRESIMO, IL VENTICINQUESIMO E IL VENTISEIESIMO

In the tenth minute of the match, Sivori whirls through a cluster of defenders just inside the Lazio area. He shoots powerfully; goalkeeper Roberto Lovati reacts well, blocking and parrying the ball out to the left of the goal. Charles is the first to it, stopping the ball dead on the corner of the six-yard box and then thumping it low towards goal from an acute angle. Perfection: one goal apiece.

In the thirteenth minute, a short pass along the ground from Stacchini to Charles. He twists his body to achieve better purchase on the ball, his left-foot strike darting past the vulnerable Lovati: 2-1.

As the sixtieth minute of the tie counts down, Sivori blasts in a half-volley to put Juventus 3-1 in front.

Six minutes from full time: a corner-kick. Stivanello takes it. Lovati bounds out from his line to try and reach the ball, only for Charles to get there in front of him. He makes the most of the straightforward task of nodding the ball into the goal, to take his afternoon tally to three goals.

◎

A case of mixed emotions for the two friends on the Turin flight back from Rome. Umberto was pleased the side had won again, but his pleasure was, unsurprisingly, tainted by the fact he had been dropped for the game. And because they had won without him, he feared his enforced absence would continue. He was right to think that way.

Charles agreed Colombo had been harshly treated, but showed only a modicum of sympathy for him. 'You carry on with the women, I'll carry on scoring the goals,' he teased. Colombo took it in good spirit; he was under no illusions – his downfalls were all of his own making.

The real reason for Colombo's omission from the team somehow reached reporters, a kiss-and-tell scandal involving a local woman. Before long the rumour wires began to overheat and warp dragging John in. One outrageous lie circulated saying that Charles was having an affair with a young – and, predictably, 'anonymous' – actress, while the *Guerin Sportivo* even accused him of frequently consorting with prostitutes and visiting notorious nightclubs. Another even more scurrilous rumour alleged that Colombo had been having an affair with a married woman. That married woman happened to be ... Peggy Charles.

John and Peggy sought the advice of the British Consulate regarding the allegations – the hurtful lies – and enquired about the possibility of suing the culprits for libel. Elsie and Alec McMillan regretfully informed them that such a process would take years, genuinely, and would cost a lot of money too. Their official advice to the couple was that they should try to forget about the matter, and take comfort from the knowledge that no one in their right minds believed a single word of the reports, and that the publications' circulation numbers were low, so hardly anyone would actually read them.

'John, those magazines aren't good enough to clean your boots with,' remarked Alec.

Charles responded, 'They're not bloody good enough to clean my ar ...' – only to change word mid-sentence on seeing the urgent and stern look his wife was giving him – '... birdcage with!'

Nervous laughs turned to genuine amusement when Elsie commented that she hadn't known the Charleses owned a pet bird.

◎

Torrential rain on Sunday 13th April pelts down on the city and hampers players' progress on the pitch. Juventus against Bologna. Bologna make this a battle for the home team – and, indeed, score the first goal – while their central defenders try to nullify the Charles threat with emphasis on force and aggression. His ankles and calves endure another battering from boots and studs ... but he will not be defeated. The referee, oblivious to Charles being a moving target for the Bologna snipers, will at least send off midfielder Humberto Machio in the second half, albeit for dissent.

The score is 1-1 by half-time, Sivori tapping in his thirteenth goal of the season.

IL VENTISETTESIMO

In the fifty-fifth minute, simple yet incisive passing and movement from Stacchini, Stivanello and Boniperti. They combine to provide the ammunition. Free in the Bologna half, Charles is forty yards from goal. Goalkeeper Attilio Santarelli, taken by surprise by Charles's speed in reaching the ball, is unsure what to do – whether to retreat to his goal-line or to advance and try to block Charles's route to goal. Ultimately, he does neither; instead he just stands still in the rain, a scarecrow in no man's land. This inaction makes it easy for Charles; he calmly strokes the ball into the net from twenty yards out. Two more goals – one each from Boniperti and Stacchini – finalise the 4-1 victory. The score-line is a somewhat distorted and harsh reflection of the game. Bologna's efforts did not deserve a three-goal defeat.

◎

One of Italy's best-known lifestyle magazines had interviewed Charles back in January and also reproduced a few family photographs to accompany the piece in the latest edition. Within it was the revelation that, in 1955, Internazionale of Milan had been close to signing Charles from Leeds and with 'money no object'; Charles had known nothing about it at the time. Eventually Inter opted for another centre-forward, the Swiss striker Roger Vonlanthen. This news explained why *Tempo*'s piece was titled 'I Should Play for Inter'.

As Charles entered the changing room before training, a copy of the magazine open at the incriminating page and a chorus of good-natured boos and whistles greeted him. And where there would normally have been a Juventus shirt or training top ready for him, there now hung a black-and-blue-striped football shirt – the colours of Inter. He smiled weakly, his spirits low. The reason for his unhappiness – his being 'down in the dumps' as he described it – was his being forced to miss the forthcoming Wales match against Northern Ireland in Cardiff. He resented having to miss *any* Wales games, but had accepted Umberto Agnelli's assurances that he would be allowed to play in the 'important' Wales matches providing they did not interfere with Juventus's season. In hindsight this was too vague a condition, and one that was embarrassing to Charles, leaving him feeling as though he were the victim of a confidence trick. This match was to be Wales's last before the deadline for countries to submit the names of the playing squad for June's World Cup finals. With those freeloading idiots in charge of Wales, Charles was afraid, dreading how they would react to him missing this match. They would probably criticise him, perhaps even *blame* him for missing the match, accusing him of arrogance and of being unpatriotic. Unpatriotic! Had Agnelli stuck to his promises then much of this stress would have been avoided. Even worse news was to follow.

Due to the Italy national team failing to qualify for those finals, the Italian Football Federation, their ruling body, decided to reintroduce their knockout cup competition this year, the Coppa Italia. The tournament would be held in June, and John Charles would be required to participate.

◎

Growing up as a boy in Swansea and as a young man in Leeds, John
Charles never encountered or had even heard of organised crime or
criminal syndicates. And until his arrival in Italy, he was ignorant
of the existence of the Mafia and the Camorra.

The Grand Hotel of Naples, where Juventus were staying on the
Saturday, was situated amidst noisy and busy streets and avenues.
Curiously, the noise actually increased as night-time progressed.
Car horns, music, shouting, chanting, whistling, clapping, metal
lids clanging ... Disturbed sleep wasn't too serious a problem for the
players, kick-off time being the next afternoon, but still, it wasn't
fair ... such dirty tricks did not belong anywhere near the beautiful
game. The local police were no help, claiming they were unable to
prevent revellers from enjoying themselves as no laws were being
broken. Those officers were probably Napoli fans too.

The keenly awaited day arrives, the weather conditions warm,
the sunshine plentiful. For numerous people, though, the joy of the
occasion will end abruptly. All of the tickets had sold out days before.
Disturbingly, thousands of forged tickets had also been produced and
sold on the black market. And combined with scores of supporters
wanting to pay to get in – as well as some trying to get in illegally –
and a powerful police presence, the chances of a disaster were rapidly
increasing. By the time the police were informed that the stadium
was full, more than five thousand people were locked out, many of
them with authentic, legal tickets.

No sympathy or compromise offered by the police officers; only
stern, aggressive orders to disperse and to leave the area. They were
not going to get into the stadium at any cost. A tide of disgust was
forming.

The crowds did not want to leave the area; they had paid good
money to see the football match. They refused to move. Why should
they move? An outrageous injustice was occurring; they had been
swindled and the police were a part of it! A few minutes went by;
people still pushed and shouted and threatened, the police officers
still kept telling them to go home. And then the police charged at
the football supporters. Screams of wounded civilians soon mingled

with the angry shouts of officers. Men, women and children were hurt, bloodied heads and broken limbs, some of them at the hands and batons of the law men, and some from falling to the ground and being trampled on. Police idiocy and brutality resulted in over two hundred casualties, some of whom were seriously injured. A convoy of ambulances would be called upon to transport the worst affected to hospital for treatment – the Cardarelli or the Loreto hospital.

Within the confines of the football ground, both teams are unaware of the scenes of chaos occurring outside. The Juventus players have more than enough on their minds already: the noise and passion and enmity from the multitude of Napoli fanatics. No black-and-white *tifosi* in the stands today, and for Juventus this is becoming a crucible of hostility.

The packed surrounds of the football pitch create an incendiary atmosphere. Apartment blocks outside the stadium, overlooking the pitch, hold hundreds of people in the balconies and on rooftops. The Stadio della Liberazione – 'the Stadium of Liberation', a misnomer on this particular day – is over-full and the terraces are uncontrolled. The human river burgeons until various areas of its banks burst, individuals struggling to escape the crush and stand on the pitch-side track or behind the goal nets.

1-0. In just the fourth minute, Garzena is tricked in the Juventus penalty area by Di Giacomo, who then mis-hits a cross, the football rolling around the penalty spot with no one attending to it. Centre-forward Luís Vinício slowly takes responsibility, kicking the ball into Mattrel's goal and then running away almost in shock at the simplicity of it all. Juventus defenders stand around feeling awkward, giving each other accusing looks, while Mattrel roars his despair to the heavens at their negligence.

1-1. Two minutes later, Boniperti is fouled by Franchini. The captain takes the free-kick himself, the cross dipping to the back post, Charles lurking. Untroubled, he jumps and heads the ball towards goal; defender Elia Greco swings at it but only grazes it with his foot … enough to deceive goalkeeper Bugatti … it spins across the line and into the net. The score should be awarded to Charles as the header was goal-bound; it should be his twenty-eighth of the season. It isn't; it is recorded officially as a Greco own-goal.

2-1. Four Juventus defenders in their penalty area, marking absolutely no one. Napoli's Luigi Brugola, receives the ball. At first nearly falling over it, he regains his composure and thumps the ball into the net ecstatically.

Half-time break.

2-2. Thirteen minutes into the second half, a low left-foot arrow from Stacchini levels the scores, pouncing amidst the Napoli defenders' confusion.

3-2. The seventy-seventh minute. A strong finish from Vinício again, against a virtually non-existent defence, a header at point-blank range. Firecrackers land on the track behind the goal; grey and white clouds of smoke linger in the weakening sunlight. Delighted fans all around, behind the terrace fencing and wires, and many in front of them too.

3-3. The eighty-sixth minute, the dramatic third equaliser. The ball, headed clear out of the Napoli area, drops to Montico. Poised, he sends it back with relish, the volley piercing a crowd of players and beating Bugatti in goal.

4-3. Three minutes later, another fine strike, the *more* dramatic winner. The left-foot shot of Gino Bertucco from the edge of the Juventus area beats Mattrel's despairing dive.

Full time, hundreds of delighted supporters converge on the pitch from all sides of the stadium to congratulate their heroes, celebrating as if they have won the league title.

Napoli's players performed as if the match had been a matter of life or death. They deserved the win not for the higher technical merit but for their endeavour and the intensity of their attacks. Juventus had been, as usual, dangerous up front – even with a lethargic performance from Charles – but woeful in defence. Napoli are eight points behind now, five games left to play. They can still do it, and on this evidence they might well do.

◎

Full-to-brimming stadia were common whenever Juventus were in town, and today is the same at the Stadio Comunale in Bergamo, home ground of Atalanta. Atalanta are near the foot of the league table; a defeat against Juventus would probably leave them closer to relegation and, as a modest-sized club, therefore closer to a disaster. After last week's troublesome defeat, a return for Corradi and Colombo to restore tenacity and energy in the side. Coach Ljubisa Brocic's main focus is on preventing Atalanta from scoring. Do that and a minimum of one point is earned. He predicts they will be desperate to score, and when a team plays with desperation they make mistakes and poor decisions. 'Be patient; they will falter, and when they do, opportunities will arise.' He instructed Charles to drop back to central defence if they came under heavy pressure from the home side. One point would be good, the two points would be excellent. Just as Atalanta needed to win the match more than Juventus, a similar onus was on Napoli, away to Bologna, and they would need to be on top form to take the two points.

Brocic sent the team out, for a moment minus Charles, onto the pitch. Charles was told to remain seated. 'John, I sympathise with your situation, and you have my support. I am confident that Umberto Agnelli is working hard for you to play for your country in Sweden. It is my view that the Federation is playing a childish game; they will not be able to stop you but because they have made the decision, they do not want to appear as stupid or weak when they have to reverse the decision. I am expecting you to be playing in the World Cup finals in June, and this is why I want you in defence, so that you can keep in good condition and, with good fortune, avoid injury. Do you understand?'

'Yes, boss.'

'Do you trust me?'

'Yes, boss.' Charles did trust his coach, but he was not convinced his coach was right.

Somewhat like the weather, the match proved to be dull and uninspiring, and while Charles had a goal disallowed in the first half – Sivori offside once again – Atalanta generally had the upper hand, though they failed to finish the job with a goal.

Charles did spend most of the match helping out at the back as an extra defender, taxed only occasionally and hardly ever out of breath. For the first time all season, Juventus failed to score. More importantly, no goals conceded either. And Napoli, as Brocic had forecast, failed to beat Bologna, drawing 1-1. Four games left and the gap between first and second still eight points. Four games left – Juventus would need to lose all their games and Napoli win all theirs for the championship title to be heading away from Turin.

16

MAY 1958

Before the football season had commenced, *I Viola* – the Purples – of Fiorentina had been widely predicted to be the next champions. Now, Sunday 4th May heralded Juventus at home to Fiorentina and the absorbing possibility that Juventus could be crowned as champions if Napoli fail to win their own match. Napoli were at home to Sampdoria. The Italian Football Federation had issued no official statements about 'the Charles situation', meaning that the player was still very unhappy. Brocic again told him to concentrate on defending and avoiding injury. 'Everything will be okay, John.'

Brocic's positive mood was not infectious; Charles was still under a cloud and he was disgusted with the Federation; his view of Umberto Agnelli was only marginally better.

While it was true that Fiorentina were the more adventurous team in the match, and Mattrel in goal the best performer, Juventus's focus was again to not concede. In a game of low drama but high intrigue, chess-like in tactics and moves, each team probed the other, trying to locate weaknesses to exploit while striving not to overheat in the hot afternoon sun. Frustratingly for some of the more critical and vocal Juventus supporters, Charles was once again employed as an extra defender. This made it easier for him in the heat, but those supporters became increasingly hot under the collar, booing what they saw as needlessly negative tactics from Brocic. They were actually booing the top team in Italian football.

In attack, South American Omar Sivori liked playing in the hot conditions; the pity was that he patently disliked sharing the football, apparently being convinced he was its sole owner. The Juventus player who seemed likeliest to score was captain Boniperti, two second-half efforts flashing so close that ecstatic cries of victory left thousands of supporters' mouths before the startling realisation that a goal had not been scored.

As play progressed and the clock advanced, the happier most Juventus supporters grew. On the terraces, and in the grandstand and the 'backstage' confines of the stadium, owners of transistor radios were suddenly very popular with fans *needing* to hear the news and updates from the concurrent match in Naples.

As full time here in Turin neared, deadlock presided. Whistling from the *tifosi* reached painful levels, all of them imploring the referee to blow the one whistle that mattered, the metal one in his possession, to declare the match completed. And then, with a dramatic flourish and a dash towards the pitch-side tunnel, their demands were met as he blew his whistle … It is full time, and with Napoli losing 0-1 at home to Sampdoria, Juventus are uncatchable: Juventus are the new champions. The players have scarce chance to celebrate or congratulate each other before hundreds of civilians overcome the barriers and obstacles in their way to invade from the *curva* and stands, waving flags and banners, clapping, dancing, singing, embracing, trying to get near their Bianco-neri heroes. No more criticism, no more booing – just relief and ecstasy.

Three happy but rather embarrassed, reluctant players are hoisted up and carried on the shoulders of overjoyed supporters: Boniperti, Sivori and Charles. More are needed to carry Charles, naturally.

This triumph signifies Juventus's tenth league title. To mark the unique milestone, the sport's rulers had decreed the awarding of a gold star. The star would be stitched onto the chest of each Juventus player's football jersey. This season, three kings by the name of Boniperti, Sivori and Charles, had followed and found that star.

Back in the dressing room, the players found crates of champagne to swig as reward for their outstanding achievement. In a few days' time they would also find a lucrative bonus in their latest pay packets, over a million lira which in English was worth over £700. Practically a normal year's earnings for John Charles, but no amount of money could sweeten the constant bad taste left by the club's and authorities' behaviour regarding his Wales career and immediate prospects of playing in Sweden. He still did not know what they had decided, if they had decided anything; they were treating him badly – they were a disgrace.

Sampdoria were level second-bottom in the table, the fight to preserve their Serie A status continuing at home in their Stadio Luigi Ferraris against Juventus. The bottom club at the season's close would be relegated, and the second-bottom club would have to endure a two-legged play-off against the team finishing second in Serie B. Whichever team won that tie would be in Serie A next season.

Sampdoria would be backed by over seventy thousand Genoese supporters. With fortune on their side too, they would be facing a team relaxing, perhaps even *recovering*, after the league title win and subsequent celebrations. After nearly forty minutes of the game, such hopes of good luck seemed foolish, Sivori putting the visitors two goals ahead in fast, flowing, stress-free football. But all was not lost for the hosts, Eddie Firmani netting to narrow the deficit to one before the interval.

And after it, they continued to build on those foundations; the second half belonged to Sampdoria. Like a cocky boxer surprised by jabs to the chin, Juventus became weaker and weaker against the strength of Sampdoria's attacks. Even with John Charles in defence, the pressure became too much and Sampdoria equalised soon after the hour and proceeded to score the winner in the seventy-fifth minute.

That night the Juventus party flew from Genoa to Brussels for a friendly match against Belgium's Anderlecht two nights later. High-profile exhibition games added to the club's reputation in world soccer, as well as to its financial coffers, but for the players there was such a thing as too much travel and too much football, and this pointless game represented more just that.

In the game staged at the Heysel Stadium, Juventus were soundly beaten 4-1, a tiny consolation being that Charles's second-half thunderbolt was the best goal of the night. No Juventus man cared much, least of all Charles himself; the goal meant nothing, just like (he suspected) the promises he had been made by the club about his playing for his country.

◎

Juventus's final two league games were both at home, the penultimate one against Alessandria, the last being six days later versus Roma.

In the first, Alessandria performed the better but somehow finished as the losers, thanks in large part to one of the two linesmen having to contend with officiating with a low sun glaring in his eyes. He crucially waved his flag for offside against Alessandria's attackers on three occasions; they had actually been onside.

The linesman was not to blame for Alessandria's deficiencies in defence, however, the decisive moment coming late on when Rino Ferrario, for once unshackled from his own defending duties, strode up the pitch and lashed a Sivori pass low into the net, making the score 2-1. The searing heat had perturbed Charles again, but it was not the high temperature to blame for his substandard display and mood like a blistered heel.

The Juventus–Roma match was to be shown on television early in the evening of Saturday 24th May. The live broadcast would be a chance for a larger audience to watch the new champions in action and proof in motion that this was the most entertaining and attack-minded team in Italian football. This Juventus side could even give the Italian national side a tough game, and with Boniperti, Charles and Sivori in attack and in good form, Juventus would be the favourites to win such a contest.

In the sixth minute of the match, a free-kick from Boniperti ... Sivori darts to it and, in flow, manages to collect, control and whack the football into the net. Delighted, he runs around excitedly, socks rolled down and arms in the air, like an urchin tasting Christmas for the first time.

IL VENTOTTESIMO

A few minutes before the half-time break, Juventus are awarded a penalty kick, defender Giacomo Losi having blocked a Sivori shot on the goal-line with his hands. Sivori and Stivanello decide between them that John Charles should be given the opportunity to score; he hasn't netted for over a month. He gratefully accepts.

He sets the ball down on the penalty spot and takes a few steps back. He does not look at Luciano Panetti, the Roma goalkeeper and, for now, his immediate, insignificant enemy.

The referee blows his whistle. Charles runs to the ball and strikes it with his right foot. A tiny cloud of chalk dust shows he has not connected cleanly, his heel scuffing the hard surface at the same time as the football is struck. Nonetheless, the strike is low, accurate and powerful enough to elude Panetti's right hand and nestle in the goal. Ball boys behind the net jump with delight and, as has often been the case this season, Omar Sivori jogs across to Charles to jump up and congratulate him.

Three minutes into the second half, Sivori expresses his creative side with a fine demonstration of football-juggling, culminating in a delightful, delicately cushioned pass that loops over hapless Roma defenders. The pass is designed for the captain of the team, Boniperti, and he pounces on it in the penalty area before calmly planting the ball in the net with his artful right foot. Three goals to nil – the three kings of Juventus scoring the goals, just like they had in the very first match of the season.

After the thirty-four rounds of matches, the final Serie A league positions were: Juventus champions with 51 points; second Fiorentina with 43; then Padova 42; Napoli 40; Roma 36; Bologna 34; L.R. Vicenza 33; Torino 33; Milan 32; Udinese 32; Inter 32; Genoa 30; Sampdoria 30; Alessandria 30; Lazio 30; S.P.A.L. 30; Atalanta 28; and Verona with 26 points.

The final chart of the Serie A top goal-scorers, the *capocannoniere*: 28 goals John Charles; 23 Eddie Firmani (Sampdoria); 22 Omar Sivori; 21 Luís Vinício (Napoli); 20 Kurt Hamrin (Padova); 19 Dino da Costa (Roma).

John Charles was now rated as the most valuable football player on earth, worth at least £150,000.

◎

On 28th May, in Milan, the Italian Football Federation's Presidential Committee met to determine the structure of the forthcoming Coppa Italia competition. Juventus were drawn in Group A along with Torino, Biella and F.C. Pro Vercelli. The teams were scheduled to play each other twice, home and away, the matches taking place on Sundays, beginning with Sunday 8th June. The committee also reiterated their ruling that each team participating must field their strongest team possible.

In the World Cup finals draw, conducted earlier in the month in Switzerland, the groupings for the tournament had also been determined. Wales would be competing in Group 3 against Hungary, Mexico and the host country Sweden, and their first game was also to be played on Sunday 8th June, against Hungary. Ferenc Puskás would not be appearing in the tournament for the Hungarian team, and it was looking almost certain that Wales would be without their own star player too.

◎

His answer of 'No, not interested' came as no surprise whatsoever to Peggy; her husband had been irritable for too many days now because of the Wales thing.

She sympathised, but sympathy has a limited life span, and she had grown impatient of his grumpiness. 'Well, I know that, if it doesn't involve goalposts and a pig's bladder, you're not interested in anything. You're going with me in the morning and that's that.'

'Why?'

'You need to forget about football for a while and clear your head, that's why.' 'That's not much of a reason.'

'It's the only one I've got; you being moody all the time is doing no one any good. Besides, I don't want to go on my own to something like that.'

'Don't go then.'

'No, I want to go and you're taking me.'

He wasn't happy to be ordered around by his wife, but here was one of those situations showing the futility of arguing. For the usually placid Peggy to get so worked up about something like this told him that there was only ever going to be one winner here, and it wasn't him! Her ability to stay calm and keep a cool head even in stressful circumstances was another quality he loved about her: strong when she needed to be – 'grace under pressure'.

One positive aspect of having to queue for something rather than being ushered through before the masses due to his celebrity status was that, at least in holy surroundings like these, no one felt inclined to pester John Charles – and Peggy – while they waited. Nobody asking for his autograph, no one asking to shake his hand, no one idolising him or wanting to give him gifts or even lend him the company of their wife. Today, late morning, he and Peggy were just normal members of the public.

With so many people in attendance, Peggy was reminded, and relieved, that the custom of queuing was not in fact entirely exclusive to England. A long line of hundreds stood outside the cathedral, patiently waiting to enter the building. It was very quiet indeed, almost funereal, the constant hum of motor traffic and trams being the most noticeable sound around. She mused that, for most of the people there, seeing the Shroud of Turin might well feel like a form of funeral, given that the shroud was believed to have been used to cover Jesus Christ's body following the crucifixion.

Finally inside the cathedral, they shuffled along until within viewing distance of the amazing exhibit. There it was, the famous – to some, *infamous* – shroud. As each person approached the closest viewing point, two priests, one at each side of the huge illuminated glass case affixed to the wall, politely and proficiently ushered them along. Each viewer had less than a minute to study it, and so to determine the distinguishing marks and impressions of the victim's body on the material was not such a straightforward task.

'Do you really think it's him?' Peggy whispered to John.

'I don't know … I don't get how it could be. Do you?'

'I wouldn't like to say. But it's amazing, even if it isn't Jesus.'

'That's true.'

'But ...' said Peggy, 'maybe the most important thing isn't whether it's really him or not but that people *believe* it could be.'

'I don't know what you mean, Peg.'

'I'm not sure I do,' Peggy admitted, embarrassed. 'I think I mean that it's a good thing that anyone and everyone can come to see something like this, even if they don't think it's genuine.'

Pleasingly for John, their viewing time was up. He was pleased, not because he had been bored – far from it in fact – but because he had made plans. As he and Peggy walked away from the cathedral, they felt more relaxed, now speaking without the need to whisper.

'What are you smiling for?' Peggy enquired. 'It wasn't that dull, was it?'

'What? No, it was interesting ... I wanted to leave; I booked us a table, specially.'

'*You* booked us a table? What for? Where?'

'A meal; what do you think I booked a table for?'

'A meal? You?'

'La Spada Reale. I telephoned Stefano; you remember him?'

'Yes, yes. I'm impressed.'

'Good bloody job!' he laughed. She couldn't recall the last time she'd seen him laugh. He went on, 'He's opening up early just for us, so we can have some privacy.'

'Brilliant, thank you.'

'And we're off to see a film afterwards, at the Lux, if you fancy it.' 'What film is it?'

'Gigi rang the cinema.'

'Is that the name of the film?'

'Bloody hell woman!' he laughed again. 'I bet you won't like it ...' 'Because it's in Italian? I'll try to.'

'No, because it's one of those horror films.'

'Oh John, a horror film?'

'I fancy it. Even *I* will be able to follow the story.'

'What is it?'

'Dracula.'

'Dracula? John, I don't think I like the sound of that.'

'I'll hold your hand if you get scared.'

◎

Concerted criticism from the British media, the Italian media, the Swedish media, the World Cup organisers and Umberto Agnelli, at last seemed to pay off: the Italian Football Federation had relented, by offering a compromise. No apologies to accompany the compromise, no regrets expressed, no reasons given for their inflexibility – just a statement. Less than five days before Wales's first match in the tournament. The statement, on June 4th, announced they would allow Charles to play in the World Cup finals providing Juventus's three opponents in the Coppa Italia agreed to his absence from their matches. There was no question whatsoever that those clubs would object to the season's top scorer missing their matches; the IFF were trying to get out of an embarrassing situation caused completely by their own officiousness.

That same day, Charles trained at the Combi training ground with his club team-mates and then caught a flight in the afternoon to Stockholm, Sweden; the Wales party had been there two days already.

THANKS AND ACKNOWLEDGEMENTS

During my research before writing *The Gigante*, I was honoured to receive anecdotal help from numerous people, all of whom I've tried to remember and list below. Sadly, during the time I was writing the book, three of those people left us, so I'd like to use this opportunity to thank them again, as it was a pleasure knowing them: Harold Williams, John Cave and Margaret Hatfield.

My gratitude to all at BBC Radio Leeds, Arts Council England, Made in Leeds Television. Special mention of course to Peggy Charles and her family, and to the gentleman and superb ex-footballer, Umberto Colombo, a fine host over in Bergamo, Italy.

Thanks to Steve Bintcliffe, Craig Bradley, Dave Brydon, Jim Cadman, Glen Campbell, John Cave and family, Ivan Cerra, Melvyn Charles, Julie Clement, Dave Cocker, Emanuele Confalonieri, Terry Crossland, Tony Crossland, Ian Daley, Cristina Demarie, Adam Digby, Jack and Norma Emery, Sam Emery, Sophie Cater-Emery, Gianluca Enzini, Mike Farnan, Giovanni Fenu, Fiona Gell, Sam Gibbard, Richard Gomersall, Dom Grace, Keith Handley, Steve Hanson, Julian Hardcastle, Sarah Hardcastle, Harry Harris, Dave Hartrick, David Hebden, John Henesy, Tony Hill, Phil Hodgson, Jon Howe, Johnny I'Anson, Juventus F.C. Museum personnel, Martin Kelner, Paul Kent, Thom Kirwin, Bryn Law, Malcolm Lawton, Johnny Lord, Peter Lorimer, Rob Mackenzie (and Larna), Peter McConnell, Chris Nickson, Kevin Nolan (the writer), Mark O'Brien, Kevin O'Rourke, Lynda O'Rourke, Jonathan Owen, Tom Palmer, David Peace, Giovanni Pedronetto, Fabrizio Pennacchietti, Adam Pope, Nick Quantrill, Ben Reid, Sharon Reid, Maureen Reynolds, Stephen Reynolds, Deborah Robinson, Peter Robinson, Alessandro Roccati, Rocky, Tom Roe, Tony Rubin, Brian Scovell, Duncan Seaman, Bobby Shields, Candida Skinner, Graham Thirkill, Dylan Thwaites, Eric Vonk, Michael White, Sarah Whitham, Richard Youle.